Lieutenant Wes James treated her as if he liked her—a lot.

That was nonsense, of course, Callie knew. She wasn't pretty in any sense. Just a plain Jane. So why had Wes given her that look?

Oh, Callie recognized the *look*. She'd seen men give it to women thousands of times—but never to her.

Shaking her head, Callie decided her emotions were skewed by the quake and the awful disaster surrounding them. That was it: she was in shock and completely misreading Wes.

Still, as she disembarked from the Humvee and ran toward the action, her heart thumped hard in her chest. And it wasn't from fear. It was anticipation at working with Lieutenant Wes James.

He liked her.

And she found that amazing. Impossible…

Dear Reader,

This August, I am delighted to give you six winning reasons to pick up a Silhouette Special Edition book.

For starters, Lindsay McKenna, whose action-packed and emotionally gritty romances have entertained readers for years, moves us with her exciting cross-line series MORGAN'S MERCENARIES: ULTIMATE RESCUE. The first book, *The Heart Beneath,* tells of love against unimaginable odds. With a background as a firefighter in the late 1980s, Lindsay elaborates, "This story is about love, even when buried beneath the rubble of a hotel, or deep within a human being who has been terribly wounded by others, that it will not only survive, but emerge and be victorious."

No stranger to dynamic storytelling, Laurie Paige kicks off a new MONTANA MAVERICKS spin-off with *Her Montana Man,* in which a beautiful forensics examiner must gather evidence in a murder case, but also has to face the town's mayor, a man she'd loved and lost years ago. Don't miss the second book in THE COLTON'S: COMANCHE BLOOD series—Jackie Merritt's *The Coyote's Cry,* a stunning tale of forbidden love between a Native American sheriff and the town's "golden girl."

Christine Rimmer delivers the first romance in her captivating new miniseries THE SONS OF CAITLIN BRAVO. In *His Executive Sweetheart,* a secretary pines for a Bravo bachelor who just happens to be her boss! And in Lucy Gordon's *Princess Dottie,* a waitress-turned-princess is a dashing prince's only chance at keeping his kingdom—and finding true love.… Debut author Karen Sandler warms readers with *The Boss's Baby Bargain,* in which a controlling CEO strikes a marriage bargain with his financially strapped assistant, but their smoldering attraction leads to an unexpected pregnancy!

This month's selections are stellar romances that will put a smile on your face and a song in your heart! Happy reading.

Sincerely,

Karen Taylor Richman
Senior Editor

Please address questions and book requests to:
Silhouette Reader Service
U.S.: 3010 Walden Ave., P.O. Box 1325, Buffalo, NY 14269
Canadian: P.O. Box 609, Fort Erie, Ont. L2A 5X3

Lindsay McKenna

THE HEART BENEATH

SPECIAL EDITION™

Published by Silhouette Books

America's Publisher of Contemporary Romance

To my dear readers
who love Morgan and Laura as much as I do.

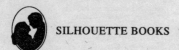 SILHOUETTE BOOKS

ISBN 0-373-24486-X

THE HEART BENEATH

Visit Silhouette at www.eHarlequin.com

Printed in U.S.A.

Books by Lindsay McKenna

LINDSAY McKENNA

A homeopathic educator, Lindsay teaches at the Desert Institute of Classical Homeopathy in Phoenix, Arizona. When she isn't teaching alternative medicine, she is writing books about love. She feels love is the single greatest healer in the world and hopes that her books touch her readers on those levels.

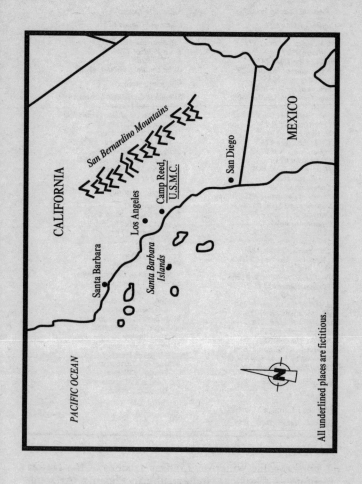

PACIFIC OCEAN

CALIFORNIA

San Bernardino Mountains

Santa Barbara

Los Angeles

Camp Reed,
U.S.M.C.

San Diego

Santa Barbara
Islands

MEXICO

N

All underlined places are fictitious.

Prologue

December 31
1600

"Oh, Morgan, this is such an unexpected and beautiful New Year's gift!" Laura Trayhern whirled around in the sumptuous suite of the Hoyt Hotel. She smiled at her husband who was grinning proudly. "I never expected this!" she exclaimed as she flew to his arms. They had just arrived at the hotel from Los Angeles International Airport. The lavish suite was a surprise—as was Morgan's plan for them to spend New Year's Eve there, just the two of them.

Morgan swept his pretty blond wife into his arms, almost dwarfing her petite form. The childlike expression of joy on her face made his heart sing. As she brushed his neck, cheek and finally his mouth with quick, wet kisses, he picked her up and twirled her around. Then, when his masterful Fred Astaire dance routine had made him dizzy, he placed her feet on the thick, white carpet, and murmured, "Happy New Year, darling. I wanted this to be a surprise for you...."

Smoothing her hands over her ankle-length, blue wool skirt, then straightening her pink blazer, Laura looked around. "The Hoyt...a five-star hotel! It's so old and beautiful, Morgan. Oh, I've always wanted to come here. This is where the Hollywood elite from the thirties and forties came to party and be seen by the press. Why, there's a gorgeous mahogany bar, trimmed with brass, where actors like Clark Gable came to drink. And so did some of the most famous writers from those eras, too!" She gazed up at her husband, who was dressed casually in accordance with California fashion in a bright-red polo shirt, dark-blue blazer and tan chino pants. "This is a dream come true, Morgan," she said, wandering about the suite, which was the best the hotel had to offer.

Laura knew the Sun King's suite, situated at the top of the old hotel, was expensive with its elegant white-and-gold Louis XIV furniture. The place looked like a palace. Gliding her fingertips across the sideboard, she gazed out through the open curtains. The Suite faced toward central Los Angeles, visible in the distance. The lurid brownish cloud of pollution that always hung across the wide basin was clearly visible. But the damask curtains, burgundy embossed with gold flowers, made the scene look like a postcard to Laura.

Fourteen stories below them, she saw the old, stately palm trees in front of the Hoyt moving in the breeze. The trees lined the broad avenue in front of the pink hotel like guardians standing at rigid attention. California was wonderfully warm compared to their icy-cold home in Philipsburg, Montana, where they'd just flown in from. Even at the end of December the temperature often reached eighty degrees here.

She felt Morgan come up beside her and slide his arm around her shoulders, drawing her near.

"Merry post Christmas," he murmured, and pressed a kiss to her mussed gold hair, which always reminded him of Rapunzel's spun-gold tresses. When Laura lifted her chin and flashed him another excited smile, he felt his heart expand with joy.

"I couldn't believe it, Morgan! When you handed me that red envelope at the Five Days of Christmas celebration we just held for everyone at Perseus, I had no idea it would contain airline tickets and a voucher for the Hoyt." She sighed happily and leaned against him, her arm going around his strong body. "What a gift! You know how long I've been dying to come here and snoop around this historic mansion, doing some in-depth research."

Morgan nodded. "I know we've been busy. Perseus has taken up a lot more of my time than I envisioned," he said, referring to the covert team of mercenaries he headed up. Now, as he looked into his wife's eyes, he found himself drowning in her dancing gaze. Even after all these years, bearing and raising his four children, she managed to retain her childlike enthusiasm and joyful heart. That ability forever astounded him, and over the years had helped heal him from the many massive wounds he'd carried from active service in the Marine Corps during the closing days of the Vietnam War.

When they met, Laura had been working as a research writer and historian, well known for her military articles, and living in Washington, D.C. They had literally run into one another.

Morgan had been at the airport and seen Laura struck down by a car. It was that accident that had brought them together, and changed their lives forever. Over the years, they had had difficult times, but their love for one another had only been strengthened as a result. Even after that terrifying time, when he, Laura, and their oldest son, Jason, had been kidnapped in an act of revenge by drug lords, Laura had emerged with her spirit in tatters, but still intact. It was a miracle, Morgan realized, because his wife had suffered horribly at the hands of their captors. The kidnapping had stolen a piece of her soul, but she battled back from the ordeal with the help of his unquenchable love and support.

Morgan knew well her penchant for research and for history. And since the Hoyt was one of the last of the elite, Gothic-style hotels built in Hollywood during the twenties, he knew she'd get a kick out of staying there. For a long time she had been wanting to depart from the military articles she still wrote upon occasion, even though she was a full-time mother, to do in-depth research on some magnificent landmarks from a bygone era.

"Well, we're going to mix business with pleasure," he told her. When he saw the crestfallen look on her face, he quickly added, "More pleasure and less business."

"Let me guess," she said impishly, turning and leaning fully against him, her arms around his waist. "Camp Reed, the major Marine Corps base in Southern California, is only a stone's throw from here— about twenty miles or so. And you're probably going to nose around over there, right? Talk to the general at the base because you've had some of his Marine Recon detachments or individual marines assigned to Perseus black ops missions?''

"Yep." Morgan breathed in, inhaling the lilac fragrance of her hair. "I have two appointments before we party in the New Year. First I'm going to see General Jeb Wilson on January first."

"He's the commanding officer of Camp Reed?"

"Yeah. More a courtesy call than anything, darling. To thank him for all his help, loaning his people out to us over the past year."

"And you're not going to be cooking up new missions with him?" Laura raised one eyebrow. She knew Morgan didn't waste time; he made the most of every trip he went on. And Lord knew, he was constantly flying here and there on the Perseus jet—checking on his mercenaries who, around the world, were involved in life-and-death missions, helping others.

Shaking his head, he kissed the tip of her nose. "Nope, for once we'll just have a drink over at the O Club—officer's club—and remember old times. I'll wish him a belated Merry Christmas and a Happy New Year."

"Okay," she murmured petulantly, pouting provocatively as she moved her hips suggestively against him. "I know there's a New Year's party at the hotel tonight and I don't want to go to it alone." She saw his eyes narrow, and slowly smiled. "In the meantime I guess I'll keep myself busy by talking to the manager of this lovely old hotel, snooping around and taking photos. Maybe I can start building a research file on it. I've already got a major magazine that wants my article. Or maybe I'll just relax a bit. Take a hot bath…"

"Hmm, you make it tough to think about leaving," Morgan said.

Her mouth drew into a knowing smile. "I sure hope so, Morgan Trayhern. Because after having fifty houseguests milling around during our Five Days of Christmas extravaganza, I think we deserve some quality downtime together. Don't you?"

Sliding his fingers through her mussed gold hair, he murmured, "Absolutely..." Laura made it tough for him to think when she started that sweet, loving assault upon him. She knew what took his mind off business—her. The years of marriage hadn't lessened his love or need of her, it had only increased his desire.

"Good, we'll be partying tonight and will ring in the New Year together. You mentioned you had two appointments. What else are you planning while we're out here for the next five days?"

Having the good grace to blush, Morgan felt the heat creep into his cheeks as his wife gave him that knowing look. "I can't keep anything from you at all, can I? I have a very brief meeting to attend here at the hotel, after I get back from Camp Reed."

Chuckling, Laura eased out of his arms. She knew that Morgan had other demands and duties. She wouldn't cause him to be late for his appointments, but she did want to know his plans. "No, darling, you can't. So—" she stood by the window, stroking the thick burgundy drape hanging there "—what else do you have to do?"

Rubbing his jaw, Morgan said, "I see Jeb on New Year's Day at 1300. He's sending a Huey helicopter over to the landing pad in back of the hotel to pick me up. We're planning on spending about an hour together, and then they'll drop me back here."

"VIP, red-carpet service," Laura murmured, impressed. Of course, Morgan had complete access to all military branches, as well as to the highest office in the land, the presidency, if he needed it in order to pull off a mission. Because of Perseus's success in solving problems globally where governments had failed, Morgan was a military heavyweight in a world that usually closed its doors to civilian outsiders. He was a megastar in some of the most powerful political circles, like a Hollywood actor on the A list. Still, Morgan never threw his weight around, and had always been humble about the power he wielded. Laura loved him for that. He ran Perseus to help people in need around the world, when authorities in those countries were unable to. And many times, the federal government used Perseus as a covert branch of the CIA. Consequently, Morgan was known by presidents and heads of states around the world, but not by the general public or media. Few people knew Perseus existed, which was fine with her.

"Well," Morgan said, "I managed to get hold of one of my old friends from Vietnam days—Darrel Cummings, a fellow officer I'd gone through school with. He's the head of a Silicon Valley computer company now, doing software work for the Pentagon and the army. I called him before we left, and I'm going to have a quick drink with him down in the bar about 2100 tonight. *After* I take my beautiful wife to the Jungle Room of this hotel for a very intimate and expensive dinner. Once I meet with Darrel, I'll come up here, get you, and we'll go find that party, which starts at around 2200. Does that meet with your approval?"

Laughing softly, Laura nodded. "Perfectly." She returned Morgan's dark, intimate look before he clasped her arm and walked into the main room with her. On the table was a massive bouquet of Hawaiian flowers freshly flown in from the islands. There were red and pink ginger, wild-looking purple-and-orange bird-of-paradise, white blossoms of plumaria, whose fragrance drifted through the suite, and red lobster-claw heliconia at the top. It was a rainbow feast of color for the eyes, Laura decided, as she watched Morgan move to the solid silver champagne bucket and pull a dark-green bottle from the ice.

There were two crystal champagne flutes on the table, and she stepped closer as he uncorked the bottle and slowly poured golden bubbly into each glass. Lalique crystal, she noted, admiring how the base of each glass was shaped like the rounded petals of a flower.

"Here, to celebrate your Hoyt adventure and our New Year together," Morgan murmured, as he put the champagne bottle back into the ice bucket. Picking up both glasses, he handed one to Laura. "Let's drink to your great writing project here. I'm sure when the manager lets you into the archives in the basement, you'll dig up dirt on every Hollywood star that ever came here." He chuckled and lifted his glass. Clinking it gently against hers, he saw Laura smile wickedly.

"Now, darling, I don't 'dig dirt' on anyone. I'm just interested in some of the wonderful old myths and legends that have drifted out of this hotel. I want to see if they're really true or not." She lifted her glass and sipped the champagne. It tasted more like a bubbly fruit juice than wine, and was sweet and delicious as she rolled it around on her tongue.

Morgan had gotten her favorite champagne—from a very small vineyard, Echo Canyon, in Page Springs, Arizona. They knew the owner, John Logan, an attorney who had worked for the federal government at one time. Morgan had brought home some of his wine over a year ago, and Laura had gone bonkers over it. She'd never before tasted such a wonderful Syrah burgundy, or the sparking champagne he'd hand-grown on sixteen acres out in the high desert, near Sedona. Morgan had made sure he had a crate of John's best flown in for their Five Days of Christmas celebration this year. Laura's favorite, however, was this incredible-tasting champagne. She closed her eyes, made a humming sound of pleasure and smiled.

"This has to be John's best year," she murmured as she opened her eyes and held the glass up, viewing it with a critical eye. "His wine gets better with every season."

Morgan chuckled. He didn't have such a sensitive or appreciative pallet for champagne or wine. "John said this was his best champagne since he's opened the vineyard ten years ago. He sent us two bottles here, to the Hoyt, as a New Year's gift."

"Wonderful," Laura said, sipping the champagne with enthusiasm. "John's wine goes for hundreds of dollars a bottle. I feel so lucky!"

As he stood near the huge Hawaiian flower arrangement, watching Laura appreciate every sip of her favorite champagne, Morgan's heart nearly burst with happiness. His wife deserved something special like this, and he didn't give it to her often enough. His work kept him on the move twenty-four hours a day, seven days a week. Although his offices were only three miles from their home, he often was so immersed in work he didn't see her much during the day. As a result, she had borne the brunt of raising their four children.

He tried to come home for lunch every day to be with her and the children. Their oldest, Jason, was now at Annapolis, the U.S. Naval Academy. Katy was seventeen and getting ready to leave for college next year. The fraternal twins, Peter and Kelly were now twelve, a wonderful age, and Morgan was trying to be home with them more often.

He frowned, knowing he'd been working too much. Jason and Katherine especially had grown up without him being there much of the time. He'd been a shadow father in their lives. Because of the mounting problems with Jason, who didn't have an easy time of it at school, and Katherine's distance from him, Morgan was trying to correct that problem. Laura was much happier that he was taking weekends off, and sending his second-in-command, Mike Houston, around the world on many Perseus missions in his place. The twins, at least, were much happier and well adjusted as a result.

Guilt ate at Morgan as he stood there sipping champagne with Laura. Nothing mattered more to him than his family. They were a close, tight-knit family. Silently, he promised Laura that he would continue to be there for their children and for her. His life wasn't all about military objectives and missions. He realized now it was about being around for his family, supporting Laura and helping her to raise their kids.

Laura eased her sensible black shoes off her feet and dug her nylon-clad toes into the plush carpet. Turning, she walked back to the window. The sun was setting.

"Look at the strange color of this sunset, Morgan. Have you ever seen anything like it?" she asked, turning as he came up behind her.

Morgan stared out the huge window toward central Los Angeles, at the needlelike buildings that seemed to be clawing the sky. "Hmm. No, it looks yellow-green, or a dirty yellow color. It is unusual…"

Wrinkling her nose as she sipped the wine, Laura leaned once more against Morgan's tall, steady frame. His arm came around her waist to keep her solidly in place. "Dirty yellow is a good description. It really is a strange, rather ugly color. We've been out to California many times in the past and I can never remember the sky looking like this." A chill went through her. She felt Morgan's arm tighten around her reassuringly.

"Cold?" he murmured near her ear.

Shaking her head, she said, "No…just, well, a strange chill just shot through me." Twisting to look up at him, she said, "Isn't that odd? Here we are at the top of the world, literally speaking, in a terribly expensive penthouse suite, drinking some of the best champagne on the face of the earth, and I get this awful feeling…."

"About what?" Morgan knew Laura was highly intuitive. With the children, she'd often get a premonition when one of them was in some kind of danger, and it always turned out that she was correct. Morgan didn't take Laura's intuition lightly. Frowning, he pressed a kiss to the top of her head.

"I…don't know, Morgan. Boy, this is strange, you know?" She forced a smile she didn't feel. "Maybe we should call home and check with the baby-sitter to see if the twins are okay."

Releasing her, he nodded. "Sure, go ahead…." And he stepped aside so she could go to the flowery couch and sit down near the ornate, antique-style phone there.

Turning to gaze out at the lurid yellow sunset, he listened as Laura dialed home. The cloud of pollution hung like a dirty brown ribbon across the sky. Stretching for a good fifty miles from north to south and roughly thirty miles from east to west, the Los Angeles basin contained millions of people. This was one of the most congested, overpopulated spots in the U.S.A. Everyone wanted California sunshine, the good life, and perfect weather conditions without snow or ice. Morgan couldn't blame any of them for moving out here, for the Los Angeles area was a powerful draw. And having Hollywood here was just another plus. Disneyland was nearby, and so was Knotsberry Farm. Los Angeles, the City of Angels, had many attractions that drew families.

As he listened to Laura talking to their baby-sitter, Julie Kingston, he didn't hear any consternation or worry in her voice. Sipping the champagne as he stood there, Morgan slid his free hand into the pocket of his chinos. The sky was a deepening yellow now, one of the oddest colors he'd ever seen. Searching his memory, he could not find a clue to this unusual meteorological event.

"Well," Laura sighed as she came back to stand with him, "everyone's okay, thank goodness. Julie said the twins are fine."

Morgan glanced at her and saw the relief in her eyes. Laura loved her children with the fierceness of a lioness and she was a wonderful mother to them.

"Good," he murmured. "Because I want you to enjoy the vacation." Pulling his hand from his pocket, he slid his arm across Laura's slim, proud shoulders and drew her close. She came without resistance, that soft look in her blue eyes once again, replacing the worry.

"Oh, you know me, Morgan. I'm such a worrywart when it comes to the kids. That's part of being a parent. You and I both know that."

Nodding, he stood with his wife in his arms, enjoying the warmth of her body against his. "I know," he whispered huskily, and placed a kiss on her silky hair. "Maybe when we go to dinner tonight, our waitress might know what this dirty yellow sky means."

Laughter burbled up in Laura's throat. "Oh, let's not ask! She'll probably think we're backwoods hicks from Montana, and get a good laugh out of it. Let's *not* embarrass ourselves that way, okay?"

Smiling good-naturedly, Morgan murmured, "Fair enough, woman of my heart. Now, let's enjoy the rest of this bottle, laze around a little and enjoy life one minute at a time with one another."

A glint came to Laura's eyes as she met her husband's warm gray gaze, which burned with desire for her. Her lips parted in an elfin smile. "I'd love to take that champagne bottle over to the huge, four-poster Louis XIV bed, lie beneath that incredible burgundy-and-gold canopy, and enjoy it with you."

Morgan raised an eyebrow. "I like your idea, Mrs. Trayhern. You're forever creative about such things..."

Giggling, Laura felt the chill and worry leave her. Slipping out from beneath Morgan's arm, she skipped across the room and slid the champagne from the silver bucket. Bottle in hand, she moved to the king-size bed and leaped onto it like a gleeful child, her laughter tinkling.

"I have a few more creative ideas we can explore together," she challenged wickedly.

Chapter One

December 31: 2150

"That sunset was an ugly yellow, wasn't it, Dusty? I always wonder what's going to happen when it's that color. It's so unusual..." Lieutenant Callie Evans squatted down in front of the cyclone-fenced kennel that housed her golden retriever, a dog specially trained for rescue missions. There were twenty-two such animals in the facility. Overhead, the pale amber glare of a sodium lamp cast deep, running shadows across the enclosed area that housed dogs of various breeds.

The U.S. Marine Corps General Rescue Unit sat a quarter of a mile away from a small lake where marines liked to fish when off-duty. The main building of the unit was on top of a knoll, sitting among rocks, dirt and cactus. The kennel area was at one side of the dark-brown stucco, single-story building. Callie spent three-fourths of her life here, and loved every moment of it. The men and women handlers were like a large, extended family to her.

Even though she was the executive officer of the unit, she considered the enlisted people family, too. In their kind of work, the walls between officers and enlisted personnel dissolved to a great degree, and Callie liked it that way. She might be a Marine Corps officer, but in her book, enlisted Marines deserved every bit as much respect. So often, out at some disaster site, rank distinctions disappeared completely. During those times, they were all just people on a mission to save whoever was trapped or endangered. Finding survivors was the sole focus for both officers and enlisted alike in this rescue unit. Whether she was searching for victims in a skyscraper fire, or after an earthquake, a tidal wave or any other type of trauma that might involve trying to find life in so much death, Callie loved her job with her whole heart and soul.

Dusty whined, his huge, golden-brown eyes looking up at her with unabashed adoration as she stuck her small fingers through the wire to pet his cold nose. Wagging his tail, he whined again plaintively.

Frowning, Callie remained hunched over, one hand on the gate and the other stroking Dusty's muzzle. For the last three days all the dogs were restless. Some whined. Others barked in a way that usually signalled danger. Danger? What kind? And where was it coming from? She shifted her worried gaze to her five-year-old friend. Giving Dusty a soft smile, she whispered, "Wish I could understand dog language better. I gotta get going, Dust, but I just wanted to stop by one more time before I left to do my rounds of this place. You've seemed so upset. What is it, boy? What's got you and everyone else spooked around here?''

The evening coolness here in the desert always surprised Callie. Camp Reed, a hundred-thousand acre Marine Corps reservation, sat on some of the most expensive real estate in Southern California. It was literally a back door to the Los Angeles basin, about twenty miles to the west. And even though Camp Reed was arid desert, with cactus, and Joshua trees dotting its rocky hills and deep, narrow valleys of ocher-colored soil and sand, it still got cold at night. Because the reservation wasn't right on the coast, it didn't benefit from the warm, humid Pacific. Consequently, Camp Reed was either broiling hot, with temperatures soaring to over a hundred degrees in summer, or marine sentries found their teeth chattering as they walked their posts during winter. No snow fell, but it might as well as far as Callie was concerned.

"Of course," she told Dusty in a conspiratorial tone, "it *is* late December, and even here in good ole California, it gets close to freezing at night." She smiled affectionately at her rescue partner and slowly rose to her full five-foot-five-inch height. Pulling her camouflage jacket more tightly around her thin frame, Callie stood on the concrete and looked around.

The dogs were really upset. As she stood there, her hands deep in the pockets of her Marine Corps cammos jacket, the cap drawn down on her head and the bill low enough to stop the glare of the lights overhead from reaching her eyes, she wondered why they were so wound up.

She'd just gotten back from Turkey a week ago. She and Dusty were still recovering from that grueling two weeks of climbing over rubble caused by a devastating earthquake in that country. Pulling her hand out of her pocket, she held up a doggy biscuit, one of Dusty's favorite treats.

"Hey…look what I got for you." She leaned down and slipped it between the wires.

Dusty quickly gobbled it up, licked his mouth with his large pink tongue and gave her a beseeching look for another one.

Callie chuckled indulgently. "Don't look at me like that. You talk with your eyes, guy." And she grinned and tucked her hands back into her pockets. Looking to the right, she saw that Sergeant Irene Anson had desk duty. The sergeant was thirty years old, married, with a little girl. Callie doted on Annie, who, at age five, just loved to come out to the kennels and pet all her "doggies." It was a time Callie always looked forward to, for she loved little kids. Irene's husband, Brad, was a Recon Marine, one of the corps elite.

Camp Reed had its own rescue dog unit, teams of which were utilized around the world in major catastrophes of any kind. Callie had been in many countries during her last two years with the rescue unit. When called to those countries for earthquake duty, it didn't hurt that she knew Spanish, plus some Turkish and Greek. Callie had taken courses in those languages because many times, earthquakes occurred in countries where those languages were spoken, and she wanted to be able to converse not only with the local authorities, but with survivors they found in the rubble, as well. One of her least-favorite duties was going to South America for the many killer mudslides that occurred during the rainy season. It wasn't something she looked forward to at all.

Dusty whined, wanting another treat.

"You are a glutton for more goodies," she told the retriever wryly. "And it isn't like this hasn't been a great day for you. We went to the beach today and we played and celebrated New Year's Eve early. You got to swim in the ocean, go after the sticks I threw, and roll in the sand while I roasted hot dogs over a fire. And then you came back and shook yourself, spraying water all over me and the food. That's how you got your fair share of the hot dogs. You ain't no dummy, are you, guy?" Callie laughed under her breath. It had been a good day, one they'd both needed. But she had no one to share this evening with, to welcome in the New Year. Even as Callie held her dog's worshipful stare, loneliness ate at her.

"Don't go there," she told herself in warning. "Don't do this to yourself, Callie...."

Dusty whined.

"I know, I know," she said aloud to the golden retriever. "Why do I do this to myself, Dusty? Why can't I just be fine with how I look? You are. Of course, you're drop-dead handsome. I mean, what lady dog wouldn't do a double take, seeing you?" Her mouth curled, but with pain, not humor. Callie hurt inside. She was twenty-five years old and single, and she knew why.

Dusty sat down and thumped his tail eagerly on his concrete slab. Callie had bought a flannel pillow filled with cedar shavings for him to lie on in the kennel. Concrete couldn't be comfortable in her opinion. Dusty dearly loved his "blankie" and joyfully slept on it every chance he got. Now he tilted his head, his intelligent eyes shining with happiness that she was still there with him.

"Why can't I just be happy like you over the simple pleasures of life, like your blankie?" Callie asked. She moved back to the kennel, rested her shoulder against it and hung her head. Staring down at her booted feet, she sighed. "Why do I always have to torture myself, Dusty? So I'm plain looking. 'Board ugly,' as I heard some jerk of a jarhead say a week ago. Dude, that hurts. You know?"

Dusty whined.

"Darn it all…" Callie whispered achingly. "I wish I wasn't so softhearted, Dusty. I need a thicker skin. I wish I could let those words roll off me like water off a duck's back, but I can't.…"

Maybe if she let her short, sandy-blond hair grow out more it would make her look more feminine. Callie had thought of that often, but in her line of work, long hair was not at all practical. She'd be filthy dirty climbing up and over buildings that had been destroyed by a killer earthquake. Or it would rain or snow and she'd be sopping wet *and* muddy. No, long hair was out. Well, how about some makeup? She had a square face, with wide-set eyes, a nose that was too big and a mouth that was even bigger. She looked…well, plain. Maybe even ugly… No man even gazed at her with the *look*. Callie had wished all her life for a man to show her some interest. She saw other women marines getting that special attention, but she never did. Sighing, Callie knew she never would.

Her hair was straight and hung limp as a dishrag around her face, even when she wasn't climbing around on rubble all day in all sorts of weather. Setting it to make it look halfway decent or using hair spray was out of the question. Hers was a brutal outdoor job. With people trapped and dying, as often was the case in a disaster situation, it didn't matter whether she wore makeup or if her hair looked feminine or not. No, the victims only wanted to know that Dusty had found them and that Callie was there to help them in any way she could, to escape and live to tell about it. To them, she was an angel of mercy.

Callie smiled a little, remembering how one man had whispered that to her as the medics had extricated him from some rubble. He'd been trapped in there for five days, and Dusty had found him. More dead than alive, the old, silver-haired man had reached out with a shaking hand and fiercely gripped hers as they carried him by on a stretcher.

"You're an angel," he'd rasped, tears streaming down his face. "An angel sent by God himself. Thank you.... You've got the face of an angel, and I'll never forget you...not ever...." And he'd choked and sobbed as they'd carried him away to the ambulance.

She wouldn't ever forget his words, either. Callie liked the idea of looking like an angel. God didn't make any ugly angels. Nope, not a chance. Smiling a little, she cast a glance at Dusty, who watched her every expression.

"Do I look like an angel to you?"

Dusty whined and thumped his tail heartily.

"You'd say yes to anything, guy." And Callie laughed. "No ugly angels in heaven, Dust." She rolled her eyes and looked up at the low ceiling of the kennel complex, made from corrugated aluminum. "Maybe that's when I'll feel beautiful. When I die."

A deep, growling roar caught Callie's ears. The dogs started baying. Where was that horrendous sound coming from? She looked around. Eyes widening, Callie hunched slightly, feeling as if she were being attacked. By what, she had no idea. The dogs' unified voices raised the hair on the back of her neck. Their baying was sharp and filled with terror. Feeling the earth shiver, Callie caught her breath in fear, and spread her arms outward. In a flash, she realized what was happening: an earthquake!

Callie didn't have time to react. One moment she was standing, the next she was knocked off her feet, slamming onto the hard concrete floor with an "oofff!" The ground bucked and heaved. As she rolled onto her back, she was thrown from one side of the kennel area to the other. The roof cracked, metal was shrieking and bending. She suddenly saw stars, like white pinpoints of lights on black velvet, where the tin had opened up.

The dogs were crying and wailing.

Callie gasped and tried to get to her feet. *Run!* She heard Sergeant Anson screaming for help. The earth still convulsed violently, its roar deafening, like a freight train bearing down on her. Callie scraped her hand badly as she tried to head for the nearest exit door. *No good!* A second undulating wave hit, and again Callie was knocked off her feet. She rolled heavily into the kennel's fence. Fear vomited through her.

This was no ordinary earthquake. No. It was a killer of incredible magnitude. Callie had been in too many earthquake-torn countries and experienced too many aftershocks not to know what was going on here. As she rolled helplessly from side to side, the earth moving like waves in an ocean, she realized that this one was off the Richter scale—completely.

December 31: 2150

Lieutenant Wes James was getting dressed for the New Year's Eve party at the O Club at Camp Reed when the earthquake struck. Although he lived in Oceanside, the nearest civilian town to the front gates of Reed, he'd taken a room at the B.O.Q.—bachelor officer's quarters—so that he wouldn't have to drive after drinking. He had just finished putting on a buttoned down white shirt, a camel-colored wool blazer and black jeans and had been sitting on the couch, tying the laces on his dark-brown Italian leather shoes, when the quake began.

Within seconds, Wes was clinging in surprise to the couch as it moved five feet in one direction, and then five feet the other way, across the cedar floor of the bedroom. As adrenaline shot through his bloodstream in response, he didn't have time to realize what was happening. But it didn't take him long to figure it out. And he only had to glance toward the darkened view out his window to realize that. The B.O.Q. was four stories tall. All the streetlights outside the military hotel had been suddenly snuffed out, along with lights inside. In the darkness, he heard his friend, Russell Burk, yelp in fright outside in the hall. Russ had the adjoining room, and they were planning on meeting to go to the O Club. The quake must have caught Russ out in the hallway.

Everything vibrated. The roar was frightening, making Wes's eardrums hurt. The furniture and floor were shivering and shaking as if someone had put the whole room—him included—into a blender at high speed. Wes pushed himself up into a sitting position and gripped the couch. As his eyes adjusted to the inky darkness around him, he watched in amazement. It blew his mind that the couch was sliding like a toy back and forth across the floor as each rhythmic wave of the earthquake rolled through the building. He heard a loud "Crack!" and jerked his gaze upward. For a moment, he feared the fourth story was coming down upon him. The B.O.Q. groaned, wobbled and swayed. The joists and timbers of this old, 1930s-built architectural wonder were not earthquake proof.

Escape! He had to get outside! But how? Wes leaped to his feet and was instantly knocked off of them. Another wave of heaving tore through the building. In seconds, he was sliding into the careening redwood coffee table. Pain arced up his shoulder as he slammed into it. The glass on top slid off, cracked and shattered on the floor. Splinters of glass glittered for a moment and then scattered wildly as the floor danced and bucked all around him.

Wes kept his gaze glued to the ceiling rocking and undulating above him. It didn't take his civil engineering degree for him to realize that if that ceiling caved in, it could kill him. He scrambled to his hands and knees and decided to head out to the hall to Russ. *No good.* Lurching drunkenly to his feet, Wes went for the door. His hand closed around the brass knob. *There!* Tumbling out into the hall, Wes slammed into Russ, who was rolling wildly, his arms and legs outstretched to try and stop himself.

The quake seemed to go on and on. Russ lay on the floor outside his room, his eyes wide with terror. Wes reached out, gripped his friend's hand and dragged him toward the wall. Every piece of furniture was on the move, many sliding through the opened doors of their rooms. The sound of cracking glass filled the hall. Some of the windows were shattering inward.

It was impossible to stand up. All Wes could do

was crawl forward on his belly alongside Russ and try to make it down the carpeted hall.

"The emergency exit!" Wes shouted. "Get to the door! We gotta get outta here or we're dead!"

Russ nodded, his brown eyes huge as they crawled toward the exit.

A grating sound started. Wes jerked a look over his shoulder. Whatever was making that noise, it wasn't the B.O.Q. There were a lot of single- and double-story stucco buildings around the huge grassy square. It could have been any—or all—of them.

"Damn," Russ shouted. He got up and scrambled wildly for the door. Launching himself at it, he clung to the doorknob as he twisted it open.

Seconds later, the two men threw themselves out the exit door and tumbled down the metal stairs.

Badly bruised, Wes managed to leap against the last door that led to the first-floor entry. It gave way and Wes tumbled through. He was out! Russ stumbled to the ground beside him.

The grass was damp with dew. As another wave of the quake hit, Russ rolled on top of him, then was swung to the left. A loud crash sounded behind them scaring Wes. As he got to his hands and knees, his fingers digging frantically into the damp grass and dirt for purchase, he saw half of the red brick building across the plaza buckle and collapse inward. Breathing hard, he gasped.

Finally, the quake stopped its deadly undulations. Silence pulsed around Wes for a moment as he sat up, his hands on his thighs. Russ slowly got off his belly, his mouth hanging open, white vapor coming out of it in sharp spurts. Then, as he looked around, Wes heard a series of explosions, too numerous to count, begin off in the distance. Fire vomited upward into the dark night somewhere off the base. The growl of the quake began again. Wes hunkered down, his arms outstretched, his fingers digging into the ground for stability.

"Oh, hell!" Russ shouted. "I don't friggin' believe this!" And he flopped on his belly again, arms spread outward.

The second wave hit, worse than the first. For the next thirty seconds, Wes was flung around on the damp lawn. More marine officers came out of the exit door of the B.O.Q., tumbling and tripping over one another to get clear of the building. In that second wave, Wes saw two of the stucco buildings in the square buckle and crash into heaps. Numerous smaller buildings caved in. Yet, half of them still remained standing including the B.O.Q. There were flashes of fire and explosions as gas lines were broken, showers of sparks from the electrical lines setting them off. Water lines broke, sending water gushing in the square like geysers. Luckily, most of the marines who had been in the B.O.Q. and surrounding buildings were now out. Anyone who lived in Southern California was used to low-grade quakes and knew the drill: get outside as soon as possible. Get into an open area where nothing could fall on you.

Breathing hard, Wes was flung savagely onto his back once again. His mind began to churn with terrifying possibilities. He'd been in California quakes before; the worst was a 6.0 on the Richter scale a year ago, shortly after he'd been transferred to Camp Reed to build highways and bridges for the Corps. But this one…hell, it was a monster in comparison. The damage it had done already was mind-blowing.

He had no idea how this quake registered on the Richter scale, but he knew as he lay there gasping with terror, while looking up at the eerie beauty of the stars in the black sky, that this one was a killer of unknown proportions. And somewhere in his colliding thoughts, Wes realized this was the earthquake that they always talked about, but no one really thought would happen: the Big One that would gut Southern California and cause hundreds of thousands of deaths and billions of dollars in damage, just as the 1906 San Francisco earthquake had totaled that city and population.

As the ground continued to shiver and shake like a horse wrinkling its skin to get rid of pesky flies, Wes slowly rolled over and got to his feet. All around him, people were crying and shouting in panic. There weren't many buildings left standing on the plaza except for the old, solidly built B.O.Q. and about five others around the plaza. On the horizon, fires were lighting up the sky with frightening speed no matter which direction he looked. Most of them seemed to be beyond the base and for that he breathed a small sigh of relief. He hoped the damage at Camp Reed would be minimal compared to the destruction he saw before him. Wes knew there was a nuclear power plant located at San Onofre, at the western edge of Camp Reed and right on the Pacific Ocean. How badly had it been damaged? From an engineering standpoint, there wasn't a question in Wes's mind that it had been. The real question was had the concrete withstood the shattering impact of this killer quake, or was it leaking radiation?

''We gotta get to H.Q.,'' he told Russ, who was a lieutenant in the motor pool, which was their transportation department.

Russ slowly got to his feet. He looked around, shock written on his face. "Yeah.... God, what's happened, Wes? Was this the Big One?"

Grimly, Wes wiped his freshly shaved jaw, which was smudged with dirt and grass stains. "Yeah, I think it was. Let's get over there. It's only a couple blocks away. I hope it's still standing." He looked around the square. The asphalt was buckled and crumbled every few feet, from what he could tell. Without light, he couldn't see that far.

Russ looked at the B.O.Q., awe written on his face. "Look at that, will you?" And he pointed up at it.

Wes turned. "I'm glad it's still standing. We're going to need a place to get some rest after putting in fourteen-hour days of rescue and recovery after this quake."

Russ nodded. Pushing his thick fingers through his mussed blond hair, he muttered, "They're gonna want every available officer over at H.Q. I know General Wilson will put the disaster plan into action."

Grimly, Wes nodded, his gaze roaming over the devastation before him. It was gonna be one helluva long night....

January 1: 0030

Callie stood among the hundreds of Marine Corps officers who had been squeezed into one of the largest rooms at Camp Reed Headquarters. Fortunately, the building had sustained only minimal damage. There was a crack running up one of the stucco walls, but otherwise, the room looked fine. At least the lights were on, courtesy of the gasoline generator outside the building.

Callie saw General Jeb Wilson, the base commanding officer, standing up at the podium. A tall, gaunt-looking man in his midfifties with short black hair peppered with gray at his temples, the general was known around the base as "Bulldog Wilson" because his face was square, his jowls set and his thin mouth always drawn in a tight, downward curve. Tonight he looked even more grim than usual.

The officers milling around in desert cammos or civilian clothes were like tall trees around her and because she was so short, Callie was jostled often. The murmuring voices were strained, and she saw stress and shock in the face of every man and woman in attendance. They were crowded together so tightly that Callie felt suffocated. Either her feet were being stepped on accidentally or someone's elbow was jamming into her back, or she was being pushed because some officer wasn't looking where he was going.

It was now 0030, just a little past midnight, almost three hours after the killer earthquake had struck. The call for all officers to meet at H.Q. had gone out an hour ago over battery-fueled radios and cell phones. Because there was no electricity available at the moment, radios, the normal means of communication, weren't available. Luckily, in this day and age, Callie thought, nearly everyone carried a cell phone.

Many of the officers were in civilian clothes. Their faces were grim, strain and shock clearly etched in their expressions, their voices low and emotional. Callie was the only one in the room from the rescue dog unit, that she could see. Standing on tiptoes, she tried to see if she recognized anyone else in the milling assemblage. There were twenty-two dogs and handlers in her unit, but most of the personnel lived off base.

She lived off base, too, but had been on duty along with Sergeant Irene Anson, who was manning their facility right now. Luckily, the quake had not harmed them and had only opened a crack in the corrugated roof above the kennels. They had checked every dog to make sure it was okay, and thankfully, they were all fine. As Callie craned her neck to get a better view, she saw an officer with short black hair, his eyes grim looking, hold up a set of blueprints before the general at the podium.

Instantly, Callie was drawn to him and instantly she told herself he was far too handsome and would never even take a second look at her. She tried to ignore the officer's gaze as it settled momentarily on hers.

Talk surrounded Callie like the sound of bees buzzing, and she longed to know what was happening. When she heard General Wilson's voice boom out, everyone stopped moving and talking. The room seemed to freeze, every officer's breathing suspended in anticipation of what he might say.

"At ease," Wilson commanded in his deep, rolling tone. He gazed across the crowded room, his brow wrinkling deeply. "I've just gotten off sat com—satellite communications—with the Pentagon. According to the experts, we have just been hit with a massive earthquake here in Southern California—8.9 on the Richter scale. According to the experts, they're calling it the Big One." Grimly, he continued in a rasp, "It has knocked out all electricity, all water and all amenities—pretty much all modern conveniences that civilian communities from central Los Angeles, southward to San Juan Capistrano and west as far as Redlands. The San Andreas Fault has moved six feet in an easterly direction." He rubbed his brow. "Ladies and gentlemen, for whatever reasons, Camp Reed has been relatively untouched, spared by this killer earthquake. As I understand it from my discussion with experts, a minor fault runs in a north-south direction under us. It saved us from major damage as a result. The Los Angeles International Airport is inoperable. All their runways have been destroyed. Nearly every airport, minor or major around it, has also been destroyed. According to the Pentagon, Camp Reed's ten-thousand-foot runways are the only ones available to start bringing in cargo planes with supplies and help. We're still receiving information via cell phone and battery-operated radios from local police and fire departments, but it looks like the entire southern Los Angeles area has been left without any way to get help to its citizens. We are sitting on top of a disaster of untold proportions.

"Luckily, the Marine Corps has worked with the Disaster Preparedness Center, an extension of FEMA, the Federal Emergency Management Agency, whose function is to restore order during just such an event." Wilson held up a thick blue book. "Our S.O.P.—standard operating procedure—is clear. If we are operable, and we are, then what it boils down to in this worst-case scenario is that Camp Reed becomes the only entrance-exit point for medical, fuel, water and food resources for this region."

Callie gasped, as did several others. The magnitude of the general's comments sent a cold chill through her. Camp Reed would become the focus point for all relief and emergency help.

"General," one officer called, raising his hand, "sir, what about the highways? The freeways? Can we—"

Wilson shook his head tiredly. "Captain, every major road has been destroyed. Every freeway. Every bridge has buckled. There is no way for any vehicle to go very far. As soon as dawn arrives, we're looking at going up in Huey helicopters to start assessing the damage. Right now, what I want to do is to break everyone into teams. Colonel Gray, here, has the disaster preparedness plan. Colonel?"

Callie waited as the silver-haired colonel came up to the podium. The urgency of the situation, the shock and terror of the picture being painted, washed like a tidal wave through the room. She stood there knowing that her team of quake rescue dogs would be on the front lines of the military's efforts.

"First off, is there anyone here from our General Rescue?" the colonel asked, craning his neck and looking over the assemblage.

Callie raised her hand. No one could see it because she was five foot five inches tall and surrounded by mostly male marines much taller than she was. Squeezing between the tightly packed officers, Callie called, "Here, sir! I'm here!"

Colonel Gray's eyes narrowed across the crowded room. "Who is here?" he boomed. "I hear a voice. Let her through, gentlemen."

Callie moved forward, twisting and slithering between officers who stepped aside to create a path for her. She approached the podium. "Lieutenant Callie Evans, sir. I'm the X.O. of the dog rescue unit. How can I help?"

Gray smiled thinly. "Lieutenant, I want you to work with Lieutenant Wes James here." He pointed to the man in civilian attire directly to the right of him. "He's a trained civil engineer. We're getting calls for help from fire and police departments all over the L.A. basin. He's in charge of blocking off specific areas into grid coordinates. In each of these areas, I want one of your dogs and a handler. We're going to be putting you on the front lines, Lieutenant Evans. Your people know how to find victims buried in rubble. You go with Lieutenant James now, and create a workable plan. We'll then fly you and your teams out by helicopter to specific trouble zones to hunt for survivors. Any questions?''

Callie gulped. Lieutenant James was the man she was drawn to earlier. Focusing back on the general, she shook her head. "No, sir."

"Good, get going—and be careful out there. Our people are a precious resource and there's no way to replace any one of you if we lose you in this unmitigated disaster...."

"Yes, sir." Callie turned and looked up into the narrowed green eyes of the officer, Wes James. He stood at least six foot tall, and was wearing a pair of black jeans, plus a white shirt that was streaked with grass stains. His black hair was short and uncombed and his face smudged with dirt. She saw the darkness beneath his eyes. As her gaze dropped to his mouth, Callie realized it was set in a thin line against a lot of emotions he was trying to hold back.

She offered him a slight smile of welcome. "Nice to meet you, Lieutenant James. Just call me Callie."

Wes nodded. He hitched a thumb across his shoulder. "Thanks for being here, Callie. Let's go into this side room. I've got my engineers and blueprints set up in there. I'm going to need your help in understanding just what you can do for us."

Despite the urgency of the situation, Wes found

himself staring at Callie Evans. She was tiny, built like
a bird. She was wearing the standard camouflage, des-
ert-colored cammos, a cap over her short, sandy-
colored hair. Her eyes were beautiful, large and intelligent looking. She didn't miss much, Wes guessed as
he created a path through the crowd and led her toward
his makeshift office. Callie followed him, almost tripping on his heels. She was too small in this sea of
men, he thought. A delicate flower among a bunch of
tall redwood trees.

Once they got into the smaller room, Callie saw at
least ten other officers standing around a huge square
table covered with blueprint maps. Most were dressed
in civilian clothes, and it was obvious they had gone
out to party the night away—until the earthquake occurred. They all stopped talking when Wes reentered
the room. He looked around to find her.

"I'm right behind you," Callie assured him in an
amused tone. She knew she was short and could easily
get lost. He managed a slight smile as he looked down
at her, his green eyes growing warm as they perused
her. And then Callie saw them become stern and pro-
fessional once again. For that brief moment, though,
she'd felt the warmth flow straight to her heart, which
pounded briefly in response. What was going on? A
wild giddiness thrummed through Callie, catching her
completely off guard.

"Good, Lieutenant. Stand over there," he ordered,
pointing to one end of the table.

Callie nodded a silent hello to the other officers,
who gave her a deferential nod back. Everyone looked
grim, and the stress was palpable in the room. Her
gaze shifted to Wes James, the officer in charge. As
he spread a roll of maps on the table with his large,

square hands, she found herself liking him even more than when she'd seen him at the colonel's side. There was a brisk efficiency to his motions; and she liked his low-key approach to this situation. He wasn't a drama king like some of the officers she'd seen out in the main room. No, he was quiet, all-business, and had that eaglelike look in his eyes that told her he was capable of handling this assignment. And he was handsome with his oval face, strong chin, and full mouth. When she noticed the laughter lines at the corners of his eyes, she smiled to herself. Obviously he had a sense of humor, and that was good in her book.

After Wes went over the grid scheme for the L.A. basin, pinpointing the largest skyscrapers that had been destroyed according to earlier reports, he began handing out assignments. Callie was able to give him one handler and dog for each of the twenty-two grid areas. He seemed pleased with her efficiency and ideas. Finally, at the end of the process, he wrapped up one roll of blueprints and tucked it beneath his arm.

"Okay, Lieutenant Evans, I'm assigning you to me. We're going to the Hoyt Hotel in southern Los Angeles. It's a fourteen-story structure that, according to the best intel we have, has completely collapsed. It was built in the 1920s, long before earthquake codes were in place, so I know it's going to be one helluva hot spot. According to the local fire department in that area, that hotel was filled to the gills with party goers. It was one of the 'in' spots." He searched her wide, flawless eyes. Her pupils were large and black, her lashes thick and long. Despite her height, or lack of it, he liked the set of her square jaw and the confidence in her demeanor. "You think you can handle it?"

Callie grinned back, once again receiving that

green-eyed warmth from him. "No question about it, Lieutenant James. My dog and I can handle anything you throw at us. We're vets of Turkey, Greece, Colombia and Mexico. This isn't going to be any worse than that." Or maybe it was and Callie just didn't want to believe it.

Satisfied, Wes gestured for her to step ahead of him. "Good enough, Callie. I've got a Humvee outside. I want you to ride over to your H.Q., grab your dog and meet me at the airport. We have a Huey at our disposal to take me and my crew—and you—to our assigned grid area. Make it back as fast as you can?"

Callie nodded. "Yes, sir, I will."

Before she hurried out, she saw Wes give her a slight, tired smile, concern burning in his eyes. This was a man who cared deeply, and that made her feel glad to be working with him. The urgency to help the thousands of victims out there thrummed through both of them, as well as the rest of the officer corps. This was worse than a war: no shots had been fired, but the death toll was going to be horrific, Callie thought.

She moved briskly toward the door at the rear of the room. Her hands were shaking. Her heart was beating hard in her chest as she trotted down the concrete steps to a dark brown and tan desert-camouflaged Humvee that waited for her at the bottom. The sky was just beginning to turn a turgid gray color. Soon, dawn would come. And soon they would all see the devastation that this quake of the century had caused.

As she rode over in the Humvee, down an asphalt road that was buckled in some places, but still functional, she clasped her hands together. Her attention seesawed from details of her duty to thoughts of the green-eyed officer with the warm, caring smile. He treated her as if he liked her—a lot. That was non-sense, of course. She was no looker. She wasn't pretty in any sense. Just a plain Jane. So why had he given her that look? Oh, Callie recognized it well. She'd seen men give it to women thousands of times be-fore—but never to her. Rubbing her hot cheek, Callie wondered if she were dreaming. But with the quake and all, it felt more like she was in the middle of a very bad nightmare, with Wes in the role of the hero she'd always dreamed about meeting. Shaking her head, Callie decided her emotions were skewed be-cause of the quake and the awful disaster that sur-rounded them. That was it: she was in mild shock and completely misreading him.

Still, as she disembarked at her unit's H.Q. and ran toward the kennel to retrieve Dusty, Callie's heart thumped hard in her chest—and it wasn't from fear. No, it was in anticipation of working with Lieutenant Wes James. He liked her and she knew it. And she found that amazing.

Chapter Two

January 1: 0700

As the Huey helicopter landed and Wes saw what was left of the Hoyt Hotel, he couldn't contain his shock. Once a proud, prestigious structure of world renown, the hotel had enjoyed a five-star rating since the twenties. Now all fourteen stories had collapsed in on one another like a house of cards. The asphalt at the intersection where it once stood had been lifted, tossed around and completely destroyed.

Wes opened the door and lifted his hand to tell his team to disembark. Leaping down, he felt the wind blast from the rotors strike him forcefully. He kept one hand on his camouflaged-patterned utility cap and gripped a large case carrying the planning essentials he needed. Head bowed slightly, he turned and saw

Lieutenant Callie Evans release her dog from the travel cage that sat in the crowded area behind the pilots. The golden retriever acted as if nothing were wrong as he leaped off the lip and onto the churned asphalt that had once been a street. Callie had him on a leash as she hurried by Wes and out of the way of the turning rotors.

Next came the supplies that they'd need to set up shop for this grid coordinate. Wes's four enlisted marines climbed out and formed a line to bring box after box out of the bird. The boxes contained tents, food, a first-aid kit, water and latrine supplies. They hurried, for time was of the essence. The door gunner handed out the last of their goods, lifted a hand toward Wes, saluted him and then shut the door. Wes returned the crisp salute and stepped away from the rotor wash.

The engine began to shriek as the pilot powered up the helicopter for takeoff. As the chopper lifted off, Wes held his utility cap on his head until the buffeting stopped. His team—the four enlisted marines, trained in the use of heavy equipment, and Lieutenant Callie Evans and her golden retriever—all looked to him expectantly for orders. Having a woman in the group was soothing to Wes. For whatever reason, he liked having women as part of his team. They seemed to lend a gentler and quieter energy that served to calm him. Right now, however, his stomach was in knots. The destruction was simply beyond anything he could have imagined. Standing with his team, Wes surveyed the area. At six lanes wide, Palm Boulevard had once been one of the busiest streets in southern Los Angeles. Now, the asphalt was so broken up it resembled rocks and pebbles. The once proud palm trees that had lined the route were lying like scattered toothpicks in every direction. Cars had been tossed into one another. Wes saw a policeman and policewoman, on foot, going from car to car in the gray dawn light, their flashlights on as they searched each car for victims.

The city blocks around Palm Boulevard contained upscale one- and two-story suburban houses. This had been a very rich enclave in what was considered the poorer section of L.A. Computer people who had plenty of money had moved in around the Hoyt, and the grid under Wes's direction, a five-mile-square area, included this wealthy suburb.

Looking at the city blocks from the air as they'd come in to land, Wes had noticed only a few houses still standing. He'd seen a lot of people wandering around the chewed up streets, clearly in shock, or standing in small groups looking at the devastation. Very few buildings of any kind still stood; most had collapsed in a shambles. The palm trees that had once inspired the proud moniker of this pricey neighborhood were uprooted and lay everywhere. Expensive foreign cars that had once sat curbside in front of these million-dollar homes were useless. To Wes, it looked as if all the cars had come from an auto graveyard, they were so damaged by the killer quake. Few appeared to be salvageable or drivable.

Grimly, he surveyed his awaiting team as they huddled with him in the cool dawn light. As he lifted his gaze, he saw that the entire L.A. basin was covered with a thick layer of black, greasy smoke. Thousands of fires were burning, the flicker of red-and-yellow flames standing out against the approaching sunrise. The air was choked with dust, debris and throat-clogging smoke from the thousands of burning buildings. Everything was on fire, including one-third of the houses surrounding the Hoyt.

There was no water available to fight the fires because the pipes had been broken by the quake. Fire departments couldn't respond because there were no roads on which to travel. No matter where Wes looked, something was flattened. A posh restaurant on the corner of Palm and Miranda Boulevard was so much debris, with part of the once-proud Spanish tile roof visible on the ground next to it. Red tiles had been shattered into marble-size pieces, mixed within gray-and-black asphalt that had been churned up by the undulating shocks.

Wes forced himself to concentrate on what they had to do. Luckily for the team, there was a construction company less than a quarter mile away, down a small side street. Turning to blond-haired Sergeant Barry Cove, who was in his late twenties, Wes said, "Sergeant, you and Lance Corporal Stevens go down to that construction company and see what you can find. Find the owner, if he's around. If he's not, break into the office and locate keys for whatever equipment he's got inside that cyclone-fence area. Get the following, if you can find it—a cherry picker, because we're going to need a crane and hook to start lifting off the top debris on the Hoyt to try and find survivors. A front-end loader with a bucket would also be useful to us. I want a list of everything he has. If you do locate him, send him to me. Right now, martial law is imposed, and we're the law. What we need, we get. Be diplomatic with him, if he's there. If not, take what we need and leave a note. Bring that equipment up here to the Hoyt." Wes pointed to the wrecked hotel, the ruins of which stood on the corner opposite them.

Sergeant Cove nodded. "Yes, sir!" And the two men started off at a trot down the pulverized street.

Wes glanced at Callie. Though he was feeling shocked by all of this, one quick look at her calm features soothed him somewhat. She was gazing toward the collapsed hotel, her full lips parted, the pain very real in her huge blue eyes. His gaze settled on his other two men, Corporal Felipe Orlando and Private Hugh Bertram.

"Corporal, take Private Bertram with you and canvass the hotel with this map." Wes handed the corporal one of the tightly rolled blueprints from beneath his arm. Orlando had worked with him for nearly a year helping to build roads and bridges at Camp Reed, which was why he and Wes had been specially assigned to the base. Orlando was in his late twenties, married, and the father of three beautiful little girls. At Wes's words, his round coppery face lit up and he nodded briskly and took the map.

"Yes, sir. Where are we putting the H.Q.?"

Wes grinned slightly and nodded to Orlando. They needed a central location to erect tents and store food before they could get busy with the rescue effort. Looking around, Wes saw a car that had been knocked around and smashed by several falling palm trees right in front of the collapsed Hoyt. With a little cleaning, the broad hood of the car could be used as a table.

"Near that blue SUV, Corporal. Once you finish canvassing the hotel, you two can get the tents up, store our supplies and get us operational. That will be our ops center until we can get reinforcement in here." There was a convoy starting out of Camp Reed, heavy trucks and Humvees bringing more tents, MREs— Meals Ready to Eat—and anything else they might need for their stay. This was a field operation, and everyone knew it was going to be a long, arduous one. Supplies that were coming to each grid area would help the local people survive.

"Yes, sir, that looks like a real good area." Orlando turned to Hugh Bertram, a soft-spoken, red-haired Southerner from Georgia. "Come on, Bertram. We got work to do."

The private nodded and saluted and, turning on his heel, followed the corporal, who was trotting toward the hotel.

"That leaves me," Callie said as Wes's warm green gaze settled on her. She offered him a slight smile, feeling as if the sun were shining around her. Throughout the trip in the Huey, she'd sat beside Wes. And she had been privileged to wear a set of headphones hooked up to the intercom. For the entire trip, she was able to converse easily with Wes without having to shout over the roar of the helo.

He hadn't known much about quake rescue dogs or what she did for a living. Callie had filled him in as quickly as possible. Every time he settled his full attention on her, her heart beat harder in her chest. She couldn't explain her reaction. Never had a man's look affected her as much as his did. When his mouth crooked slightly upward at the corners, she felt a little breathless because he was smiling at her. The look that lingered in his sharply assessing eyes made her feel giddy and unsettled at the same time.

Callie decided crazy things happened during disasters and her feelings could only be attributed to her skewed, unreliable emotional state. During times of trauma, most people were in shock and nothing made sense to them. Even though she was a trained rescuer, that didn't mean she could just shut off her emotions and do her job; far from it. Callie had lost count of how many times she'd cried while out on a grid search for victims. Whenever she thought about what the families of the victims went through, she was ripped apart inside. No matter how difficult it made her job, Callie didn't ever want to lose her capacity for sympathy and empathy with others; she would rather suffer the consequences. She knew herself well enough to know that her reaction to Wes was not normal, and probably a symptom of what she called "earthquake mode" emotions.

Maybe Wes was in the same mode; she wasn't sure. As he stood there, tall and straight, his broad shoulders thrown back as he assessed the Hoyt, he seemed rock solid emotionally. Callie was grateful for his quiet, unobtrusive style of command. Right now, with panic rampant, a calm voice and clear thinking were hard to find. She was glad he was in charge of this operation.

"Let's get over to the hood of our H.Q.," he told her wryly. "You need to commence a grid search in that mess, right?" he asked, hooking a thumb toward the pulverized Hoyt Hotel.

Callie nodded and fell into step with Wes. Dusty got to his feet and walked obediently at her side, his body swinging comfortingly against her leg. "Yes, the search grid has to be overlaid on your blueprint of the hotel, and then I'll search each square foot with Dusty. Hopefully, he'll locate someone who's still alive. He'll also pick up the scent of those who have died. He's been trained to whine if the person is dead and to bark if he finds someone alive. If they're dead, I'll put a bright-red plastic square in that place so everyone knows there's a body under the rubble. If we find

someone alive—'' she gave him a hopeful look
''—I'll be radioing down to you and asking you to
bring the construction equipment to try and help us
unearth the person ASAP.''

Wes nodded, absorbing the information. ''I hope
you find a lot of live people. Our number-one priority
here is to recover survivors. Secondly, we're charged
with getting tents, food and water to the people of this
area, as we get supplies delivered here.''

''You've got a tough job ahead of you,'' Callie admitted. Their arms brushed together as they walked.
She moved away slightly to ensure that didn't happen
again. Though she liked touching him, Callie knew it
wasn't appropriate. Still, her heart had pounded a little
harder in her breast when she'd made contact with
Wes. And he didn't seem to mind the accidental touch.
In fact, he'd slanted a glance down at her, a slight hint
of a smile playing at the corners of his mouth.

He snorted softly now. ''I'm a construction guy, not
a rescue trained military officer. I hope I can do justice
to this mess, but I'm not sure.'' He held her gaze.
''And I'm looking to you for help, Callie. You're the
real disaster expert here. I hope you don't mind if I
call you often on the radio and ask for help and guidance when I need it?''

What a delightful surprise, Callie thought, happy
that Wes didn't have trouble relying on her. Usually
that was the case when she was paired up with a man.
''Sure, I'll try to be of help to you in any way possible,
Wes. No one is ever trained well enough for something like this....'' She looked around, sadness enter-
ing her voice. ''No one could *ever* imagine the scope
of this disaster. I mean...I've been in some pretty awful places, especially Turkey, but this is even worse

because it has affected such a *large* region—not just one city, a few square miles. No, this is a horse of a different color, Wes, and frankly, I don't think General Wilson at the base realizes how bad it is—yet. He will.'' Lifting her arm, she gestured toward the suburbs surrounding the Hoyt. "This is a nightmare come true. And we're in it as it's unfolding. All we can do is help each other, hold one another, do a lot of crying when people aren't looking, and pray we make the right decisions."

Wes slowed as they approached the vehicle. "I know," he told her worriedly. "Being a civil engineer, I've worked in a lot of rough environments, and the one thing that strikes me more than any other with this quake is that the people of this basin are not going to have enough water to sustain them."

"Right," Callie murmured unhappily. "Within the week, water is going to be the number one factor in who lives and who dies here. If we can't get enough water in, people are going to start dropping like flies. It will be babies and the elderly first."

"You've seen situations like this before, haven't you?" Wes found himself fascinated with Callie. She seemed easygoing, soft-spoken and very responsible. That told him of the steely emotional strength she must have within her heart. And it drew him. She was a woman of incredible compassion and substance, and he'd never met anyone quite like her in his life.

"Yes," Callie admitted haltingly. "In Turkey, in the major cities we've been in to help locate survivors, the pipes carrying water from the reservoirs were all broken up. At first, we saw people working together to collect water and food. But later they began to steal from one another. The fabric of society comes undone real fast in a life-and-death situation like that, Wes, and we're going to have the same thing happen here. I hope you're prepared for it. People will turn on one another. They'll steal, lie and cheat to get water. And if that doesn't do the trick, then they'll resort to any means to take what they want.'' Her mouth quirked as they stopped at the vehicle. ''Later, they'll start killing for it. That's when the situation turns ugly and dangerous.''

''You carry food and water on you when you search. Were you a target then, too?'' Wes turned and studied her saddened face. For a moment, her eyes glimmered with what he was sure were tears. But she forced them back.

''Oh, yes…we had to have Turkish troops, armed to the teeth, accompany us over the search areas to make sure we didn't get robbed of the canteen we carried…or the food we had in the pockets of our cammies. We didn't have much, but when parents see their children dying of dehydration or lack of food, they'll do anything they have to do to save them.'' She saw his eyes flicker with surprise. ''Earthquakes bring out the best and worst of humanity, Wes. Sometimes you find that, if you scratch the surface of most human beings caught in such a situation, they're savages underneath.''

Tilting her head, she added, ''And then, when you think humans really are mere savages who have no regard for law, order or society, you'll run into a man or woman who is positively saintly. I've seen miracles happen…and it restores my belief in humanity. I'm sure we'll see it here, too.''

''Well, whatever happens, this rescue is not something I'm looking forward to.'' With a grimace, he added, ''I usually work with concrete and steel and it's pretty unemotional.''

''Yeah...'' Callie answered, seeing the pain in his eyes. ''Now you'll be dealing with flesh and blood. A whole 'nother ball game.''

Wes wanted to talk more, but their mission was desperately urgent. Every person buried in the Hoyt Hotel rubble must have a mother, father, brother or sister— some relative frantic with worry. His conscience ate at him. What if someone he loved was buried in that heap of debris behind them? How would he be feeling? Pretty awful, especially if he couldn't determine if that person was dead or alive. All lines of communication were down, with the exception of battery-operated radios and cell phones. And cell phones were only as good as their batteries. There was no electricity to recharge any batteries once they died.

Wes scanned the area, noting a number of people sitting on the edge of the chewed-up boulevard near the Hoyt. They had to be survivors from the hotel. One man was up on the heap of rubble, calling a name repeatedly and looking for someone. ''This is bad. I've never seen anything like this in my life. I just hope I can do a good job of leading this detachment. Do the right thing at the right time, with all the limitations we face.''

Hearing the edge in his deep voice, Callie gave him a compassionate look. His eyes were alive with feelings as he surveyed the Hoyt. ''Yes, it's terrible. But I know in my heart you can do this, Wes. I think you're perfect for it. You're calm, cool and collected.''

Chuckling dryly, he said, ''Bane of the engineer breed, you know? We're numbers and figures people, not very glamorous, exciting or dazzling on a scale of one to ten.''

"You're all those things in my eyes," Callie declared, then stopped abruptly, shocked at what she'd just said. Where had that come from? Feeling heat crawl into her face, she stammered, "I—I believe in you. You're a Marine Corps officer and we get the best training in the world, especially for difficult and changing situational operations." She saw his eyes glimmer at her praise, and it made her feel good.

They continued toward the hotel, and silence fell between them as they surveyed the devastation. Dozens of palm trees lay scattered all around them. The once beautiful Spanish-tile entrance to the Hoyt was gone; there was nothing more than concrete, shattered glass and twisted steel visible now. Though neither of them said it, Callie knew many lives had been lost here. Because the Hoyt was a landmark building, once a gathering place for Hollywood stars, it was always filled to capacity, especially on New Year's Eve. The Hoyt threw one of the grandest, most publicized New Year's parties in California. Anyone who was famous was here for it. Callie stopped herself from thinking any further than that.

When Wes reached the blue, dusty SUV, he used the arm of his coat to wipe off the hood. Dust and rubble flew in all directions. He laid the maps down and unrolled them. Dawn was upon them and the growing light made it easier to read the blueprints.

Looking around him, Wes picked up small pieces of asphalt and placed them on the corners of his maps to keep them flat on the hood of the vehicle. Only then did he notice that Callie was too short to read them.

"Hop up on the bumper here," he said to her, half

in jest, "so you can draw your grid. This is the blue-print of the hotel. It doesn't look like it used to, but you can still work out the parameters so you can begin your search." He handed her a black felt-tip pen.

"Okay, hold on. Let me get my safety gear on." She gave Dusty a hand gesture and the dog sat down. Then she placed a bright-red vest that said RESCUE in bold yellow letters on the front and back. It was actually a flak jacket. If she fell on sharpened objects in the rubble, the jacket would protect her from being pierced and possibly killed. The familiar chafing and weight actually felt good to her as she used the Velcro tabs to close it snugly around her torso.

The bright-orange helmet that hung from a hook on her olive-green web belt was next. She settled it over her camouflage-colored utility cover, which was shaped like a baseball cap, and strapped it into place beneath her chin. Last came the hard leather knee pro-tectors in case she fell in the rubble or had to get down and crawl into tight places. Her knees would take a beating, and the leather absorbed the shock that would be guaranteed if she started poking around between slabs of concrete.

She'd already placed a bright-red cotton garment over Dusty. It held four large pockets, two on each side, holding small bottles of water, as well as human and dog food. Dusty carried roughly ten pounds in the specially made Marine Corps vest. His uniform was edged in bright yellow, with RESCUE DOG printed in large letters on each side. A leather harness was then fitted over it. Callie had also placed thick, soft leather "booties" on his feet held on by Velcro. Dusty was just as susceptible to cuts, gouges and scratches on the sensitive pads of his feet as she was.

Taking off her thick leather gloves, Callie took the pen Wes held out to her. When their fingers met, she felt a brief flash of warmth. Wes was amazingly calm and matter-of-fact, despite all the carnage around them.

Looking up, she saw a group of civilians, some with children in their arms, straggling toward the hotel rubble where Corporal Orlando and Private Bertram were waiting. Wes saw them, too. He knew they would be asking for help. The other part to his mission was to bring order to this chaos. He had a lot of responsibilities to carry out. Engaging the help of the survivors, all of whom were dazed looking, their faces drawn with shock and strain, would be his next order of business. By using the construction equipment, Wes could help locate other victims. But there were many things he couldn't supply the survivors with yet, such as medical help, water and food. All he could do at this point was murmur empty platitudes.

His stomach tightened at that realization. He was an engineer, used to ordering people and equipment around to get things done. But in this situation, everything was difficult. He had neither the people nor the supplies to help survivors as he wanted to. Would they understand that? The expressions on some of their faces were heartbreaking. Some people were bloody, others simply disheveled and dirty. Two children had dust-covered faces, and even from this distance, Wes could see the tracks of their tears through the filth.

Right now, everyone in this neighborhood would be drawn to Wes's camp, for he and his teams were the only authority around. Feeling helplessly overwhelmed with the magnitude of his mission, he looked down at Callie. Wes needed her serenity, gazed almost desperately at those guileless blue eyes that held the hope of the world in them. She was so strong right now; he felt it and sensed it in how she held herself.

As Callie hoisted herself up on the bumper so she could study the map and draw a quick sketch of the Hoyt's rubble, Wes stood back, studying the group approaching. He counted at least ten people, very dirty and dusty, heading slowly toward Orlando and Bertram. The silver-haired man leading them, picked up his pace as Corporal Orlando waved him closer. Wes saw the man's face light up with hope. Standing there, Wes didn't feel the least bit hopeful. The pressure of people's expectations weighed heavily upon him.

He lowered his eyes and watched Callie, hungrily absorbing her profile as she worked over the blueprint. She was like a breath of fresh air compared to the hell surrounding them. A wisp of her sandy hair had slipped free and was lying across her rosy cheek. Although she was no raving beauty, Wes found her face intriguing, especially her wide, soft mouth and those very deep, dark-blue eyes that he didn't think missed a thing.

He found his heart opening, and that shocked him. Every time Callie was near him, or he thought of her or pictured her face, the same feeling overcame him. That scared Wes. The only other time he'd felt like this was when Allison, his fiancée, had been with him. Sadness overwhelmed him momentarily at the thought. She had been a firefighter. She'd died in a ten-story building fire, and his love for her had gone up in those flames, in that black smoke.

Wes had sworn he'd never again be drawn to a woman who did dangerous work for a living…yet here he was once more, with the same kind of tantalizing joy creeping through his heart. It told him he was powerfully drawn to Callie. But she had a dangerous job, dammit, and he simply couldn't love her as he'd loved Allison. No, his heart couldn't stand such a risk again.

Wes found himself wrestling with the past. Looking at Callie, he wanted to forget the stern promise he'd made to find a woman in a safe job. Callie was so beautiful in his eyes. That outgoing warmth she'd automatically established with him seemed to ease all his burdens, made him want to reach out, pull her into his arms and hold her tight until the air rushed from her lungs. That was the effect she had on him.

Trying to shake off the desire and need he felt for her, Wes tried to focus on what she was doing. She'd quickly drawn her grid with expert strokes and was now numbering each area.

"Okay, Lieutenant…" She laughed apologetically. "I mean, Wes…"

"I'd like to use first names when we're alone," he told her in a gritty, intimate voice, stepping close to her. "We're both the same rank. I don't have a problem with it—unless you do?" Sexual harassment was something today's military was working hard to eradicate. The U.S. Navy had a color-coded warning system in place, and since the Marines Corps was technically a part of this service, they employed the same criteria.

"Green" meant that the person receiving the comment felt it was appropriate. "Yellow" meant that the comment or choice of words made the recipient uneasy and unsure of the sender's intentions. "Red" meant that the sender had crossed over the line and the receiver considered the comment or gesture sexual harassment. Ever since the Tailhook 2 scandal in the early nineties, the navy used this three-color system to help everyone understand what was and was not sexual harassment.

Callie glanced over at Wes. She wanted to simply stare at him. His face was strong, and she liked the life that glimmered in his forest-green eyes. "Sure. Callie is fine. It's a green, Wes." Pleasantly surprised by his intimacy and friendliness, Callie knew he was questioning whether she felt his demeanor toward her was harassment. It wasn't; his warmth was welcome under the circumstances. Saying it was a green situation told him that. It also meant she was leaving the door open for a much more potentially intimate relationship with him, but that had yet to be verbalized.

Her heart pounded briefly at her boldness. Could she say it to his face? What a coward she was! Callie felt incredibly drawn to him and unable to stop the energy that seemed to pulse between them when they were together.

She handed Wes the pen and leaped down off the bumper. As she picked up the leather leash, Dusty instantly stood up, his tail wagging. He was ready to go to work.

"Callie is a nice name," Wes murmured. "Kind of old-fashioned. I like it." And he liked her. Heart pounding in fear, he added, "Listen, green can mean a lot of things, Callie. I know we've got this emergency we're handling, but from a personal standpoint, I'm really drawn to you. I'm not promising a forever relationship, but I'd really like to explore what we might have between us. Maybe see where it leads?" Wes gulped unsteadily. His words were brazen, he knew. He saw her eyes widen in shock. And then he saw them glisten. With tears? No. Impossible. Just as quickly, her eyes darkened slightly and whatever emotions he'd seen, were gone. Waiting tensely, because he wanted her to say yes, Wes compressed his lips as he held her stare.

Callie reeled internally from his bold and unexpected suggestion. Was Wes a mind reader? Jumpy and yet anxious to pursue what she felt toward him, she whispered, "Gosh, I thought I was the only one feeling something since we got together."

Giving her a wry smile, Wes said, "It's mutual, Callie. Like I said, I'm not promising forever, but I'd really like to know you better."

Callie was embarrassed and befuddled. Men simply didn't come on to her. She wasn't good-looking. Yet Wes was making it clear he was interested.

Oh, she knew it wouldn't be forever. He was offering her passion, but not his heart; she got that. Because of her past, her lack of male relationships, Callie found his honesty refreshing. He wasn't playing games. Okay, she'd like to know Wes on a passionate and personal level. Callie had never fallen in love, so didn't expect that to happen now. Just the fact that he saw her as *worth* knowing more intimately made her giddy and frightened at the same time.

Wes was standing there, patiently waiting, as he watched her through hooded eyes. Managing a partial grimace she opened her hand and said, "To be honest, just being asked to go for a walk on a beach with a guy, or maybe to dinner, is wonderful…and something I'd like," Callie admitted. Where was her courage coming from? She felt the hard pulsing beat of her heart in her chest. Was it Wes giving her this incredible bravado to express what lay in her heart? Joy threaded through her as she saw him give her a slow smile filled with promise.

"A walk on the beach? Dinner? You bet. That's something you can count on from me, Callie."

Looking past her, Wes suddenly saw a tall, older man in a dark-blue pinstripe suit rapidly approaching them. He was covered with a film of gray dust from the shattered concrete, and his hair was disheveled. Wes had seen the man earlier, climbing around on the rubble of the hotel and calling out for someone. The look on the man's face was one of shock, anxiety, and Wes could see that his eyes were red-rimmed from crying.

"We've got company," Wes warned as he turned to meet the stranger.

Callie watched the man hurrying toward them from the ruins of the hotel. His suit was torn in several places and there were a number of bloody cuts on his massive hands. What made her stomach clench was the terrible look in his eyes and the slash of his mouth that spoke of the pain alive inside him.

"Someone he loves is still trapped in that hotel," Callie warned Wes quietly. Her heart went out instantly to the man. She could sooner stop breathing than protect her emotions from any one of these people who had suffered such a shocking loss. This was the part of her job that Callie never got used to: experiencing the depth of loss in the survivors, seeing the awful anguish in their eyes, just as she saw it now in the man approaching them.

Chapter Three

January 1: 1100

Wes studied the man as he came to a stop in front of them. He was tall and carried himself like an ex-military officer; Wes would recognize that kind of bearing in anyone, regardless of whether the person was in uniform or not. "Yes, sir? How can I help you?"

"I'm Morgan Trayhern," he said, his voice deep and shaken. "Are you the rescue crew for this area?"

"Yes, sir, we are." Wes quickly introduced himself and Callie.

"My wife, Laura, is somewhere in that hotel," he stated, his voice breaking. Battling back tears, he rasped, "I'd gone down five minutes earlier to the bar on the first floor to meet an old friend for drinks."

Rubbing his dirty, unshaved face, Morgan closed his eyes for a moment. When he opened them, he looked directly at Callie. "When the quake hit, everything exploded around us. I made it out the front door just before…before the building collapsed." Morgan turned and looked at the fourteen floors of concrete and steel that were stacked like pancakes on top of one another.

"You were lucky, Mr. Trayhern," Callie said soothingly. She saw that Wes was uncomfortable. He had no training in working with survivors, but he was going to get a crash course in how to talk to them, help them, lend a shoulder for them to cry on.

Wes frowned. "Wait a minute…you're *The* Morgan Trayhern? You were in the Marine Corps?"

"Yes, that's right, Lieutenant James."

Eyes widening, Wes glanced at Callie. "You remember him, don't you? It was part of Corps history to study Morgan Trayhern and the Vietnam War. He's a living legend among us.…" Wes felt his heart contract for this man, who had obviously been digging for his missing wife since the earthquake had occurred. Wes pulled the canteen from his web belt.

"Here, sir. You must be thirsty. Have some water."

Gratefully, Morgan took the canteen and drank deeply. Beads of water collected at the corners of his mouth and his Adam's apple bobbed as he relished the cool liquid.

Callie knew of Morgan Trayhern from the history she'd learned during boot camp. She was stunned and anguished by this turn of bad luck for him. As Trayhern capped the canteen and handed it back to Wes, she asked, "What floor was your wife on, Mr. Trayhern?"

"The fourteenth floor, Lieutenant Evans. Why? Does it make a difference?"

Nodding, Callie said, "Yes, sir, it often can. When floors pancake on top of one another like this, more survivors are found in the upper floors than lower ones, because of the crushing weight." She saw hope suddenly ignite in his bloodshot gray eyes. Holding up her hand, she added, "I can't guarantee you she's alive, sir, but it's hopeful."

Rubbing his face tiredly, Morgan rasped, "It sounds good to me, Lieutenant. Is there anything I can do to help? I've been digging through that rubble all night calling out for Laura. So far, I haven't heard her..." He stopped, his voice choked.

"Voices don't carry well through rubble, sir, so don't take that as a good or bad sign," Callie said softly. She patted his shoulder gently. "Why don't you sit down here by Lieutenant James and rest for a while? Let me and my dog start a grid search. I'll talk to those other survivors near the hotel and try and get information from them before I go up there and begin my search."

Morgan shook his head. "Rest? When my wife might be alive?" He wiped his reddened eyes. "No...I'll keep hunting, calling for her until I know...for sure...one way or another. I won't leave her up there alone. I need her.... I love her and I won't desert her now...."

Trayhern was ready to keel over, but Callie said nothing. She gave him a sympathetic look that she hoped spoke volumes to his torn and bleeding spirit. Giving Wes a warm, heartfelt glance, she pulled on her thick, protective leather gloves and said to him, "I'll see you after I'm done with the first grid."

"Be careful up there," Wes warned in a low tone. "The aftershocks are almost as bad as the original trembler." Suddenly, he was afraid for her. He remembered losing Allison and felt his heart reaching out automatically to Callie, wanting to protect her. She was incredibly courageous to be climbing up on that slippery, sliding stuff. If the rubble moved, it could kill her. A piece of concrete weighed tons and would slide quickly in an aftershock. Anxiety flowed through him. He wanted to reach out, grip her by the shoulder, touch her, but he couldn't...not under the circumstances.

She grinned sourly. "No one knows that better than me, Wes. Thanks for being concerned. See you in a couple of hours..." Callie felt warm again as she saw the look of anxiousness in Wes's eyes. He was genuinely concerned for her safety. As she and Dusty picked their way through the rubble toward the small knot of people opposite the hotel, Callie wondered if Wes's concern was for all people under his command, or something special aimed at her. In her heart, Callie sensed that it was more than just a commander wanting his team to stay safe in such a dangerous, volatile situation. Her head, however, whispered nastily that she was too plain and that no one, especially a handsome officer like Wes James, could ever be interested in the likes of her.

January 1: 1400

The sun was high and the temperature in the seventies as Callie carefully climbed down off the rubble with Dusty. The air was thick with black smoke and dust. Sweat trickled from beneath her uniform as, watching every step she took, she left the first grid area she'd covered. Many survivors were continuing to try and find their loved ones. Watching them was heart wrenching.

Once on the ground, the shattered glass crunching beneath her booted feet, Callie found her spirits rising as she rounded the end of the building and saw a cam-ouflage-painted Humvee parked next to the blue SUV where Wes had set up his temporary headquarters. About an hour ago, a marine Super Sea Stallion heli-copter had landed nearby at a park, where a Humvee had been off-loaded, along with crucial supplies Wes would need. From Callie's vantage point, she saw that the Humvee was going to be useless. There were no highways to traverse. Although the Humvee was sup-posed to be an all-terrain vehicle, nothing would go far with all the glass and twisted steel lying around. The tires would be slashed in no time. Callie saw that Wes probably realized that, because he'd made a desk out of the hood of the Humvee instead.

All the tan-colored tents had been erected in a row where a sidewalk had once existed. The good news was that Wes's men had gotten the cherry picker and other construction equipment, and had already begun to slowly remove debris in order to try and find sur-vivors. The noise and growl of the heavy engines, the creaking of the crane arm, the sound of steel cables being wrapped around huge slabs of concrete all com-bined in what to Callie's sensitive ears was a musical cacophony.

Wes felt a warm unexpected tug at his heart at the sight of Callie approaching with Dusty. He straight-ened from studying the maps of the surrounding area he'd laid out on the hood of the Humvee. A wave of heat rushed through his body when he saw Callie was all right. His pulse pounded as he perused her. She'd been out of sight all morning and early afternoon, working on the other side of the hotel. As she reached him, a slight smile pulled at the corners of his mouth.

"Don't take what I'm going to say the wrong way," he told her conspiratorially as Callie halted near him at the Humvee, "but you're a sight for sore eyes."

Instantly, heat shimmered up Callie's neck and into her face. Avoiding Wes's warm, engaging look, she dropped her gaze to her dust-covered boots. "Uh, thanks... But I must look like a fright right now." She managed a short, nervous smile and gave Dusty the hand signal to sit. Placing the leash on the ground, Callie removed her helmet, as well as her vest, which was now chaffing her flesh because she was sweating. Then she shrugged out of her heavy cammo jacket. The cold morning chill had dissolved into a warm winter day.

Wes tried to keep from staring at her. Callie was built like a slender bird beneath all that heavy military garb. As she stripped down to her olive-green T-shirt and cammo pants, he had a hell of a time looking away. The inconstant breeze ruffled her damp, blond-streaked hair, and he was almost relieved when she put the bright orange vest back on and resettled the cap on her hair.

"Was that a yellow flag?" he asked her seriously. Yellow meant that a man had overstepped his bounds, was getting too familiar with a woman, and she was feeling uncomfortable with such attention. Wes couldn't help himself; the words just flew out of his mouth. Her innocence and unawareness of her own attractiveness as a woman was throwing him for a loop.

He watched her soft mouth curve upward. She was so damned kissable. Did she know that? He wanted to know everything about Callie, but now was certainly not the time for private, intimate conversation. How could he have been at Camp Reed for a year and never run into her? That stymied him completely, because if he had seen her, he'd sure as hell have pursued her passionately and relentlessly. Of course, he would have been careful to keep his heart out of the equation. He couldn't risk his emotions again.

"No...it was a green," she assured him shyly. Taking the canteen from her belt, Callie knelt down in front of Dusty, cupped her hand and poured a little water into it. Instantly, the dog began eagerly lapping it up.

Just being near Wes, she felt the force of his desire for her. Oh, it was a giddy, terrifying experience. But one that Callie was absorbing like a thirsty sponge.

Wes stood there, hands on his hips, watching Callie. She had to be dying of thirst, yet she was giving her dog a drink first. That said something good about her, in his book. "I was worried about you," he said, looking toward the Hoyt and studying it from beneath furrowed brows. Specters of Allison being on the roof of the burning structure, and then the roof caving in and killing her and her partner, haunted him. The Hoyt reminded him of that terrible day in his life. "I didn't see you at all. When that aftershock hit at 1200, I sent Private Bertram around the hotel to see if you were still standing."

Touched by his concern, Callie continued to dribble water into her cupped palm until Dusty had gotten his fill. "I'm used to aftershocks, Wes. They're a part of our trade. It knocked me off my feet, but I was okay." Callie looked up at him and melted beneath his thoughtful green stare. "How are you doing down here? And how is Mr. Trayhern doing? I see the survivors who were around this morning are gone. You must have handled their situation okay?"

Wes drowned in her wide blue eyes. He wanted to find time to spend quietly in Callie's calm company. "He's asleep in the back of the Humvee here," he said, hitching a thumb across his shoulder. Wes had long ago shed his jacket, and was dressed in his olive-green T-shirt and cammies. "He was keeling over with exhaustion. I talked him into having an MRE and some water. As soon as he finished eating, he fell asleep. I'm leaving him there until he wakes up on his own."

"Did he find his wife yet?" Callie asked, standing and then taking a deep draft of the water herself. "He was working on the other side of the hotel from us, so I couldn't hear or see anything going on."

Shaking his head, he said, "No...the guy's beside himself. When the helicopter brought this Humvee, they brought a navy corpsman along with it. I managed to talk Mr. Trayhern into getting his hands taken care of. He's been ripping through piles of concrete and glass, trying to locate her, and his hands were looking like so much ground meat." Wes didn't add that if it had been Callie instead of Laura Trayhern trapped somewhere in that hotel, he'd have done the same thing Morgan was doing. He wouldn't allow a loved one to just lie there alone, without help. Just as abruptly, Wes reminded himself that he desired Callie, he didn't love her. No, love was far too great a risk to take with a woman in a dangerous profession. Yet Wes felt a wave of warmth when she looked up at him again.

"Maybe we can loan him a pair of our leather gloves?" Callie said, putting the canteen back into place on her web belt. Her stomach growled and she knew she and Dusty had to eat before they continued the search.

"Yeah, good idea." Wes grinned a little as he watched the equipment working in the distance. "You have a lot of common sense, Callie. We need you around here. I'm sure I can scare up a pair of gloves for him when he wakes." Damn, it was hard not staring at her. Wes's fingers positively itched as he thought about removing her cap to run his hands through her short, golden hair. Would it feel like warm silk? How badly he wanted to find out.

She nodded and opened one thigh pocket of her cammos. Reaching deep into it, she found a couple of protein bars and pulled them out. "Common sense is what I live on during this kind of work, Wes. It's feet on the ground, not head in the clouds. One wrong move and Dusty or I could be history." She handed Wes one of the foil wrapped bars. "Hungry?"

The word stuck in her throat. Callie was hungry for Wes. The moment she'd come over to him, she'd seen that officer's look disappear, to be replaced by the intense gaze of a hunter—trained on her. The sensation was uplifting. Scary. Beautiful. And Callie wanted more of it…and him.

He took the protein bar. "Thanks. They say the Huey is going to be bringing in a supply of MREs for us shortly. We gave all we had to the survivors. They'd been without food or water since the quake. I couldn't stand to see the starved look in the kids' eyes, you know?''

Taking a deep breath, Callie said, "You have a soft heart, Wes. It's dangerous to let all your supplies go. What if that Huey has engine trouble? Or the supplies ran out completely? Do you have *any* food or water for your team?''

"A little," he said. "And I hear you." Rubbing his face with his hand, he muttered, "I guess I'm not used to seeing hungry and thirsty American people. It was the kids that got to me. I'm guilty as charged. I've learned my lesson.''

"I understand. The kids *always* grab you by the throat and never let you go." She reached out and briefly touched his darkly tanned arm, her fingers grazing the dark hair on his forearm. Because Wes was a civil engineer by trade, Callie imagined he loved being outdoors in any kind of weather. His flesh felt damp as she trailed her fingers along it, probably due to the fact that the sun was high and it was hot. His eyes glimmered when she touched him, and a thrill moved through her, erasing some of the strain and dread that always haunted her during rescue operations.

"Yeah," Wes griped good-naturedly, "I'm a sucker for a kid. You learned to carry this emotional stuff a long time ago, didn't you?''

He found himself amazed by Callie. She was so different from most of the women he'd ever known, even Allison. There was something refreshing about Callie. She didn't play games. All she knew how to be was honest, and that made him want to explore her fully—even more deeply than he'd wanted to at first. His injured heart warned him that all he could feel for her was desire and passion. That was it.

Callie grinned and leaned against the front of the Humvee, peeling back the red-and-silver foil wrapper of her protein bar. "Oh, yeah…" Digging in her other pocket, she produced a handful of dry dog bones, which she gave to Dusty, who was staring up attentively. He quickly gobbled them, and Callie gave him another handful.

Wes leaned against the hood, leaving a foot of space between them. The temperature was rising into the sixties. The sky was a freakish mix of gray, black and yellow with the sun appearing blood-red through the pollution caused by the quake and continuing fires.

"How long have you been stationed at Camp Reed?" He munched gratefully on the tasty protein bar. Again, Callie's sense of sharing, of caring for others, struck him as a wonderful attribute.

"Two years. Why?"

He smiled a little and savored her closeness. At least she didn't move away from him. "I've been here a year building roads and bridges on the base. The ones that have been here were forty or fifty years old—well overdue to be replaced and modernized. I was just wondering why I never saw you over at the Officer's Club. I thought I'd danced with every woman on the base. I have a reputation as a party goer when I'm not working. And pretty women don't escape my attention. Or…are you married?" He held his breath as she turned, and was surprised to see shock written across her face. Had he overstepped his bounds? Wes hoped not.

"Me? Married?" Callie laughed heartily. "No… I'm not married. I wouldn't have given you the green light if I had been. And the O Club? I never go there." She didn't add that she had heard of Wes. He ran with a group of single officers that liked to party a lot. While searching for survivors all morning Callie had combed her memory, trying to remember where she'd heard his name. Now she knew. Yes, Wes was a party animal, no doubt about it. They called him the ''golden boy'' over at the O Club. Groupies from off base had spoken glowingly of him—what a great dancer he was, and how they loved his drop-dead good looks. Because Callie had finally placed Wes and his party-animal reputation around Camp Reed, she was even more perplexed as to why he'd be interested in pursuing her. Still, the idea made her feel breathless and more than a little excited.

''But…why?'' Wes demanded. ''The O Club has a great dining room. There's dancing on Friday and Saturday nights. I'm always over there on weekends and I've never once seen you.''

Callie finished off her protein bar and began a second one. Climbing around like that for hours on end burned up a lot of energy. ''Yes…I remember that you are well known for partying over there on weekends.'' She grinned and added, ''I'm kinda shy, Wes.''

''You dance, don't you?''

''Well…sure, I love to dance. But…'' Her heart flip-flopped as he smiled boyishly and held her gaze. There was such genuine warmth and sincerity emanating from him that Callie didn't know what to do or how to handle this intimacy.

''But what? You look like you could dance all night.''

Callie avoided his probing look. ''Yeah…well, I just don't go over there.…''

''Why not? How could I meet someone like you if you don't come out of hiding?'' he teased. Now that he'd found her, he was stymied by her behavior. She was young—in her twenties like him. Everyone he knew who was single showed up at the O Club. It was a place to meet people and have fun. And he didn't mind the reputation he'd accrued. He liked living life. He liked women.

Waving her hand, Callie muttered, "Oh, I just don't think I fit in, I guess...." Her voice fell. "No...I don't fit in."

Wes heard hurt in her softened tone. He saw Callie's arched brows wrinkle as she looked away from him. Sensing something was wrong, he tried to step more carefully this time.

"You're single. You're in your twenties. You're pretty. Why wouldn't you be at the O Club?"

Her, pretty? Callie snapped her head upward to meet his gaze. His face had lost a lot of its officer's facade. The man she was looking at now was open and vulnerable. She was ready to toss him a blithe comment, but it stuck in her throat. Swallowing convulsively, Callie nearly choked on the protein bar. Wes thought she was pretty? It had to be a line. A come-on. There was no way on earth she was the least bit pretty.

"I'm as much of a plain Jane as you get," she managed to answer in a strangled tone. "Ever since I can remember—through school and college—boys have avoided me. I'm not pretty, Wes. Not even close. I used to go to dances with my girlfriends because they forced me to. But I got tired of sitting against the wall waiting for someone—anyone—to ask me to dance. I got the message."

Wes heard the raw hurt in Callie's strained voice. It took everything he had not to reach out, brush her cheek and tell her that she was not plain at all. Just the way her lips pursed and she avoided his look told him plenty. Feeling her pain caught him off guard. There was no way Callie should have suffered like that. She was an incredible person, courageous and responsible.

"Well," he rasped, "there's the problem."

Callie glanced at him. Wes seemed untouched by her opinion of her plain looks. He had placed his large, square hands on his narrow hips and was looking at the hotel. There was a slight hitch to one corner of his generous mouth.

"What problem?" she asked.

Cocking his head, Wes held her upraised gaze, which was riddled with shyness and hurt. "They were boys. What the hell did they know? Any man worth his salt would see you differently, believe me." And how Wes wanted her to know that! He saw his compliment strike Callie like a bomb going off. Eyes widening and lips parting she turned away from him.

His heart thumped with regret. The last thing he wanted to do was hurt this brave, courageous woman. *Damn.*

"I'm as plain as that slab of concrete over there," she told him emphatically, leaving no room for disagreement. She pointed at a huge portion of flooring sticking out of the flattened hotel.

"Not to me, you aren't," Wes said as lightly as he could. He bit back a lot of questions. Who had made Callie think she was unattractive? He wished they had time…lots of time, so that he could sit down and tell her how each inch of her was beautiful in his eyes. But time was not on their side. Already he saw more civilians making their way toward the Humvee.

"I'll bet you think I'm giving you a line about how pretty you are. Don't you?"

Frowning, Callie said, "Yeah, I do."

"I'm not." Frustrated, he stood there looking at her squared jaw and set lips. "Listen, we're not done with this conversation," Wes warned her in an intimate growl as he stood up and leaned over so that only she could hear him. "In my eyes, my heart, you're an angel. Your care for others makes you beautiful to me. Okay? Okay. Good. I'm glad you agree. Now, I gotta do some more calling on the radio. Are you going up on grid two?"

Callie felt overwhelmed by his intensity. She nodded and watched as Wes picked up the radio that sat on the hood of the Humvee. "Yes…"

"Just be careful. Remember I want that first dance with you back at the O Club at Camp Reed when this disaster is over. And I'm already working on a picnic basket for that walk on the beach you suggested earlier. Promise?"

Chapter Four

January 2: 2100

Laura Trayhern forced herself not to panic. She lay in the dark, on her back, shivering. All she could hear was the grating, shifting sounds every time the earth trembled with aftershocks. The pain in her right leg was constant and in part, it helped her keep clarity of mind. All she could feel was rubble around her as she slowly swept her right arm outward in an arc. There was a tremendous rush of wind from her right that chilled her. Because she was unable to move, it was impossible to stay warm. She lay in the dark, the concrete cold and sucking away what heat she had.

How long had she lain here? The last thing she recalled was hearing a frightening, roaring sound, as if a jumbo jet was bearing down on the hotel and coming right through the window of their penthouse suite. And then the hotel had convulsed as if something as large as a plane had hit it. Laura closed her eyes and tried to lick her dry, chapped lips. Only bits and pieces of what came next were clear to her. She remembered that hellish roar. And being knocked off her feet and crashing to the floor of the bathroom where she had gone to put on her makeup. She was still in her plum-colored wool suit and had just started to unbutton it when the earthquake struck. Morgan had left minutes earlier to meet an old Marine Corps friend in the bar on the first floor for a quick drink before he came back to take her to the New Year's Eve party in the Jungle Room.

How was Morgan? Was he dead? A sob escaped Laura. She gripped a piece of what she thought might be concrete, the sharp, jagged edges biting into her palm. No! He couldn't be! He just couldn't! She loved him too much. Too much. The years hadn't dulled what she felt for him only heightened what they had together, made it even more exquisite and beautiful.

The Hoyt Hotel had been one of Morgan's favorite haunts early in his career as a Marine Corps officer, and he'd come to this hotel to party often. He'd been stationed at Camp Reed for three months before shipping out for Vietnam, and this hotel had been a refuge for him. And now… Once again the ground trembled around her. Laura held her breath. Every time there was an aftershock, panic seized her. She could hear the grating and grinding as steel and concrete shifted around her. Would it slide enough to crush her? When she'd regained consciousness, Laura had tried to pull her right leg free, but discovered it was trapped. Her left leg was hitched up on top of the rubble that had her right one pinned, but she could at least move it. And her arms were free. But she couldn't sit up. No, the space she was trapped in seemed to be the size and shape of a coffin, judging from the exploration she'd done with her hands. There was lots of room to her right. She'd rolled as far that way as she could, but the pain in her right ankle when she shifted prevented her from doing much exploring in her dark cave.

Dust sprinkled down constantly from above. Coughing violently, Laura pressed her cut and bloodied hands against her chest. Oh, how she needed a drink of water! Her mouth felt like cardboard.

Her heart veered to Morgan. Was he dead? Had he died in the elevator on the way down to the bar to meet his friend? Or had he died in the bar itself? No! She couldn't allow her mind to go there. She just couldn't.

Somehow, Laura knew she had to escape. But there was so much rubble around her. She'd picked up a lot of the broken concrete and moved it to one side. The roof of her cave was low, yet she could roll from her back to her side. If there was wind, that meant there might be an escape route to the outside. Her mind spun with ideas and ways to get free. But every time she tried to pull her right leg in any direction, pain shot up it, making her lose consciousness for minutes at a time. She had no idea if she was bleeding from her leg injury. There was no way to lean down to touch it. The whole lower leg was numb below her knee, so she had no idea of the extent of damage.

Laura thought of their children, and pain of a different sort blazed through her. She couldn't die! They needed her! What must they be going through? She knew an earthquake had struck. Did their children know she and Morgan were involved? That she was trapped? Did they think their parents were dead? Laura's heart thrashed with such agony she began to sob. Despite her anguish, no tears came, because she was so dehydrated.

Did Jason know? Had the authorities contacted their oldest son at the naval academy in Annapolis? Oh, dear God, why had Morgan argued with Jason before they'd left town? Jason had stormed back to the academy after his short visit home, angry and upset. Closing her eyes, Laura's hands curled into fists against her breast. That was the last meeting between her husband and her son, a hot and angry one. Morgan was worried that his firstborn was throwing away his burgeoning military career, refusing to study hard and make the good grades he needed in order to stand out at the academy and groom favor from the higher-ups.

Jason had accused his father of constantly expecting him to shoulder the load of Morgan's own past—the accusation of treason that had plagued him when he'd returned to the States after Vietnam. It was as if Jason felt the burden of dispelling lingering doubts about the family name and upholding the long history of honor. Well, Jason was tired of Morgan pressuring him and tired of his classmates expecting heroic things from him because he was the son of a living hero. At Annapolis, Morgan Trayhern was a legend. He was held up as a model of what a true marine was all about. Most marine officers went through the naval academy. Morgan had. And now Jason was expected to, also. Only Jason was tired of trying to live up to his father's illustrious legacy. He could never be his father, never live up to the expectations Morgan had of him. Laura tried to get Morgan to understand that, but Morgan's determination where his son was concerned was fueled by a two-hundred-year family legacy in which the first born son went into military service. Laura had seen the identity crisis building in her son. Intuitively, she knew he didn't want a military career and he was going through all the motions to appease his father. All Laura could do was helplessly watch as neither father nor son could truly separate themselves from the Trayhern family heritage. She felt Jason was at a breaking point but she couldn't do anything about it. She wasn't sure what the pressure was going to do to Jason. Worse, what actions he'd take to rid himself of his father's expectations. Though Morgan loved Jason, he refused to see his son as an individual. That was the crux of the problem.

Sighing raggedly, Laura opened her eyes. No tears came, but her heart was breaking. Rightly or wrongly, Morgan had pressured their son to be all that any young man could be expected to live up to. Jason couldn't be his father. He couldn't be a legend, something even his classmates seemed to expect of him. No child could possibly carry that kind of weight on his shoulders and survive. Laura knew that Morgan had only dimly begun to realize that their son had to be his own person, not a replica of Morgan.

Jason had stormed out of their house, caught a bus to Anaconda and then a flight back to Annapolis five days earlier than his leave dictated because he couldn't stand the fights he and his father had gotten into during his stay.

"Oh, Jason…my poor little boy…" she whispered tremulously. What must Jason be feeling now? He'd known that they were going out to Southern California for New Year's. He knew they'd be at the Hoyt Hotel. How was he handling this awful news? Laura pressed her hands against her closed eyes, her elbows brushing against the ceiling of her coffin. Somehow, she had to get out of here. Somehow, she must survive—for their children's sake. But how?

January 2: 2100

Callie staggered with exhaustion as she carefully climbed down off the heap of debris. It was completely dark, except for the thousands of fires dotting the landscape as far as the eye could see. Dusty hopped down to the ground, his tail wagging. She followed, leaping the last couple of feet, flashlight in hand, and then patted his head gently.

"Good boy. Let's go see if Wes got those MREs in. I'm starving and you must be, too." They walked around the perimeter of the ruined hotel. Callie tried to keep her emotions at bay. They'd searched five grids today and had found no sign of life. They'd discovered twenty dead bodies so far. As she walked tiredly down Palm Boulevard, she saw that much had changed with their H.Q. since noon today. She'd been working the backside of the massive hotel, so hadn't seen what was going on with Wes and his group until now.

There were lights—bright lights—standing on steel stilts and powered by a gasoline-fed generator nearby. She saw Wes bending over a blueprint on the hood of the Humvee, talking with two of his men. Instantly, her step became lighter. Her heart hammered briefly. Just seeing Wes infused her with a happiness that drove away the sadness she carried. Nearby, she saw the two bulldozers and buckets. A number of civilians, people who had lived in the area, most likely, were also huddled around the Humvee, talking animatedly to Wes. Callie's heart expanded with such wonderful emotions that she felt suffused by a warmth that loosened the cold knot in her stomach. Finding dead people might be a part of her job, but it was the worst part of it, and over time, Callie had begun to feel like a wrung-out dishcloth. She felt so depressed by the fact that Dusty had found no one alive that now she clung to anything that looked halfway uplifting or positive. And seeing Wes was a huge high for her.

As she got closer, she recognized Morgan Trayhern. Someone had given him a marine cammo jacket. It was cool tonight, in the fifties. The sky was turning cloudy, and Callie wondered if it would rain. That wouldn't be good; it would only make what they had to do more miserable to endure. Right now, there were few places to hide from the rain, few homes standing. Everything had been flattened in the quake. There was no shelter for anyone except for tents that had been helicoptered in during the day. Now tents doted the lawns of nearby homes, forming a small tent city around the destroyed Hoyt Hotel. No, they didn't need rain on top of all of this.

Callie saw the grim look on Morgan's face as he stood next to Wes. The older man's hands were swathed in white dressings. In one hand, Morgan held the pair of leather gloves he'd worn. All day he'd been digging and searching for his wife, Laura. From time to time, Callie had heard him calling for her. It was all so sad. Callie knew from experience that few people would survive this hotel collapse. The man's eyes burned with a look of anguish that made her wince.

How much he loved his wife! Callie wished that she might someday meet a man who loved her as fiercely as Morgan loved Laura. That kind of love, she knew, was in short supply nowadays. People didn't know how to make a relationship work; at the first sign of trouble, they usually bailed out and divorced. That's not what she wanted. She wanted something like Morgan Trayhern had with his Laura, a marriage where love deepened over time. Callie had no doubt that Morgan and Laura had their ups and downs. But they loved one another enough to persevere, work through the bad spots and keep growing as individuals within the framework of their marriage.

As Callie approached, the group broke up and went back to their assigned jobs. She saw Wes twist to look in her direction. Unaccountably, her heart thumped once, hard, in her breast. She smiled at him tentatively, noting how the garish lights emphasized the strong lines of his face. As she met his gaze, his officer's facade melted and a smile shone through. A smile for her. It lifted Callie's flagging spirits even higher.

"Any luck?" Wes asked, rolling up the plans. Callie looked disheveled and exhausted. Her face was covered with smudges of dust and dirt. Yet it was so good to see her again. There wasn't an hour that went by when Wes didn't stop what he was doing and look at the hotel, wondering how she was. When she was working on the opposite side, he couldn't see her, and that ate at him. They'd suffered several aftershocks, and she was the last person he wanted to see hurt.

His pulse bounded as she smiled softly up at him. Callie reached up just then, unsnapped the helmet she wore and took it off. Because she still had her thick gloves on, the chin strap slipped between her fingers and her helmet bounced a couple of times on the ground near her boot. Wes leaned down and retrieved it for her.

"No luck," Callie said quietly, taking the helmet from him. "Thanks…"

"You look tuckered out." For two days now, Callie had worked relentlessly, in nearly eighteen-hour shifts, in her search efforts on the Hoyt. The only time she came down off the rubble was to feed herself and Dusty. Those were precious, stolen moments to him. But even then, Wes was usually inundated by civilians wanting help or asking questions.

He reached into the opened driver's side door of the Humvee. "We just got a fresh supply of MREs in this afternoon." He grabbed one and handed it to her. The packaged meals could be eaten after hot water was added, making them highly practical in such chaotic times. The food was better than nothing, but a long way from a gloriously hot, homemade meal. But that probably wasn't going to happen for them in the coming days.

Callie took the package. "Great. Lotsa MREs mean more choices. I'm tired of macaroni and cheese." She grinned as he smiled.

"How are *you* doing?"

"I'm beat. How's it going down here? I see the civilians starting to create their own tent city?" she asked as she carefully placed her helmet on the hood so it wouldn't roll off. Callie knew that Camp Reed H.Q. was trying to create a constant stream of incoming supplies to the grid areas in the Los Angeles basin. That meant the helicopter crews were flying long hours to keep food, water, medicine and other supplies funneling slowly but surely into these devastated communities. Without the chopper supply lines, people would already be rioting, starving, dying from lack of water. It wasn't the best of all worlds, but it was better than nothing. She knew from talking to Wes this morning that there was a huge effort underway to create dirt roads into the basin with bulldozers from the Marine Corps facility. Once roads were in place, huge diesel trucks filled with a lot more supplies could reach those who needed them the most.

"Good, under the circumstances," Wes murmured. "We're lucky because we've got construction equipment. I talked to the owner of the outfit down the street and he's got a small crane. We're going to put it into operation later tonight. Our main problem is gasoline, but the owner, Bob Dorffman, has a huge underground tank with ten thousand gallons, so we're set that way. Somehow, it survived the quake. Don't ask me how, but it did. That gasoline is going to be like gold in the future."

Callie smiled a little. "That's great. And yes, I've seen people kill for a gallon of gasoline over in Turkey. Do you have a sentry guarding it yet?"

"No…not yet. I'm getting more personnel in tomorrow. I've requested two sentries, and they'll do twelve-hour shifts over in that gas storage area."

She looked up at the lights. "Good. You're thinking right, because these people will be desperate for protection sooner or later." Callie looked around. "Any chance of some hot water?"

Grinning, Wes nodded. "Yeah, Bob's got a hot plate set up over there." He pointed across the street. "We found a huge steel pot, and Corporal Stevens found a leak from a water main that had been pushed above ground by the quake. He's keeping us supplied with water and is in charge of boiling it. Boiled water means no germs, so we can safely drink it and make MREs with it, too. Right now, the civilians are coming over to get the water and things are moving along pretty smoothly in that area.'' With a grimace, Wes added, ''Of course, if one of those aftershocks busts up the underground water pipe, then we'll go into an emergency situation, because there is no other water source around here.''

''We're lucky to have that pipe,'' Callie said. ''And I wouldn't count on it giving us water in the future. The aftershocks around here are hitting 6.0, from the feel of things.''

''Yeah,'' Wes said unhappily, ''I agree with you. I'm feeling helpless, Callie. If we lose this water source…well, so far, there's five hundred survivors we're dealing with, and I don't know what we'll do if that happens.'' He took off his cammo cap and ran his fingers through his hair, frustrated by that very real possibility.

''The Hueys could possibly carry in a load of water,'' she suggested.

''Yes, they're already doing that for other grids in the basin.'' He gestured broadly. ''I've talked to Logistics about getting a plastic pool liner set up so water can be dumped in it, but I'm not hearing that there are any more available. The support people at Camp Reed have an emergency call out for liners that are used by volunteer fire departments, and they'll get them.''

''It's a question of when,'' she murmured, ''and if it will be soon enough.'' Though there were many concerns to be dealt with still, Callie cherished the moment standing and talking with Wes. He looked exhausted. In part, she knew, it was simply from lack of sleep, as well as all the demands of leading the detachment. The other, more insidious and tiring facet was the emotional toll this disaster took on everyone. No one was immune to the suffering. And it was only going to get worse. Callie knew firsthand how the general panic would escalate sharply after the first three days. Food and water resources might hold out for that time, but after that, things became dicey. The look in Wes's eyes told her that he was more than a little aware of the crowd mentality, and that when, not if, survival mode kicked in, the most placid civilians could become an unruly, perhaps even savage mob, ready to steal, lie, cheat and maybe kill to get supplies in the tents nearby. The team was armed, but Callie knew that not one of the marines wanted to hurt anyone, especially desperate civilians. No, it was going to get a lot worse as the nightmare continued to unravel. She was sure Wes's crew was equally tired and knew the potential problems to come, as well. In a disaster like this, there was little time to rest for those on a rescue team.

Wes could see that Callie was punch-drunk with fatigue. He took her MRE from her and gripped her elbow. "Come on," he urged her quietly, "come and sit down over here and I'll make up this meal for you. You're in need of a little care right now yourself...."

Callie was touched by his generosity and sensitivity to her plight. Never one to complain of how she felt, she realized Wes had seen her own exhaustion and wanted to help. Callie felt the strength of his hand on her elbow as he guided her across the rubble-strewn street. "I've got to feed Dusty first," she protested.

Giving her a slight smile, Wes said, "Does he eat MREs, too? They didn't bring any dog food in on that

Huey flight—just a lot of crates of MREs.'' He guided
her to a section of the curb that had survived, next to
their makeshift kitchen arrangement. Locating a beat-
up tin cup, Wes opened the food packet, dipped the
cup into the boiling water and poured steaming liquid
into the pouch.

Callie sat and Dusty laid at her feet, his pink tongue
lolling out the side of his mouth. ''Yes, he can. Actually, out on a site, he'll eat anything that doesn't
move.'' She dug into her thigh pocket and took out
the last of the dried dog biscuits. Leaning down, she
placed them before Dusty, who eagerly lapped them
up. The hard physical work they did required they eat
on a regular basis, but Callie hadn't eaten since noon
today, and it was now 9:00 p.m. She watched gratefully as Wes prepared the MRE for her. When it was
done, he handed it to her, along with plastic utensils.

''I'll get one for Dusty,'' he told her. ''You just
stay put.''

Too tired to speak, Callie saw that she had the
chicken and noodles meal. Dusty was giving her a
longing look. He could smell the luscious odors drifting out of the opening.

''You'll get yours in a minute,'' she promised him
with a pat on his shoulder.

Spooning a bite of food into her mouth, Callie tried
not to think of possible survivors somewhere in that
heap looming darkly above them. In the distance, she
saw the crane swinging into place, its huge steel legs
extended so that it wouldn't tip over and kill someone
when lifting a heavy concrete slab.

Meanwhile the bulldozers and front-end loaders
were working away relentlessly. At the moment one
was trundling loudly down the chewed up boulevard,

heading for the area Callie had just covered. Instead of tearing into the hotel ruins indiscriminately, they waited until she and Dusty had thoroughly searched a grid. If no survivors were found, they would begin to dismantle the hotel to locate bodies of the dead and bring them to the surface.

It was gruesome work. So far, with her and Dusty's help, twenty bodies had been recovered. Wes had started a morgue of sorts on the other side of the hotel, near where she had been working. He didn't want people to see the bodies, and tried to keep the area sealed off from the populace. The odor, however, was becoming worse. As Callie worked the rubble, the breeze would often bring the smell of decay to her and she would gag. Between the dryness of the concrete dust plugging her nostrils continually, the odor drifting up from the rubble, and the morgue nearby, her stomach was roiling.

As she ate the food, which was tasteless to her, Callie watched for Wes. Her heart expanded with euphoria when he came toward her out of the shadows, another MRE in hand for Dusty. The look on his face made her pulse speed up. Again, that mask, that officer's veneer, was gone. He was allowing her to see him—all of him—the human being behind the marine. The man. There was nothing to dislike about him, Callie realized. As he approached, she said, "Are you sure you aren't a throwback to the knights of yore?"

Grinning, Wes opened the pouch and poured hot water into it. "Maybe. But what about you? You're the one out there climbing around on that hotel. You're the real rescuer." And then his mouth curved. "Maybe an angel of mercy?"

Wrinkling her nose, Callie avoided his probing look. "Angel…"

"That's what I've been calling you in my mind— Angel. You look like one," he said conspiratorially as he sat down next to her, their elbows brushing momentarily. He tested the contents of the packet, wanting to make sure it wasn't too hot for Dusty to eat. The dog didn't need to have his sensitive mouth burned on the food, so Wes opened the MRE wider to allow it to cool.

"That's a nice compliment," Callie murmured shyly.

Wes's mouth crooked. "And it wasn't a line, either, if that's what you're thinking."

He saw her give him a tired smile. "I'm beginning to think your compliments are genuine, not lines, okay?"

His smile increased and he held her dark, exhausted gaze. "Good, because they are. They are inspired by my desire for you." He refused to use the word *heart* because he wouldn't—couldn't—give his heart to Callie. It was simply impossible because of his past loss.

Heat rushed up Callie's neck and into her face. Unable to keep holding his warm stare, she turned her attention to her meal, despite the fact that she could barely taste it. Just being close to Wes made her heart open up like an icy pond being showered with sunlight and warmth. She warned herself that he'd used the word *desire,* not *love,* and she mustn't under any circumstances mistake one for the other. "Once, when Dusty found this older man in Turkey buried in a three-story apartment building, and they rescued him, he called me an angel. Of course, he was English, from Britain. Most of the people in Turkey are Muslim. I don't know if they have angels or not in the Muslim religion. But as they brought this man out and put him on a stretcher, he gripped my hand and called me an angel." She sighed. "That was nice. It made my whole week."

Nodding, Wes set the MRE, which had cooled enough to eat, in front of the dog, who promptly started gobbling up the contents. "I'm sure it did." He scowled and studied the hotel. "What do you think, Callie?"

She liked the way her name rolled off his tongue, and she felt her cheeks turn pink with pleasure. "About the hotel? The possibility of survivors?"

"Yeah. I have no experience with this stuff." Wes gave her a wry smile. "I build bridges and highways for the Corps, I don't usually tear into buildings destroyed by earthquakes." In the lights that chased the darkness away, he noted that Callie's cheeks were flushed. He liked the dancing lights in her eyes when he'd called her Angel. Yes, she was an angel—to him and a lot of other people. Her hair was disheveled and he had the maddening urge to slip his fingers into the gold-brown strands and tame it into place. He resisted, barely.

Wes was discovering that Callie's quiet, unassuming presence was prying loose all his bad past experiences and tempting him to try again in a serious relationship—with her. He laughed to himself. Impossible. That's why he was such a party animal at the O Club. Dancing, dining, a few stolen kisses... well, that was okay. That was desire. Not love. Somehow, Callie was different from most women he met. Very different. And he found himself eager to reach out, make a connection with her, find out who she was and create an ongoing dialogue with her. That scared him. Usually, at the O Club, he was the king of social patter, his glib tongue always ready with a comment or a line. Around Callie, he couldn't give a damn about polite, empty talk. He wanted to dig into her background—find out who she really was. She was endlessly intriguing to him. No woman had ever triggered this desire in him before, so Wes was very, very wary of it…and her.

"When I'm done eating, I'm going to take advantage of the lights over here and explore grid number twenty-four, on this side of the hotel."

"You need to rest, Callie."

Shrugging, she finished the MRE. Placing the plastic bag and spoon on the ground nearby, she said, "If you were trapped in the rubble, Wes, would you want me going to sleep right now? What if Dusty finds someone? We've got the equipment, the person power to help extricate them." She looked up and searched his scowling features. Callie felt his concern. "Thanks for caring…. It's a nice feeling. Usually, everyone is telling us just the opposite—get out there, keep looking. They forget we're human and animal—that we need to eat and sleep, too."

Wes nodded and looked glumly at the ruined building. "I don't know how anyone could survive that quake, Callie." He gestured toward a lone figure working near the base of the hotel. "I feel sorry for Morgan Trayhern. The man is fanatical about trying to locate his wife."

"He loves her, that's why. Love drives you to do anything for your family. I've seen this so often.…"

"Yeah…I found a woman like that once.…"

Callie frowned. She heard the wistfulness in Wes's

voice as he watched Morgan digging in the rubble. She wondered what had happened. Wes James was so handsome, articulate and intelligent that Callie felt amazed he didn't have a wife or significant other. The golden boy of the O Club must have a lot of women who desire him. So why hadn't Wes married one of them? Or gotten engaged? That didn't make sense to Callie. "So why didn't you marry her?"

Taking off his cap, Wes rubbed his short, dark hair self-consciously. "Time for some honesty, I guess," he muttered. Giving Callie a dark look, he said, "I was engaged to be married several years ago. Allison was a firefighter." Wes grimaced and then went on in a low tone. "I fell in love with her. But she had a risky job, and I found myself worrying about her constantly. Allison just laughed it off." Shrugging painfully, Wes said, "She died in a fire about four months before we were to be married."

"Oh, no…" Callie's voice cracked. "How *awful.* I'm so sorry, Wes. I can't imagine what it would be like to lose someone you loved like that.…"

"Yeah…it wasn't the best part of my life, believe me." Throwing back his shoulders, he said in an off-key voice, "I'm over that now, though. I've sworn off women in dangerous professions. Maybe that's why I have the reputation of being a party animal. I like women. I enjoy them tremendously. I just don't want to give my heart to anyone, that's all."

"I see." And Callie did, with stunning clarity. Wes had used the word *desire* with her. Not *heart.* Now she knew why. And she realized the rules to any relationship he might want with her. She, too, was in a dangerous profession, which explained his worry about her climbing over the Hoyt. Maybe he cared more than he would admit. But then Callie shrugged the thought off. She shouldn't mistake his worry as anything other than one human caring for another. No, since he'd lost the woman he obviously loved, Callie could understand clearly where he was headed with her in their budding relationship.

"Well, you're doing better than I am," she said wryly as she got to her feet. Maybe her own dark honesty would make him feel better. Leaning over, she made sure that Dusty's leather boots were firmly in place, and then took the dog's MRE pouch and put it with hers. As she straightened, she saw Wes give her a perplexed look. Pointing to her face, she said, "This isn't a big secret, you know? I'm plain looking. Guys go for the glitz and glam gals, not someone like me. I don't wear makeup. I don't wear fancy clothes." She gave him a silly grin and pointed to her hair. "And I don't do a thing with my straight, mousy hair." She settled her cap back on her head. "I gotta get back to work. Since the lights are shining over the end of the site, I think I'll join Mr. Trayhern."

Wes sat there as Callie walked back across the street, her golden retriever at her side. She picked up her helmet and put it on, then turned toward the hotel. He felt her hurt even though she'd said the words teasingly.

How could Callie think she was plain? That was a revelation to him. There was so much about her that was beautiful to him. As he slowly got to his feet, Wes wished the times he spent with Callie could last longer—a *lot* longer. He craved having privacy with her, to talk on a personal basis. But that was nearly impossible under the present circumstances.

Sighing, Wes knew it was time to get back to work. Callie was right: rescuers were expected to work twenty-four hours a day....

Morgan looked up from where he was climbing across the rubble. ''Lieutenant Evans?''

''Hi, Mr. Trayhern.'' Callie watched him steady himself between two slabs of concrete. ''We're done searching the grids over there. Now, we're starting over here. I thought I'd come over with Dusty and search this grid with you.'' She patted the head of her dog and smiled up at Morgan. ''Maybe that will help you. If Dusty doesn't find anyone in this square, you might try another area.''

Gratefully, Morgan nodded and straightened up, one hand on the corner of what had once been a piece of floor to steady himself. ''Yes, that would be great, Lieutenant. Thanks for your help. I really appreciate it.'' Morgan had already learned that rescue work was done in search grids. It was systematic and thorough. That way, no section of a structure was accidentally missed, no survivors left undiscovered. He had no idea where Laura might be and was grateful for Callie's help. Having her with him buoyed his hope of finding Laura.

''Call me Callie, sir. And it's an *honor* to try and be of help to you. Us folks in the Corps have gotta stick together.'' She gave him her most hopeful smile, though inwardly she didn't think anyone was likely to have survived this carnage. Still, on former searches it wasn't unusual for her to find one or two people alive every day, for the first few days, at least. Then the challenge was getting to them fast enough to pull them out alive.

Callie didn't share any of her thoughts with Morgan

Trayhern. The man's eyes burned with sudden hope when she'd come over to help him. Callie didn't want to take that hope away from him. Still, her heart bled for him because she knew the odds of finding anyone alive at this point, were diminishing rapidly with each day.

"I'm grateful, Callie," he said, his voice cracking with emotion.

Callie eyed this section of the structure, where at least three floors had pancaked down upon one another. To her left was the dark void beyond the reach of the floodlights set up near the Humvee. She called to Dusty and the dog leaped up on the rubble, scrambling for purchase. Callie followed, being careful where she placed her gloved hands and booted feet.

They worked from the top left side of the area and began to crisscross it slowly, one step at a time. Callie was careful where she walked for a fall could send one of those twisted steel rebars, which stuck up like needles, into her body, or that of her dog. Dusty, too, moved with careful precision as he hunted and sniffed through the rubble.

They spent the better part of an hour covering half the grid. The other part was bathed in shadows or darkness. Morgan walked behind her and occasionally helped her to gulf the chasms between concrete barriers, because she was short and didn't have long enough legs to span the space. She was grateful for his help.

As they reached the top, Dusty suddenly lunged forward. His move nearly toppled Callie, for the leash snapped taut in her hand, jerking her forward unexpectedly.

Dusty began barking. He strained on his leash.

Morgan helped Callie up. "What is it?"

Clambering to her feet, she grinned. "Dusty's on the scent! He's found someone alive! He only barks if he sniffs someone living. Let's go!"

They hurried, scrambling over twisted rebars, dodging jagged edges of concrete as they headed down into a black abyss ten feet below them. Breathing hard, Callie leaped to another concrete wedge that stuck out like a wing on an aircraft. Dusty again jerked hard on the leash, which slipped out of Callie's hand. He disappeared below them, his barking sharp, loud and joyful.

Her heart pounded and her breathing was labored as she followed, moving as quickly as she could. Alive! He'd found someone alive! Switching on her flashlight, Callie climbed down off the slab of concrete and dropped into the crevasse. Dusty had disappeared, his high-pitched bark echoing. Flashing her light downward, Callie wondered what he'd found.

Morgan was right behind her, breathing in gasps. Since he was a lot taller, he was able to lift Callie up when she wedged her ankle in a crack, and set her free. Flashing the light around the space, Callie saw twisted lengths of mangled steel. Gray powder from pulverized concrete fell as her booted feet found purchase. Regaining her balance, Callie stepped aside as Morgan eased himself down beside her.

"What is it?" he gasped, gazing around in the darkness.

Callie's beam of light stabbed through the blackness toward where Dusty was barking. The golden retriever stood beside what looked like the entrance to a tunnel. Dropping down on her hands and knees, Callie praised the dog.

Instantly, Dusty sat down next to the tunnel opening. He was wagging his tail and panting heavily.

Callie patted him. "Good boy!" she exclaimed. "Sit, Dust. Sit and be quiet."

The dog sat, stopped barking, though his tail thumped wildly with elation. His brown eyes shone.

Morgan squeezed down into the narrow space next to her, their shoulders touching. Callie felt her face break out with perspiration as she studied the small tunnel entrance, an opening barely larger than she was.

"What?" he gasped. "What do you see?" She could feel his heart thundering, as hers was. Someone was alive! Could it be his wife? His heart must be bursting with agony and hope.

"Shh," Callie cautioned. In the distance, she could hear the growl of the bulldozers and the chuttering of the gasoline-fed generator across the street. "Just a moment…" She hunkered down even closer, careful not to go into the tunnel itself. With the aftershocks, the whole thing could shift and crush anyone who went in there.

"Hello!" Callie called, flashing her light into the abyss. "This is Callie. I'm here to help you. Can you hear me? If you can, call out." Her voice was absorbed by the tunnel. Her flashlight revealed that it sloped gently downward about six feet and then curved sharply to the right. It was a big enough opening for either Dusty or herself to crawl into, but there was no guarantee it stayed that large. The shaft might suddenly stop or narrow further.

"Help…!"

The voice was weak, yet Callie heard it distinctly. It was a woman's voice, she was sure. The strong draft rushing past them made it hard for her to hear. Callie eased into the tunnel, her shoulders brushing concrete and rebar as she strained forward.

"I hear you! What's your name?" Callie called strongly. Again her voice was absorbed by the tunnel, muffled by the wind rushing past. Callie heard Morgan shift restlessly, and felt him nearby.

"...Laura..."

Gasping, Callie called back, "What's your last name, Laura?" Her heart pounded. She heard Morgan gasp behind her.

"...Trayhern..."

"Oh, my God!" Morgan cried softly.

Callie grinned hugely and twisted to look up at him. His face was taut with relief, his eyes glittering with tears.

Heart pounding with joy, Callie called back. "Okay, Laura Trayhern...hold on! We're gonna help you! Just hang on...."

Chapter Five

January 2: 2200

Wes huffed as he worked his way down to where Callie and Morgan were hunched in the narrow space between two concrete floors. Getting a call from Callie on the battery-operated radio had made his day. They'd found a survivor! He saw the hope burning in Morgan's eyes. There was a wide, joyful smile wreathing Callie's dirty, strained features. What touched him most were the tears he saw glimmering on the cheeks of both.

"She's alive!" Callie crowed triumphantly as Wes knelt down near the tunnel where she was crouched.

"What's the protocol on this?" he asked her.

"Get in there and find out what kind of medical shape she's in," Callie answered. "Give her water right away. She'll be dehydrated. And I'll need a blanket, because quake victims are usually cold, sometimes hypothermic.'' When they'd called Wes on the radio to tell him the news, he'd told her Sergeant Cove and Corporal Orlando would be right with him. Now she was glad Wes's men were coming. They were going to need some muscle on this rescue.

Scowling, Wes switched on his light, knelt down and studied the twisting tunnel. It was small, too small for any of his men to get into. Callie could do it; so could her dog. But was it too dangerous for either to go in there? ''You sent Dusty in already?''

Callie grinned and hunkered down beside him, their bodies wedged together. ''No, we never send our dog in. I'll go in.''

''What if we get an aftershock?'' Fear ate at Wes.

Callie's face was shining with hope, her eyes wide with eagerness and excitement. She was already taking off her helmet and her thick cammo jacket, stripping down to her green T-shirt and pants. She adjusted the web belt around her slender waist, shifting the canteen to one side so that it rested on her left hip, less likely to snag on something when she crawled into the tunnel.

Shrugging, she said, ''That's the chance we take, Wes.'' Glancing over at Morgan, whose face was alive with fear and hope, she reached out and gripped his hand. ''I'm going to try and see if I can reach her, sir. If I can, I'll assess her condition. I've got water on me, and I'll give that to her if she's conscious.''

The area where they stood was large enough for six people. To Callie, it was perfect for the rescue effort. The tunnel lay below two huge slabs of concrete that bracketed the area. That was why the tunnel had remained hidden until Dusty discovered it.

"Wait…" Wes took his small hand-held radio off his web belt. "Take this in with you." He saw Sergeant Cove approach along with Corporal Orlando, and asked the sergeant for his radio. Immediately the officer took off his belt and handed it over. The hope on the marines' faces was very real. Wes understood that hope, but so much could go wrong; they'd just had an aftershock an hour ago. But he focused on the task at hand, ordering Cove to retrieve some blankets from the tents and bring them back to the site.

"Thanks," Callie said, affixing the radio to her web belt so it, too, would remain out of the way when she crawled in on her belly. Kneeling down at the entrance, she said, "Those aftershocks are about one hour and fifteen minutes apart. So I figure we've got ten or fifteen minutes before the next one."

Wes placed his hand on her small shoulder. When he touched her, she twisted to look up at him, her eyes wide with surprise. He suddenly didn't care what his gesture looked like to the other men. Fingers skimming her shoulder, he said, "Yeah, you've got ten minutes, Callie. Then you have to get out of there. And I don't know how long it will take to get to Mrs. Trayhern."

She sobered. "Or if I can." Tearing her attention from the feel of his warm, protective hand on her shoulder, she studied the dark tunnel before her. "Pray that I can get to her in time.…"

"Be *careful*," Wes said in a low, raspy tone. Then he leaned down and whispered, "I want that first dance over at the O Club when we get back to the base and things settle down. Remember?"

His voice was husky with feeling. Gulping unsteadily, Callie realized that Wes was very serious about her and whatever relationship was growing between them. Her heart opened, and she relished the feel of his fingers digging briefly into her shoulder, signalling his concern for her.

"Okay," she whispered. Callie glanced down at the watch on her left wrist, studying its luminous dials. "Call out to me every minute, will you? Once I get in there, I don't know how much room there will be to lift my arm and check the time." She gave him a crooked smile. "A dance, huh?"

"Yeah. Promise?"

"Promise," she whispered. She gave Morgan, who stood off to the side and out of the way, a hopeful smile. His eyes burned with urgency, spurring her on as she moved gingerly into the tunnel.

Darkness instantly closed around Callie. She was on her belly, her leather-padded knees propelling her forward inches at a time down the shaft. Every movement, no matter how careful she was, brought a jab or a poke from some jagged debris. The strong draft brought fresh air whistling past her. Callie was so sweaty she could smell her own fear, and longed for a hot bath. With her flashlight on, the light stabbing through the inky darkness, Callie could see many pieces of broken glass, jagged concrete and bars of steel sticking out like porcupine quills along her route. It was like trying to slither slowly and carefully over a pincushion. The air hissed around her as she crept on her knees and elbows around the tight right turn. The tunnel abruptly plummeted into a nearly vertical descent for six feet.

Callie was breathing hard. "Laura?" she called,

then waited. No answer. Gulping, her mouth dry, she blinked as sweat ran into her eyes. Again she hollered into the tunnel. "Laura? Can you hear me? It's Callie. I'm coming in to find you...."

"I...yes I hear you. You're close...."

Good. Gasping, Callie grinned and got ready to move on.

"One minute."

Wes's voice reached her just as she wriggled around the corner. Jabs of pain shot up through her elbows. Unlike her knees, they were unprotected. Ignoring the pain, she saw to her relief that the tunnel widened considerably on the down slope. Stifling the urge to hurry, Callie carefully chose where she would hang, one gloved hand anchoring her, so she didn't tumble forward on the steep decline. The possibility of slicing open an artery in her hand or arm was very real if she fell, or didn't watch where she placed her hands and feet.

She could smell so many odors, all of them obnoxious. The faint scent of natural gas scared her. Excrement and urine drifted toward her flared nostrils. Sweat leaked into her eyes again and she blinked rapidly to clear her vision. Breathing harshly, she saw the tunnel flatten out. *There.* The shaft ran horizontally once more. As she flashed the light ahead, Callie spotted a small space, a little over four feet in width and about three to four feet high. Obviously, one floor had settled on top of another in the collapse, leaving this small air space between two huge chunks of concrete. On the right, she saw a woman's white hand and slender, graceful fingers covered with gray dust.

Callie moved gingerly into the space, quickly crawling the last five feet. She flashed the light, and Laura

Trayhern looked back at her, her eyes huge with hope and terror. The woman lay on her back, with barely two feet between her and the ceiling hanging threateningly above her.

"Two minutes," Wes called.

"Hi, Laura," she whispered, grinning, "I'm Callie." And she reached out and gripped the woman's bloody hand.

Laura's grip was strong. "Hi…thank you—thank you for coming.…" And she began sobbing.

Callie maneuvered around in the tight space and pulled the canteen from her belt. "Here, let me give you some water. You gotta be dehydrated." She was able to move into a half-kneeling position, and, sliding one arm beneath Laura's neck, brought the canteen to her puffy, bloodied lips. The woman drank for a long time. As she did, Callie heard a loud groaning sound around them—the rubble straining again, threatening to shift. Would it settle on top of them, flattening the space? The threat was great.

When Laura stopped drinking, Callie took the canteen away and capped it. "Where are you hurt?" she asked in a breathless voice. Picking up the flashlight, she ran it across Laura's unkempt blond hair and down her prone body.

"My right ankle," Laura whispered, pointing toward it. "I'm trapped. I can't reach it. Can you?"

Moving closer, Callie hit her head on the ceiling, causing a flash of pain. Biting down on her lower lip, she suppressed a groan. When warmth began to trickle down her head, Callie knew something had scored her scalp and opened it up. "Yes…I see it. Hold on…let me get down there.…" She forced herself forward.

"Otherwise, you okay? Any other medical problems?"

"I—I think I'm okay. Just my ankle, Callie."

"Hey, did you know your husband is right outside this tunnel? He's alive and well. He's been looking for you nonstop."

"Morgan?"

Callie heard the pain in her voice and declared, "Yes, ma'am. Your husband. He's fine. He escaped the earthquake."

Laura sobbed and pressed her hands to her lips. "Oh, thank you…thank you! He's alive. He's alive!"

Laughing softly, Callie said, "Yes, alive and well." She pressed upward with her hand and began to shift big chunks of debris from around Laura's ankle. As she did so she saw dark stains there on the woman's wool skirt.

"Three minutes."

Damn. Callie saw a piece of rebar that had arced over, trapping Laura's ankle beneath it. Hunting around with her flashlight, Callie found another piece of rebar, about two feet long, behind her. She grabbed it.

"There's a piece of steel rebar looped over your ankle, Laura," she explained, breathing hard. "I'm going to try and leverage it up so we can get your ankle free. It might be painful. I don't have much room to get to it."

Sobbing, Laura whispered unsteadily, "Do what you have to, Callie. I want out of here. I just want to live.…"

"Four minutes."

Grunting and groaning, Callie slid the rebar into place on the slab. She heard Laura take in a breath.

"I'm sorry," Callie whispered, and she gripped the lever with both gloved hands and pushed up. Nothing happened. Damn! It was a one-inch-thick steel bar, and it wasn't going to bend easily. Callie pushed again, straining against it. She heard Laura moan in pain. Wiping her brow with her shaking hand, Callie glared at the rebar that had Laura trapped.

"Five minutes."

Gasping for air, her mind spinning, Callie stared at the steel bar, trying to think of another way to loosen it. "You know, at times like this I hate being small. I don't have the muscle I need," she told Laura.

"I'm small, too. Hey, what we don't have in muscle, we make up for in brains."

Callie grinned. She liked Laura's courage under the circumstances. "Right on, ma'am."

"Call me Laura, Callie. What are you going to try and do?"

Callie explained her next idea, painting a verbal picture of the impediment that kept her trapped.

"What if you use a piece of wood under your lever? That would give you more force, wouldn't it?"

"Yes...you're right. Hold on...." Callie quickly flashed her light around.

"Six minutes."

"Why are they calling out the minutes to you?" Laura asked.

Callie located a four-by-four length of wood. "Aftershocks have been occurring every hour and fifteen minutes. That leaves about five minutes until the next rumble. They want us out of here before the next one hits. We don't know how unstable this place is and they don't want us trapped down here if the rubble starts to shift."

Laura nodded. She knew what Callie had left unspoken: that any aftershock could bury and kill them. "I—I understand, Callie. You get out of here, then, when your time is up. There's no sense in both of us dying if this space doesn't stand the pressures of another aftershock."

Callie chuckled as she placed the wood beneath the lever next to Laura's ankle. "Well, I didn't tell them this, but I don't care how long it takes, I'm staying here until I free you. I just told my lieutenant that to give him something to do because he's afraid for me."

"Sounds like a nice guy." Laura smiled a little. "You might be petite, but you're mighty, Callie. I'm glad you're here...."

"Okay...here we go, Laura...." And Callie placed her shoulder beneath the rebar. Gripping with both hands, she pushed up hard, throwing all her body weight against it. *Move! Damn you, move!* Gasping, she shoved with all her might.

"Seven minutes."

Gasping hard, Callie lunged again into the rebar. Her shoulder hurt, bruised by every lunge she took. Every muscle in her body screamed in protest as she kept pushing, pushing, pushing until finally, the loop of rebar grudgingly gave way.

"There!" Laura cried.

"Eight minutes."

Panting, Callie dropped the lever and pulled out the block of wood. "Okay, Laura, here's what you need to do. Listen to me carefully and do exactly as I ask, okay?"

"Okay," Laura whispered. Pain was stabbing hotly up her leg and past her knee. She felt faint from it, and her stomach rolled with nausea. Laura knew high levels of pain could make a person throw up, and it was the last thing she wanted to do right now. Trying to concentrate on Callie, who had crawled back over to her and placed her hand on her shoulder, Laura opened her eyes. The gray light in their coffin made Callie's sweaty features shine.

"I want you to slowly roll over on your right side. I need to get you down off that table you're lying on. As you roll, I'll pull your upper body forward and down to the floor. I'll catch you in my arms as you come toward me. But you gotta be careful. There's a lot of glass and sharp objects here."

Callie quickly took off her gloves and fitted them onto Laura's hands. Then she took off her protective knee pads, strapping them around Laura's knees. Finally, placing her hand protectively on the woman's small shoulder, she grinned.

"You wear the equipment to get out of here. I know how to do escape stuff in my sleep. You ready?"

Laura gulped. "Y-yes…I'm ready."

"On the count of three. One, two, three…" Callie used all her strength to pull Laura off the table as she rolled to the right. The woman was as small as she was, which was good.

Laura's face became a mask of pain. Callie tried to support her right leg as she moved from the slab to the floor.

"Nine minutes. Callie?"

"We're coming!" she shouted back. "Laura's free! Get ready for her to come out!"

Laura was shaky and weak so Callie helped her maneuver, urging her into the tunnel.

"Okay, okay," Callie whispered, her hands on the other woman's hips as she half guided, half pushed her into the tunnel. "Just take your time, Laura. It's okay. You're going to make it.... Just be careful...." She flashed the light so Laura could see the climb ahead of her. Could she make it with that broken ankle? Callie wasn't sure. The vertical ascent was steep. Did Laura have the upper body strength to pull herself up? Gasping raggedly, Callie followed her out, one painful inch at a time.

Sobbing for breath, Laura gripped the jagged edges of concrete and tried to hoist herself upward. She could only use her left leg to push with, as her right one was useless. Pain was keeping her mind clear.

She felt Callie on her heels. They had to escape! Her children needed a mother. She needed Morgan! Love for her family kindled a resolve so deep and strong within her that it gave her the strength she needed to haul herself up into the other part of the tunnel, where the rescue team waited to assist her.

Callie crawled quickly behind Laura once she'd passed the vertical shaft. She heard a growling roar.

Aftershock!

A cry tore from Callie's lips as she felt the entire tunnel quiver sickeningly and groan. The shivering, rhythmic movements slammed her from side to side in the tunnel. At the same instant, she heard the cries of joy as Laura and Morgan were reunited. Callie continued to squirm forward on her belly as the earth shook around her. She didn't care how badly she was cut; she didn't want to be stuck by a cave-in after this latest tremor.

As if the hounds of hell were at her heels, Callie shot forward. Using her feet, she launched herself the last few yards and thrust upward. Hard. Throwing out her arms, her hands extended, Callie grunted as she hurtled forward like a cannonball being shot from the tunnel's mouth.

Relief shattered through Wes as he saw Callie come barreling out of the darkness. "Hurry!" he pleaded, his voice cracking. The thunder of the aftershock roared around them, swallowing them up with its wild, savage growl. He felt the shivering and bucking of the rubble beneath his feet as he stood hunched over in the confined space, waiting to grab Callie. Morgan had hauled his wife into his arms, and two marines were helping them climb off the hotel ruins to the ground below.

Seconds later, Callie plummeted into Wes's arms, warm, alive and small against his bulk. The earth shook hard. One moment they were standing, the next, Wes was falling backward with Callie in his arms. Above all, he wanted to protect her. He heard her cry out in alarm as the aftershock, which was a lot bigger than they'd anticipated, struck them with full force.

A second later Wes had hit the hard, unforgiving wall of concrete. His arms were strong and tight around Callie, whose head was buried against his neck and jaw. He lay there breathing hard.

"It's okay…okay," he rasped near her ear. "We're okay. Thank God you're safe…safe…." The terror of almost losing her tore through him, reminding him of his past pain. He could have lost Callie just as he'd lost Allison! The terror he felt, like ashes of the past, tasted acrid in his mouth. He was so scared! But for the moment, all he could do was hold Callie.

Callie was stunned by the aftershock. She had heard the tunnel crunching and exploding behind her as she'd lunged out of it. Thick clouds of dust filtered down around them as she and Wes hit the floor of the rescue area. She felt his arms, strong and caring, wrap around her body like steel bands.

She remembered how he had grunted out in pain when they'd hit the ground. Alarmed that he might be hurt, Callie struggled to free herself from his arms. But their bodies were melded against one another, the shifting rubble pressing them tightly together. Gasping for air, Callie heard the growl begin to recede as the aftershock rolled on by. Coughing violently from the thick dust raised by the tremor, she felt Wes sit up dragging her with him. Small against his bulk, Callie relaxed and let him do so.

Wordlessly, Wes released her and framed her dirty face with his hands. "Callie?" His voice was ragged with fear. With longing. Where did desire begin and end, or weave into a greater feeling?

To hell with it.

Wes knew they were alone. No one could see them down in this crevasse, out of the gray wash of the floodlights. Right now, his men were focused on getting Laura Trayhern over to the medical tent, to give her the best attention they could under the circumstances. Wes and Callie were alone. Finally. And that's just the way he wanted it.

Looking down into Callie's eyes, he saw the fear, the terror and hope burning in them as she clung to his gaze. Holding her face with his shaky hands, he whispered harshly, "You almost died in there, Callie...." And he leaned down...to kiss her.

Callie was stunned as his strong, warm mouth met and moved against her parted lips. She'd seen the need in Wes's narrowed eyes, the desire in them—for her. The fact that she had nearly died moments ago and now was in the arms of a man who wanted her made her emotions seesaw violently. Life was what mattered. In that moment, Callie capitulated and told her screaming mind to shut up. For whatever reason, even if she was plain, Wes found her desirable. She knew his kiss was fueled by desire, not by love. He'd lost the woman he loved because of her risky occupation. Callie knew he was rattled because of that. Yet, as his mouth glided firmly against hers, she drank his moist breath deep into her lungs. His hands were cherishing as he tilted her face so that he could drink even more deeply of her.

Callie had been kissed infrequently in her life, and never like this. She felt such strength in Wes, such love as his mouth hotly claimed hers. Her breath was stolen, her heart pounded wildly in her breast and her hands opened and closed spasmodically against his broad, powerful shoulders. She felt so loved, so nurtured and protected. As she surrendered to Wes in every way, her breasts pressed against his broad chest, her mouth clinging wetly to his, the disaster and terror dissolved around Callie. So this was what it was like to be desired—really desired. She was lost in the exploding brightness, light and heat of his commanding mouth as it took hers without apology. Yet his kiss was tender and searching, too, and invited her to respond and share with him the glory of that private moment together. Callie did, unashamedly, wanting to claim the life she felt in his arms over the death she'd just narrowly escaped.

The seconds melted between them. When Wes tore his mouth from hers, Callie's eyes opened slumberously, and he saw desire in them—for him. His entire body exploded with raw need. As he caressed her warm, pink cheeks and threaded his fingers tenderly through her dirty, uncombed hair, he whispered unsteadily, "You're so brave, Callie...an angel. I swear, you're an angel...."

His words fed her lonely soul as nothing ever had. She hung on his every word, part of her utterly disbelieving and part of her suspended in a heaven she had thought she'd know. Wes was so handsome! He was successful. He had everything.

Callie tried to shut off that insidious voice inside that always sliced into her negatively. The narrowed, heated look in his green eyes shook her deeply. His hands, brushing smudges of dirt from her cheeks and jaw, then riffling gently through her hair to tame it into place, brought tears to her eyes.

"I—I never realized..." Callie began lamely, her voice cracking.

Wes studied her, his gaze falling to her parted, well-kissed lips. "What? What didn't you realize?" He caressed her hair again and settled his hands on her small shoulders. Shoulders that had just rescued another woman from sure death. He searched her eyes. "What, Callie? Tell me what's in your heart. I can see it in your eyes. Talk to me...."

Tears welled up then. Callie was going to cry, and she knew it wasn't right for a Marine Corps officer to do that. But the continuing caress of Wes's hands against her face, neck and shoulder was stripping her of all her armor. With each touch, her heart opened more.

"Y-you're so gentle...so kind...." She shut her eyes tightly, the tears drifting from beneath her sandy-colored lashes and making thin, clean trails down her cheeks.

"My beautiful angel," Wes whispered, and he

brought Callie fully against him once more. When she nestled her face against his neck and jaw, he sighed raggedly. Lips near her ear, he rasped softly, ''I've never met anyone like you in my life, Callie. You're so different. So wonderful. Every time I look at you, my heart explodes. And I get scared. Scared all over again.'' He laughed a little nervously and ran his hand across her back. The T-shirt she wore was damp with sweat, and he became concerned that she might become chilled. ''I feel like someone cold-cocked me with a sledgehammer. The first time I saw you, my world stopped. There you were—those big, blue eyes of yours, and that soft mouth.'' He sighed and pressed a kiss into her tangled, damp hair. ''Here we are, in the midst of just about the worst disaster the U.S. has ever had...and the fact that we've met under these circumstances... It's crazy. It's scary.'' Wes wanted to tell her more, because he knew they were all living on borrowed time. Suddenly he realized that he wanted to live every minute as if it was his last. But he couldn't. That would mean giving his heart to her, and he simply couldn't do that. Fear warred with desire within him.

Callie lay against him, her heart beating wildly in her breast. His words were like balm to so many old wounds that had never healed within her. Wes thought her beautiful! That was so foreign to her, and yet Callie had heard the simple sincerity, the emotion in his voice when he'd told her how he felt about her. Moving her hand shyly from his chest and up his arm, she lifted her head and drowned in the green fire of his gaze.

''I don't know what's happening, Wes.'' Her voice was unsteady. ''And I'm scared, too.'' He desired her, yet he didn't love her. Callie was having difficulty keeping the two separate, and knew it was dangerous to think they were one and the same. Wes had never promised his heart to her. And he wouldn't. The past was indelibly stamped upon him.

"So am I. Scared that I'll chase you away by being so damned bold with you so fast. I don't want you to think I'm handing you a line. I'm not.... I couldn't ever do that to you...." Wes laughed a little unsurely and looked around them. "A helluva place to find someone like you...."

"We've got jobs to do...."

"I know. They—the people who need our help— come first."

Callie nodded and slowly sat up. Her lips tingled with the power and desire of his kiss. Wes had crashed into her life like a thunderbolt, as powerful as the earthquake that had devastated Southern California. What was real? What wasn't? She touched her lower lip with her fingertips and then gazed shyly up at him. The shadowy darkness made his face more angular and powerful-looking as he watched her in the throbbing silence. "I feel crazy inside, Wes. I can't separate this disaster from you...and me...."

"Yeah, I know...it's rather sudden." One corner of his mouth lifted. "All of this is."

"I'm exhausted," Callie admitted quietly.

"I can see that. You almost died a few minutes ago...." He glanced toward the tunnel, which was all but closed due to the aftershock. Wes turned and gazed down at her. "You're one of the bravest, gutsiest women I've ever met. Your job is so dangerous...."

The warmth of his voice filtered through her. Callie was chilled now by the coolness of the night air against her sweaty body, and Wes took off his jacket and pulled it around her, as if realizing she was getting cold. That stunned Callie. ''Do you read minds, too?'' she asked, hugging the coat gratefully around her. She was touched by the boyish smile he gave her as he stood up and held out his hand to her.

''No. Not usually…but you're an exception. Come on. We've fixed up a makeshift bed in the back of the Humvee. You can curl up there and get some sleep.''

Callie patted Dusty, who sat dutifully nearby. He thumped his tail. ''Sounds good. He needs to rest, too. Thanks.''

She gripped Wes's outstretched hand. Dusty came to her side and she picked up his leash. Looking up at Wes, she saw him studying her critically in the gray light that washed the area.

''What?'' she asked.

''I'm not sorry I kissed you. Or that I desire you.''

She avoided his hawklike gaze. ''I'm not either, Wes.'' And she wasn't, but her heart was afraid as never before. As they climbed down over the rubble to the littered street below, Callie wondered if their relationship was created by this disaster. She knew from long experience and observation that people did wild and unexpected things during such a crisis, made impetuous choices they'd never entertain ordinarily. Was this what was happening to them? Was it a mixture of desire and danger that had created such a powerful alchemical mixture of such unexpected intensity between them?

Chapter Six

Drunk with exhaustion as she headed back to the camp, Callie saw Sergeant Cove creating a makeshift splint to stabilize Laura Trayhern's badly broken right ankle. They had spread out two cammo jackets for her to lie upon near the curb where the Humvee was parked. Blankets had been laid across her to stave off hypothermia. Anyone trapped for days, unmoving and without proper protective clothing, was susceptible.

Callie liked Sergeant Cove, a calm, competent medic who seemed to roll with the punches, no matter how serious the circumstances. He didn't have a gurney to lay Laura on to stabilize her broken leg, so he used the soft flat grass in front of the tents instead, splinting it properly with any material he could find.

Morgan Trayhern was kneeling at his wife's side, his expression anxious as he held her slender, dirty hand between his. He gently pressed it against his chest and murmured words of comfort as Sergeant Cove worked on her ankle.

Callie felt Wes place his hand beneath her elbow as they walked across the street to see how Laura was doing. Feeling beyond fatigue, Callie wanted to lean on Wes, but that wouldn't be wise according to regulations. The military frowned on any overt show of affection between two people in the service. Lifting her chin, she drowned in his concerned gaze instead. Her lips tingled softly as she recalled his branding, heated kiss.

As they drew near, the bright lights making everything look surreal and garish, Callie saw Laura open her eyes slightly. Wes remained at Callie's side, but dropped his hand reluctantly from her elbow. He was the commanding officer here, and as such could not risk such affectionate displays around the rest of his team.

Mustering up a smile, Callie halted beside Morgan. "How are you doing, Laura?" she called down to her.

Laura managed a wan smile. "Much, much better… Thanks, Callie. You saved my life.…"

Callie patted Dusty, who stood at her side, his tail wagging. "No, he did. He found you, after all. Give Dusty the thanks."

Wes moved over to the other side of Morgan. "Just as you got clear of the tunnel, Mrs. Trayhern, it started collapsing. And by the time Lieutenant Evans leaped clear of it, the tunnel was destroyed. She and her dog *did* save your life. Literally. If they hadn't found you before that last aftershock, the whole place would have caved in on you. We got lucky.''

Morgan looked down at his wife and tightened his grip on her hand. "My God..."

Laura sighed tremulously and closed her eyes. Tears trailed from the corners. All she could do was cling weakly to her husband's large, warm hands.

Morgan raised his head and looked at them. "When this disaster gets straightened out, you can count on a big check coming to your unit, Callie. It's our way of thanking you. You deserve a medal for what you did. If you hadn't gone in there, Laura would be dead now." His voice broke and he looked down at his wife, reaching out to try and smooth her filthy, un-combed hair away from her face. "I can't even think what our lives would be like without her...."

The look that Callie saw pass between them reso-nated deeply in her heart. She glanced at Wes, who gave her a wink and then moved away.

"Corporal Orlando?" Wes called.

Orlando was standing on the driver's side, a radio in hand. "Yes, sir?"

"Did you contact the Huey at Camp Reed? Do they know we have a medical emergency here?"

Orlando nodded. "Yes, sir, I did." He looked at the watch on his hairy wrist. "We're gettin' lucky, sir. There's a Huey diverting from its regularly scheduled grid drop and heading our way. They're going to drop off supplies meant for another grid, and pick up Mrs. Trayhern." He grinned. "Extra supplies can be a big help here, sir. Once we off-load the tents, food and water supplies, they said they'll have room to fly Mrs. Trayhern and her husband back to the base and get her to the emergency room of our naval hospital for treatment.''

Wes nodded. ''Good enough, Corporal. Thank you.'' Although he wanted to stay and keep Morgan and his wife company, Wes couldn't. He saw another group of civilians, people who had lived nearby, straggling down the street. Throughout the day he'd sent his bulldozers, cherry pickers and front-end loaders into the surrounding neighborhoods to help out people who had loved ones trapped in the rubble of their homes. Since Callie hadn't found any more survivors in the hotel ruins, he could pull the equipment from there to help others in equal need until—or if she— found more. It would be easy enough to bring the equipment back.

Out of the corner of his eye, he saw Callie sit down on the curb and give Dusty water. Her face was gray with exhaustion. His jacket was huge on her small but courageous frame. His chest expanded fiercely with a tidal wave of emotion, making him afraid. Yet at the same time Callie's quiet, calm presence seemed to settle over the scene, affecting all of them.

He watched as the sergeant finished splinting Laura's ankle and stood up, a pleased look on his face. Morgan made sure his wife was bundled up in olive-green wool blankets, keeping her warm.

Opening the rear of the Humvee, Wes eyed the makeshift bed his men had made out of blankets. The tents they'd been given thus far had to be utilized to keep the radios, batteries and supplies protected. With this Huey coming in unexpectedly with extra tents, that meant Wes could have them erected for themselves. Before this, his men had taken turns getting a few hours of shut-eye in the rear of the vehicle. It was better than nothing.

He saw Callie stand and walk toward him. As she came around the corner of the vehicle, he said, "Climb in. This is your home away from home. You're going to get some sleep before you drop."

Callie looked at the blankets spread out in the rear of the Humvee—plenty of room in there for her to curl up and sleep. "Can my dog sleep with me? He's bushed, too."

Grinning, Wes nodded. "Yeah, no problem. Do you sleep with him at home, too?"

Giving him a wry look, Callie patted the end of the Humvee, and Dusty leaped up into the vehicle. "No. Dusty stays at the unit's kennel facility when I'm not working with him. I'd love to take him home with me, but that's against regulations. I have an apartment in Oceanside, but there's no way I'll be able to get to it under the circumstances."

"Yeah, I know that one," Wes muttered. "Most of us live in Oceanside. I heard over the radio earlier that they're putting grid teams up at the bachelor officers' quarters back at camp. It's basically a hotel, with rooms, beds and bathroom facilities. A nice little perk to look forward to after spending days out here."

Callie climbed into the Humvee. "It could be a lot worse," she agreed. "The B.O.Q. is a great place to get cleaned up and grab a good night's sleep on a nice bed." She began to slowly unlace her black, dusty G.I. boots. "A bed. A hot shower. Wow. What'd I'd give for a hot shower right now." She wrinkled her nose and gave him a silly grin. She smelled of sweat, dirt and grime.

Wes reached out and briefly squeezed her shoulder.

"I've got good news for all of us. They're organizing another team to come in here and spell us off, Callie. We'll be relieved for twenty-four hours of R and R, rest and recoup, back at the base. You'll get that hot shower, a soft bed and real food...." He wanted to say, "and a night in my arms," but he didn't.

"That's *great* news. Will they be sending out another rescue team?"

"Yes, they will. A sergeant Lucy Perkins will be flying out on this flight and she'll continue where you left off."

"Wonderful!" Callie said.

Then Wes saw her brows fall and her soft mouth purse. There were dark circles beneath her eyes, and her fingers trembled badly as she tried to loosen the double knot on her boot. Leaning over, he said, "Let me...." He quickly loosened the laces.

"Thanks, Wes.... I'm feeling like a slow motion klutz right now. I'm whipped...." Callie wanted him to stay near her. Her heart pounded briefly when he gave her that narrowed, burning look that she'd seen seconds before he'd kissed her and breathed his life into her. Did he know how much he'd given her with that unexpected, beautiful kiss? Probably not.

"Okay, get some sleep."

Callie looked forlorn as he stepped back to close the doors on the Humvee, to give her privacy. If he accurately read the look on her drawn features, he knew that she wanted him beside her, holding her, loving her as he dreamed of doing. Hesitating, his hands on the doors, Wes said in a low, growling tone, "If you give me that look back at the B.O.Q., you're going to end up in my bed, in my room and in my arms...."

The doors closed.

Callie sat there in a daze as Wes's quietly spoken words spilled across her like a wonderful, warm embrace. He'd read her mind again! That amazed her. She saw him round the vehicle and move forward. In the distance, she could hear the Huey helicopter approaching from the west. Good. Laura and Morgan Trayhern would be taken back to the base. Laura would get the best medical attention from the specialists at Camp Reed's medical center, which hadn't been damaged in the quake.

Lying down, Callie snuggled up against Dusty, who was already sleeping deeply. The night was cool. She pulled up the wool blanket and placed one arm beneath her head. In moments, Callie plummeted into a hard, healing sleep.

January 3: 0600

Wes jerked awake. He'd been sleeping in the driver's seat of the Humvee for the last three hours. The dawn was a turgid gray-brown color. Ugly looking. Sitting up, he rubbed his face. He needed a shave, but there was no way to get one at the moment. Water was precious and conserved for drinking only. Last night, the Huey had delivered the new rescue team, along with tents, cots, a few more medical supplies, food and water. At the hotel, he had seen a woman and her German shepherd moving carefully throughout the rubble, and he had figured it was Sergeant Lucy Perkins. The last thing Wes had ordered his sergeant to do before he knocked off and got a few hours of badly needed sleep was to erect the tents.

As he sat up, Wes saw that the camouflage green-

and-brown tents, which held two cots, had been erected next to the Humvee, on the other side of what had been a sidewalk. Wes had given orders not to be woken up. He saw the booted feet of his men at the open flap doors. Everyone needed to sleep.

Rousing himself, Wes quietly turned around in the seat. Directly behind him was Callie. She lay on her back, her hand gently curled near her head. She was an angel, he decided. Even as dirty as she was, he saw the soft beauty of her parted lips, the shallow rise and fall of her breasts beneath the blanket, and the way her thick, pale lashes fell against her cheeks. She was so small, tiny yet courageous. Who would have thought she'd risk her life as she had last night?

Wes smiled slightly. Dusty, her dog, lay snoring loudly at her side. The dog was as much of a hero as she was. Without him, they'd never have found Laura Trayhern.

Wes couldn't help himself; he wanted to touch Callie again. He wanted to kiss her awake. He wanted to make love to her..to satisfy his desire for her and share everything with her.

Reaching between the seats, he grazed her uncombed hair before forcing himself to stop. If he didn't, well…he was the C.O., and military-wise, it wouldn't look good. No, he'd have to suffer in eloquent silence while other, more important things were attended to.

Easing out of the Humvee, Wes closed the door quietly in an effort not to waken Callie or Dusty. Stretching in the damp, cold air he looked around. The sky heralded another murky day, and that depressed him. Odors from a nearby burning oil refinery clogged the air. He saw small fires on some of the lawns of civilian homes down the block, the people huddled around the flames for warmth. Walking over to the first of the newly erected tents, Wes shook his sergeant's boot to wake him. They had to saddle up. Time wasn't on their side in terms of finding survivors. Every hour that ticked away, could mean another life lost. And he wanted to introduce himself to the new dog rescue marine as soon as possible.

January 3: 0700

"Hey, sleepyhead…"

Callie groaned. She heard Wes's voice nearby. When she felt his hand settle on her shoulder to give her a slight shake, she barely opened her eyes. Feeling Dusty get up, she groaned again.

"Uhh…what time is it?" she muttered thickly, forcing herself to sit up. The blanket fell away and pooled around her lower body. She had a lot of aches and pains.

Wes was leaning in the rear door of the Humvee. He looked dangerous with his face unshaved, his cheekbones accentuated. The expression in his eyes, however, was one of humor laced with desire. Callie ran her fingers through her mussed hair and wished she had a comb.

"Time to get up. It's 0700. I let you sleep for as long as I could. Sergeant Cove has MREs with eggs in them from that supply that was dropped off to us last night. Come on, join us for breakfast?"

How badly Wes wanted to take Callie in his arms. She looked so innocent and desirable upon wakening. Her eyes were slightly puffy, her lips parted, and she seemed excruciatingly vulnerable in those moments. What would it be like to have her wake up in his arms?

Never had he wanted anything more in his life. Forcing himself to move away, he allowed Dusty to leap down to the roadway. Callie followed and picked up the leash. She drew Wes's jacket around her, the chill pervasive.

"I'll join you in a few minutes," she said in a sleep-ridden voice.

Nodding, Wes moved aside. Yesterday, he'd had two latrines set up. His men used them, as did the people who lived in the area, and that was fine by him. One of the big problems after a disaster was disease. Anything that could be done to contain it was a wise precaution. No one liked digging latrines, but it was one of the first things he'd had done with the big machine the day they'd arrived. Good sanitation measures meant less likelihood of disease breaking out.

Callie felt drugged with tiredness as she trundled into the first tent and joined her team. There were two cots there, one on either side of the tent, which was large enough to stand up in. Two marines were sitting on the plyboard floor of the tent, another two on one of the cots, with Wes sitting opposite them on the other cot.

"Ma'am," Sergeant Cove said in greeting as she entered, handing out an MRE, "you and your dog have the last tent down there." He smiled. "You got a cot, blankets and pillows. How about that?"

Callie sat down on the deck near the entrance. She wanted to sit next to Wes, but that would have been too obvious. Seeing the same wish in his eyes, she tucked his warm look away in her heart. He would agree with her prudent decision to not join him on the cot. "Sounds like heaven to me, Sergeant. Thanks for getting it set up for us.'' She eagerly spooned into her rations. The eggs weren't real; they were a dehydrated form and she really didn't care for them, but they were better than nothing. The sergeant had thoughtfully made Dusty an MRE beef dinner, and put it into a tin bowl for him.

Wes was eating slowly from his MRE with a plastic spoon, hardly tasting the cardboardlike eggs. But it wasn't lost on him how Callie's feminine presence made a difference here. Men and women worked together in the military these days, but the effect women had on the men was obvious. And it was positive.

Callie looked over at Wes, who stood nearby. ''What's on the drawing board today?''

''More of the same. You go ahead and continue your grid work on the Hoyt and fill Sergeant Perkins in. She's already hard at work up there. I'm having my men take the equipment and work with homeowners in this area who need our help and muscle. If you find anyone, dead or alive, radio me, and I'll send someone over with the appropriate equipment to get them out.''

''And if Dusty finds someone alive, you'll bring back the equipment we need to extricate them?''

''Count on it,'' Wes said. Raising his head, he looked at the sky. ''It looks like rain.''

Glumly, Callie stared at the darkening clouds drifting in off the Pacific Ocean. ''Rain only makes our work more dangerous. Concrete and broken glass get much more slippery when you're trying to walk across it, hunting for survivors.''

Wes stopped himself from telling Callie to be careful. Again, from a military standpoint, he couldn't be seen favoring Callie like that. It was important his men didn't realize anything was going on between them. So he gave her a short, hard look that spoke volumes. Wes hoped Callie would understand his nonverbal message.

"Okay, everyone, let's saddle up," he told them in an authoritative tone. "Every minute counts. Meet me back here at noon and we'll chow down and make plans for the afternoon. Private Bertram, you stay with the Humvee and work the radios between us and the base. I'm going to be down on Marshal Street with the rest of the team and the equipment." He patted the cell phone on his web belt. "Call if you need me."

Bertram nodded. "Yes, sir, I will."

Wes knew that their cell phones were prized possessions right now. The only problem was he didn't have the means to recharge them. The gasoline generator made them some electricity—just enough to keep the radios and the computer in the tent working and the lights burning at night.

Callie finished her meal. The next order of business was placing the protective leather boots back on Dusty's feet. She dressed him in his bright-red vest, then got up and went to the Humvee to retrieve her safety helmet. As she picked up the leash and got ready to leave, it began to rain. That was a bad omen for her day. She'd found her jacket lying on a cot in her newly erected tent, and put it on. Although water resistant, it wasn't waterproof. With the cool January temperature hovering in the fifties, she knew they'd get soaked, and then slowly become more and more chilled as the day wore on.

Giving everyone a smile, Callie lifted her gloved hand to the team as she walked by. "You guys be careful. I'll see you at 1200."

The look Wes gave her was swift and intimate, making her heart pound with joy. She treasured that warm glance, his care and concern, deep within her. It made Callie feel as if she were walking on air.

January 3: 1200

Everyone had crowded into two of the five tents to eat their noontime MREs. Callie huddled next to Wes on one of the cots. Opposite them was Sergeant Cove and Corporal Orlando. The rain was steady outside the tent. The rest of the group, including Lucy and her dog, were in the other tent. She shivered involuntarily as she spooned the hot, tasty chicken and noodles into her mouth. Dusty lay at her feet lapping up the MRE that Corporal Orlando had provided for him earlier.

"How're things going?" Wes asked her. All morning, he'd been on Marshal Street with his men and equipment. He'd worried about Callie and Lucy being cold and wet up there on the rubble. To make matters worse, they'd experienced fifteen major aftershocks. And after each one, Wes had wanted to run back to the hotel, which was out of his line of sight, to see if they were all right. He'd tried to curb his worry and remain focused on his task of dismantling the broken houses to find survivors.

"No luck," she murmured unhappily. "Lucy and I are going to concentrate on the front side of the hotel now. All the grids in the back have been completed."

"I think we're lucky to have found one person alive in that hotel," Wes told her as he hungrily ate his MRE. He liked the fact that Callie had come and sat next to him. He wanted to put his arm around her, hold her and kiss her, but not here. Not now.

"I know." Callie sighed. "But I hold out hope for the hopeless." She found it impossible to be immune to Wes and the intense, dark looks he gave her. Each glance was like the soft rose petal touch of his fingers upon her flesh. Yearning, hot and sweet, filled Callie.

"In something like this," Corporal Cove asked her, "do you often find survivors?"

"Maybe one to five," Callie said. Worriedly, she looked out the flap of the tent. The rain pelting down on the waterproof fabric made a soft drumming sound. "This weather isn't going to help. Rain and cold temperatures produce hypothermia in people trapped in rubble. It just hurries their death."

"Yeah." Orlando spoke up in an unhappy tone. "We just saw that happen."

Callie looked over at Wes. "You found someone?"

Nodding, he finished off the MRE and tossed the plastic bag into an awaiting trash can. "We're three to one so far. Three people have been dug out and are alive. The last one...well, he was elderly and didn't make it."

"I'm sorry to hear that," Callie whispered. She gave them all a slight smile. "Still, you've rescued three survivors. That's great."

"The other problem is getting them medical help," Wes said darkly.

"We barely have any medical supplies," Orlando said sadly, "aspirin and that's it. No antibiotics, no painkillers...no nothing." He gave Cove a look. "Not that you aren't helping, Sergeant. We're lucky to have your EMT skills available."

Cove nodded. "I know what you mean. All those people are out there in the rain with no shelter. Sir, is there anything else we can do to help them?"

Wes felt the brunt of their frustration. "Unfortunately, no. The local people have gotten together and are now searching around for pieces of wood and fallen walls that they can use to make shelters." Logistics was just beginning to formulate a disaster relief effort. What little drugs the naval hospital could spare had been distributed to the affected areas. Wes found out that they were scrambling to get more in, but that it would take days. The whole west coast was being geared up to help the beleaguered L.A. Basin. When the precious antibiotics and pain-killing drugs arrived on daily helicopter shipments, Wes knew they'd be used in a hurry. Until then, everyone suffered.

"Mrs. Daltry over on Marshal Street has started a soup kitchen," Orlando noted with pride. "What a saint she is. The people of this area are banding together, bringing all their canned food and other stuff they can find, over to her house. They're beginning to work together to survive."

"They're going to have to," Wes muttered. He glared out at the gray day. "According to the Huey pilot I talked to this morning, there are *no* roads leading into the basin yet. No vehicles can get supplies in to them. These people are really on their own. Teams from Camp Reed have got road work going on right now, but it's going to be weeks before they reach this grid area. Once they can get dirt roads bulldozed and graded, we can get trucks carrying in a lot more supplies than a Huey can. Until that time, it's going to be rough on people."

Callie nodded. "I've seen a lot of this over in Turkey and in Mexico. The people either band together or they fight among themselves and steal from one another...and sometimes even kill for food. It can swing either way."

"I wish to hell someone had written a procedural manual on this," Wes growled. "Right now they're all looking to us for resupply, medical help, food and water. And we can't supply nearly enough of it. The medical center at Camp Reed is taking only the worst cases. We're on a triage footing. And I heard the pilot say that they're becoming swamped with medical emergencies at the base. They've got C-141 and C-130 Hercules cargo planes from the Air Force flying in and out of the airport now. The worst cases—the ones that need surgery—are being flown out to San Diego or ten other cities along the West Coast."

"It sounds like Camp Reed has become the heart of the rescue effort," Callie murmured. She reached down and patted Dusty's damp head. The dog looked up, an adoring expression in his soft golden-brown eyes.

"It is," Wes said. "But we're being overrun. There's no way one military base, no matter how big it is, can handle millions of people left homeless in the wake of a quake like this." He shook his head, his voice becoming grim. "No, we've only seen the start of this nightmare. As water and food run out, people are going to get desperate."

"Don't forget disease," Sergeant Cove muttered. "I know people in this area are drinking water without boiling it first. And as an EMT, I know that means disease is next. He clasped his large, callused hands together, a worried look wrinkling his broad brow. "Cholera and typhoid will spring up so fast it'll make people's heads swim. They won't listen to us. They'll die from diarrhea and loss of fluids and electrolytes.

And what food they have isn't refrigerated, which means food poisoning is going to take its toll unless they're using canned goods. This is a bad situation that is only gonna get worse with time.''

''You guys are real uppers,'' Callie teased lamely. She more than any of them knew the score on long-term disasters of this magnitude. It was enough to depress even the most hopeful person.

Wes studied his weary crew. They had been working at maximum effort helping people pull beams, bricks and other debris from their destroyed homes, trying to find quake victims. Physical strength went only so far. His marines were all fatigued; he could see it in their faces. Wes also saw the bulldog look in their eyes. They would work themselves into exhaustion, without whining or complaining, in order to try and save people still trapped in the area.

Glancing over at Callie, Wes saw the same deep exhaustion written in her face. Just looking at her made his heart fill with hope. Her soft-spoken manner, her obviously gentle nature, were healing and uplifting to all of them. He could tell by the look on the marines' faces as they sat surrounding him that Callie had a healing effect on everyone, whether she knew it or not.

''Okay,'' Wes said, placing his hands on the damp thighs of his camouflage cammos, ''let's saddle up. We've got work to do.''

Chapter Seven

January 3: 1600

Callie's teeth were chattering as she slipped and slid over the hotel debris with Dusty. Rain continued to fall, but it was much lighter now. It really didn't matter. She was wet to her skin and, despite all the physical exercise, was getting colder by the moment. Below, she could see the activity, which was ceaseless now, across Palm Boulevard. Wes was becoming a veritable traffic cop as more and more civilians wandered into their small camp for help, guidance and supplies.

Callie knew Wes must be feeling a lot of pressure to do something to help them, yet he could do very little. Because she had found no more survivors this afternoon, all the heavy equipment had been pulled from the hotel and was being used in an adjacent three-block area west of the Hoyt. Wes had donated his own tent as a medical facility because more and more people were in dire need of such help. Callie wondered where he'd sleep. The thought crossed her mind that her own tent had two cots in it, and she wasn't sharing with anyone else. Would he, because he was an officer, share her tent? More than likely, because in the military now, men and women in the same squad slept together. That thought sent a sheet of heat and delicious anticipation through her.

Just then Dusty lunged. He barked sharply.

Instantly, Callie followed, carefully balancing herself as, with sharp tugs, the golden retriever clawed and scratched his way up and over a jutting piece of concrete, then leaped down into a shallow dip on the other side. Heart hammering with hope, Callie scrambled after him, slipping and sliding on the wet surface. Her hands had garnered a multitude of cuts and nicks when she'd climbed out of the tunnel behind Laura Trayhern, and they burned and smarted as she landed with a jolt. Losing her balance, Callie fell awkwardly. Dusty was digging furiously and barking joyfully.

Getting up on her hands and knees and breathing hard, Callie peered about her. Stacked-up concrete, glass and twisted steel met her gaze.

"Sit," she ordered Dusty.

Obediently, the dog found a fairly level spot and sat down, his tail thumping.

Callie lifted her head and studied the area. Above her was part of a hotel floor. It looked promising. The possibility that the flooring was supported by concrete beneath meant that there could be a space where a person might survive.

"Hello...!" Callie called, cupping her hands to her mouth. "Anyone in there?" Her voice was muffled by the thick humidity and gently falling rain. She tilted her head and listened for a moment.

Nothing.

Again, Callie called.

Dusty whined.

"...Help...!"

Callie heard a woman's weakened voice floating toward her. Grinning, she felt her hopes soar. She was practically yelling in return, but she knew that the rubble soaked up the sound, as did the rain.

"I'm Callie. I'm here to help you. What's your name?"

She waited. Nothing. Callie sat back on her haunches, hands resting tensely on her wet thighs. The woman could be badly hurt, maybe drifting in and out of consciousness. Heart pounding, Callie held her breath. Finally, she heard the woman's voice again.

"...Tracy Fielding...help...my baby. She's only five months old...you have to help us..."

Gulping unsteadily, Callie called back, "I hear you, Tracy. Hang on. I'm calling for help. What's your medical condition?"

Her hands were slippery and wet with the thick leather gloves on. Callie wasn't able to release the cell phone from her web belt, so she jerked off one glove. Leaning over, she opened the precious cell phone and placed it beneath her jacket to protect it from the rain.

"...Can hardly breathe...baby...baby needs milk. I don't have any! Oh, please...help us...."

Dialing Wes's number with numbed, shaking fingers, Callie hunkered over the cell phone and waited.

"Lieutenant James."

Wes's voice washed over Callie. Instantly, her heart responded to his growling tone, which was filled with raw fatigue.

"Wes? This is Callie. We've got two survivors up here in grid area four. A woman and a five-month-old baby. I need your help. Can you get over here right now?"

Callie heard his intake of breath before he answered. And when he did, he sounded excited and hopeful. "You bet. Hang on, we'll be right there. Out."

She shut off the cell phone and carefully eased it back into the protective leather carrier on her web belt. Buttoning up her jacket again, she slipped on the wet leather gloves and stood up so Wes could locate her easily. The day was coming to a close. In front of Callie was the crane. It stood idle at the hotel site because Wes needed his men and the smaller construction equipment to help locate civilians among the smashed houses in the neighborhood.

Her heart pumped violently as she saw Wes come trotting across the boulevard toward her. As he drew closer, Callie felt joy sweep through her. His face was dangerous looking with that dark growth of beard. He quickly climbed up the rubble. Leaning over, Callie petted Dusty's head and waited for him to arrive.

"Good work, Dusty," she praised him.

Dusty thumped his tail, his pink tongue lolling out the side of his mouth.

As Wes made his way toward their location, Callie's spirits lifted even further. Because they were in a dip, her head could barely be seen. They were, quite literally, in a pocket, with debris piled up like unstable walls around them.

Wes grinned unevenly as he leaped into the dip with

her. "What did you find?" Hungrily, he gazed down into her wet, exhausted features. Callie's eyes shone with such hope...and desire? Gulping hard, Wes steadied himself above her, his hands outstretched. The wet concrete was incredibly slippery and unstable.

Callie matched his grin. "Dusty found them. A mother and five-month-old baby. Her name is Tracy Fielding. She's having trouble breathing. There's no milk for her baby."

Looking around, Wes quickly surveyed the debris. "How far down do you think she is?"

"Judging from her voice," Callie said, kneeling and pointing to the area where she'd heard the woman's voice, "I'd say six or ten feet. But I think she's semiconscious, and her voice is soft...so that might mean she's closer—maybe six feet down?"

Crouching beside her, his arm and thigh against hers, Wes saw Callie point to the spot where Dusty had halted and barked. Again he critically inspected the area. The rain was stopping and that was good. Pushing against the rubble in front of him, he sighed.

"What?" Callie demanded, afraid as she saw worry etch his brow.

"We're going to have to use the crane." Pointing upward, Wes said, "See that piece of flooring?"

Callie followed the line of his index finger. "Yes."

"We're going to have to lift it off. The question is will the slab prove to be too big and heavy for the crane to lift?"

"And if we can't lift it, we can't get to them, right?"

Rubbing his jaw, Wes stood up. "Right." He studied where the crane was positioned. Perfect. "We're good to go here." Gazing down at her, he absorbed

Callie's serene beauty. He knew she must be very cold, because her cammos were soaked. Her eyes were red-rimmed and he knew it was from physical exhaustion. They were all pushing themselves well beyond their limits now. "What can we do for Tracy and her baby? Anything?"

"While you're getting your men over here to start removal operations, I'll try to find out more about her medical condition."

"Good." Wes pulled the cell phone from his belt and called Sergeant Cove, who was spearheading search efforts on another block. Snapping the phone shut after the exchange, Wes turned to her. "Okay," he growled, "let's get this show on the road. I'd like to finish our day off with a mom and baby pulled alive out of that pit."

January 3: 1900

As night fell, Callie couldn't and wouldn't stay away from the unending efforts to dig Tracy Fielding and her baby out of the debris. The rain had stopped, but now a cool offshore breeze was blowing, chilling everyone even more. She reminded herself, as she climbed into the pocket with two other marines to help throw rubble out to the street below, that Tracy and her baby were even colder than they were. Luckily, the crane had been able to lift off the massive chunk of concrete, enabling them to continue digging.

No one had stopped to eat, either. With Sergeant Cove on the crane controls and Private Bertram manning the front-end loader below, they were working at top speed to clear the rubble. The pocket was now two car lengths long. Wes kept checking the rubble and adding metal supports here and there in hopes that their widening trench wouldn't cave in and trap them, too. Each time debris was peeled off to expose a new layer, Callie would call to Tracy and tell her what they were doing. Rarely did Tracy answer her, and that scared Callie.

Teeth chattering, she heard Wes give the order to stop. Dropping carefully to her hands and knees, she waited impatiently as they moved a set of lights up on one edge of the work area. She could now see a hole about half the size of her body opened in front of her.

A sudden aftershock occurred. Callie hunkered down. She threw her arms out to steady herself as the ground rippled. The roar always scared her; it sounded like a freight train speeding toward her. In seconds, it was over. The lights above her swayed but didn't fall. Thankfully, none of the mass had shifted around her, or filled the opening.

Breathing hard, her teeth chattering, Callie peered into the hole. Getting down on her belly, she took off her glove and stretched her arm as far as it would go into the maw. Her fingers grazed twisted steel and concrete. Then her fingers touched something warm and soft. Tracy!

"Tracy? Am I touching you?" Callie called excitedly, her voice cracking. She grunted and tried to reach farther into the hole. Yes! She could feel what she knew was a woman's arm hanging limply. There was about a foot and a half of debris between her and the inert form.

"Tracy?"

Callie held her breath for a moment, hoping to hear from her. As she waited, she ran her fingers down the woman's cool arm. Twisting a little, Callie managed to hook two fingers over Tracy's wrist to check her pulse. Releasing the air from her lungs, Callie frantically tried to find a beat. Maybe she had her fingers in the wrong spot. Groaning and pushing with her feet, she tried to maneuver another inch or two forward. There! She was able to grip Tracy's limp wrist. This time, Callie knew she'd placed her fingers over the pulse point. She waited what seemed like an interminable amount of time to feel that soft, pulsing beat occur.

Nothing happened.

"No!" Callie resituated her fingers on the woman's wrist. Again, no pulse. Releasing it, she moved her hand upward. Almost instantly, Callie felt a soft, warm lump on top of the woman. It had to be the baby!

There was a whimpering cry as her hand collided with the little body. Callie gulped. She could feel movement beneath her trembling, searching fingers. Yes, it had to be the baby. She could feel the damp fleece of what was probably a romper the infant was wearing.

Scrambling back out of the hole, Callie cried, "Hurry! There's about a foot of debris between us and them. I have contact. Tracy isn't answering and I can't get a pulse on her. I heard the baby crying. We've got to get to them fast!" And then Callie turned and began to grab at the rubble, flinging handfuls over the side faster than ever.

Wes slid down into the pocket. Lance Corporal Stevens joined them. Suddenly, everything began to heighten with urgency. Adrenaline pumped through Wes as he worked at Callie's side. She was like a madwoman tearing into that pile of shattered glass and steel. The hole grew larger. Within twenty minutes, they had exposed half of Tracy's body.

Wes ordered Stevens to stand back as Callie got down on her hands and knees and leaned into the hole. Breathing hard, he wiped his mouth. Sweat was running in rivulets from his temples. His heart was banging away in his chest as he waited. Waited and prayed that the two would be alive. He watched as Callie pulled her flashlight from her belt and snapped it on.

"Tracy?" Callie's voice was urgent as she reached in and gripped the woman's dusty, bloody arm. She flashed the light upward. "No!" Callie's heart sank. Tracy Fielding's face was a grayish color, with no sign of life in it. Gulping, Callie sobbed, "No! Oh, no…dammit.…"

As she flashed the light toward her midsection, she saw the baby for the first time. It was lying across the dead mother's chest in a filthy, yellow fleece, booted romper. Tears blinding her, Callie sniffed. She felt Wes come to her side. As he leaned over her, his body against hers, she absorbed his unspoken support.

"The mother's dead," Callie choked out. "I'm going to get the baby. Hold my flashlight.…" She turned it off, twisted and pulled it out of the hole, then handed it to him.

Moving into the hole as far as possible, Callie wormed and wriggled her way forward, her arms stretched toward the infant. Hands shaking badly, she closed them gently around the child and pulled it off the mother's body. Carefully, Callie drew the baby out through the hole. Getting to her knees with Wes's help, Callie opened her coat and placed the little body inside for warmth and protection.

''The baby?'' Wes asked hoarsely, helping her to her feet.

''Okay...I think,'' Callie sobbed. She tried to check her tears as she looked up into Wes's grim features. ''The mother's dead. No doubt about it.''

''I'm sorry,'' he said, voice rough with unshed tears.

Callie squeezed her eyes shut and fought against her own tears. She felt the infant wriggling against her. That was a good sign. ''Have Sergeant Cove confirm the mother's death. He's an EMT, I'm not. From what I could feel, there was no pulse. Her skin's cool to the touch.''

Nodding, Wes kept his hand on Callie's elbow as she spread her feet apart to anchor herself in the debris. She held the baby with such care, her arms wrapped around it outside the jacket. As they learned what had happened, the faces of the other marines were filled with sadness and hope. They'd lost the mother, but they'd save the baby. At least, Wes hoped the baby would survive.

''Okay,'' he whispered unsteadily to Callie, ''let Private Bertram and Lance Corporal Stevens help you down off this heap of rubble with the baby.''

Callie was grateful for the hands that reached to help her as she negotiated her way to the street below, her precious cargo in her arms. They escorted her across the street, and she went directly to her tent. Private Bertram ran to retrieve several dry blankets from his cot to give to her for the baby. The air was cool and damp. Callie gently laid the infant on her cot and knelt down beside it. Worriedly, she carefully moved the baby's arms and legs, looking for any sign of injury. Sergeant Cove checked the baby and proclaimed her uninjured. The infant, who had black, curly hair and wide blue eyes, began to whimper as Callie carefully stripped off the dirty yellow romper and soiled diaper. It was a little girl, she discovered. A soft smile pulled at Callie's mouth as she heard Private Bertram galloping toward the tent. He arrived at the flap opening, breathing hard and thrusting two blankets into her outstretched hand.

"Thanks, Private."

"Yes, ma'am...." He eased into the tent to look at the baby. "A little girl? Isn't she cute, ma'am?"

Callie swaddled the baby girl in the dry blanket. "Yes, she's beautiful." Easing her back into her arms, she pressed the baby against her chest. She saw Wes arrive. The private moved aside to allow him entrance. Wes's eyes were narrowed upon her. The look in them sent a bolt of heat through Callie as she held the baby to her. Lips parting, tiredness making her groggy and dizzy, she wondered if the feelings she had right now for this orphaned infant would be similar if it were her own baby she held, and Wes were its father. The thought was so far from out of left field that Callie knew she must be hallucinating because of extreme exhaustion. Wes desired her. He didn't love her. He'd told her that from the beginning....

"I need some milk," she told them, her voice slurring. "And a baby bottle?"

Bertram beamed as he stood just outside the flap. "Hey, ma'am! There's a lady over on Beechwood Street that just had a baby a few weeks ago. I'll run over there and get you a bottle. She's got several, and I know she'll loan us one."

Frowning, Wes studied Callie and the baby as she stood in the center of the tent, rocking her in her arms.

"What about a milk source? Could we use the dry milk packets that come with the MREs? Would that be okay for the baby, Callie?"

She smiled tiredly. "Sure, it's a great idea."

Turning, Wes ordered Bertram to hotfoot it over to that woman on Beechwood Street. Instantly, the marine saluted, turned on his heel and took off at a fast run down the avenue.

Dizziness swept over Callie. She sat down on the cot and continued to gently rock the baby. "Use that boiled water to mix up the milk," she told Wes. "And use about half the amount of water so that the milk is strong. If you have any sugar around, you can put a teaspoon in it."

Nodding, Wes turned and called out through the tent flap. "Lance Corporal Stevens?"

"Yes, sir?" The marine halted and looked into the tent. He grinned widely when he saw Callie holding the infant. Resuming a more serious look, he came to attention in front of Wes.

"Grab the dehydrated milk packets from three MREs in the supply tent. Mix them two to one with boiled water, and then cool it enough so the baby can drink it once Bertram comes back with a bottle."

Steven's face lit up with pleasure. "You bet, sir." He hurried off toward the supply tent.

Wes entered the tent. They were alone, if only for a few precious minutes. Hungrily he absorbed Callie's soft look as she held the baby in her arms. Kneeling down on one knee, he reached out and caressed her cheek. Her flesh was cool and he was concerned for her.

"You'll make a beautiful mother someday," he told her in a low, gritty tone.

Shaken by the intimacy he effortlessly established with her, Callie closed her eyes and absorbed his fleeting touch. She was starved for Wes—in so many ways. Moments of privacy were like gold to her. "This baby wouldn't be here with us now if not for you," she choked out softly, opening her eyes. Drowning in his dark, burning gaze, Callie added, "I don't know what's happening between us, Wes.... I need you, and yet we just met. It's all so crazy. I find myself out there hunting for survivors and you pop into my mind and heart out of nowhere." Her brows knitted. "What's going on? Has this ever happened to you?"

Reaching out, Wes helped to cradle the baby in her arms. "No...not ever. I can't explain it, either, Callie." Tiredness lapped at him. Wes struggled to find the words for how he felt, but it was impossible. "It's the same for me, Angel. There's so much ongoing trauma around us, so many people who are needy and desperate...and even in the middle of this crisis, I'm seeing your beautiful face and those incredible blue eyes of yours haunting me." Wes gave her a lopsided smile drawn with exhaustion. "Just know this, Callie—we'll both have the time to explore our desire for one another. I know we're in a helluva crisis right now...."

As he grazed her wet cheek, Callie sighed. "Too much is happening too fast. I'm too tired to sort it all out and so are you...."

An ache settled in his heart, one he tried to ignore. He smiled slightly. "I've got some good news for you and the rest of our team."

Sighing, she pressed her cheek into his cupped hand. "I could use it. What's the surprise?"

Wes removed his hand from the infant and looked

at the watch on his left wrist. "In another hour, a Huey is bringing in a replacement team for us. Lucy will stay here with her dog and continue rescue efforts. We're going to be flown back to Camp Reed for twenty-four hours of R and R. How's that sound for a nice surprise, Callie?"

Gasping, she whispered, "Really? In just an hour?" Wes had mentioned it before, but Callie hadn't known when it would occur.

Wes suddenly felt silly, like a teenage kid once again. He wanted to laugh but clamped down on the desire. Knowing that his emotional state was shredded by the quake and the long, grueling days of work, he met and held her wide eyes instead. "Yeah, it's for real, Callie. They are finally giving us a break." He reluctantly removed his hand from her soft cheek. What he wanted to do was kiss her senseless. The maternal look on her face as she rocked the baby gently in her arms nearly overwhelmed him. Callie might be a woman marine, but that took nothing away from her femininity, or the fact that she was all woman.

Because he knew Bertram or Stevens would be coming back soon, and he wanted no one to eavesdrop on what he had to say to Callie, he whispered carefully, "What I want—and this has to be mutual, Callie—" He drew in a deep breath and held her glistening blue eyes. "When we land back at Camp Reed, I want you to share my room at the B.O.Q. I want to take a hot shower with you…I want you in my bed and in my arms. I need to hold you…and I need to be held."

His words touched her like warming rays of sunshine. Callie bowed her head and closed her eyes. Wes was honest in a way that she'd never experienced with a man.

The baby moved and she opened her jacket to allow her tiny black-haired head to appear. With trembling fingers, she caressed the little girl's curly strands.

"Talk with me, Callie. What do you think about this? How are you feeling about it?" Wes asked unsteadily. He got to his feet and stood across the aisle from her, knowing his men would arrive shortly. It was important for appearance's sake that the others didn't know what existed between him and Callie. Anxiously, he perused her features. Just the way she caressed the baby's soft, damp hair made him long for her touch. The quake had ripped his armor from him. Wes was finding himself even more vulnerable to the worsening conditions at the camp, the incredible human suffering around them. And somehow, his heart knew that Callie could soothe him, heal him, and give him some of that quiet, unending strength that he saw burning in her glimmering eyes.

"I—I'm afraid, Wes," Callie managed to stammer in a low, strangled tone. Forcing her gaze upward, she met his shadowed eyes, which burned with desire— for her. "I—it's me, you know? I've just never had a guy want me like you do. It's nice in one way, but scary as all get out in another. I'm not pretty.... I just don't understand your attraction to me, I guess...."

"Callie, you're beautiful to me. Shouldn't that count?"

Managing a grudging smile, she gazed down at the little girl, who was sleeping now. "Yes, it does. I'm just afraid, Wes, that's all." Afraid that her heart longed for him and he would reject that because of his past. Wes offered only a fleeting relationship, nothing substantial to build over time. At first Callie had thought she could do that—just respond to Wes on a level of mutual desire. But something else was taking root in her heart and she was even more confused and unsure.

"That's okay. I don't want to pressure you, Callie. That's not what my honesty is all about. This is a two-way street, and like I said, we have time."

Her heart burst with ripe pain and need. "I owe you an explanation, Wes. I'm afraid I haven't had much experience in relationships. In high school, I was shunned. They called me a lot of names and made fun of me."

"Why?" His voice went off-key with anger—an emotion he wasn't concealing as well as he would like. The hurt in Callie's tone, and the anguish in her eyes, tore at him.

"My parents were very poor, and I couldn't afford the 'in' clothes. My mother made our clothes. My dad was a farmer in Minnesota until he broke his back. He's now stuck in a wheelchair for the rest of his life. We had to go on welfare and we lost the farm. We lost everything…and my dad, well, it broke him in another way, because he was an outdoors man. He loved nature. He loved working outside." Tucking her lower lip between her teeth, she hesitated. Wes deserved the whole truth, so she pushed on in a hushed tone.

"I worked after school to bring in enough money to feed the family. I was the oldest. That was my responsibility. My mother had to stay home to raise the little ones. I tried to make things better for everyone, Wes. I had two jobs after school, but we couldn't afford clothes or shoes for everyone. We ended up buying things at the secondhand clothing store. But even though we had some hard luck, we were always clean and our clothes pressed and spotless.''

Grimly, Wes settled his hands on his hips. ''But the kids at school, being kids, they knew. And they made fun of you.''

''Yes…kids aren't exactly nice to those who have hit some hard luck,'' she agreed wryly. Callie saw the anger banked in his eyes and in the harsh line of his mouth. ''Kids that came from the wrong side of the tracks, like we did, were outcasts, too.'' She smiled slightly. ''You don't strike me as coming from a dirt-poor farm family.''

His hands slipped from her narrow hips. ''No, I've never had to scramble or scrape by like you or your family had to, Callie. My father is a very well-known architect back in Hartford, Connecticut.'' He sat down on the plyboard floor and wrapped his arms around his upraised knees. Just getting to talk to Callie, to find out about her as a person, was an unexpected gift to him.

''And he wanted me to follow in his footsteps. I guess that's where the trouble began.'' Wes offered her a sour smile. When he saw the corners of her soft mouth move upward, he felt almost dizzy with need for her. The lights outside dimly illuminated the tent interior, accentuating the planes of her square face and emphasizing those wide, intelligent eyes.

''You went into the Marine Corps instead?'' Callie guessed.

''Yeah…'' Wes gave a bark of laughter. ''I wanted to help build a better world. I guess I inherited my dad's engineering skills, but I wanted to help others. I came from a privileged background, Callie. I've never known what it's like to starve or have to scramble to make a buck to buy food to put on the table. I went to Harvard, just like my dad. I didn't have to worry about scholarships or anything having to do with money, because my father paid for it all. From there, I went through officer's candidate school, and after graduation, I joined the Corps."

"He wasn't too happy about that?"

Shaking his head, Wes said, "No, but I've been in the Corps awhile and he's getting used to the idea."

Rocking the baby, Callie gazed down at her as she slept soundly in her arms. "Brothers and sisters?"

"No, I'm a spoiled only child." He grinned.

Laughing quietly, Callie said, "There's six in our family. Three boys and three girls. I send half my paycheck home to my parents every month. It's helped them out a lot. They're not on welfare anymore, and that's helped my dad's pride. He's a proud man and he never in his life wanted to ask for a handout."

"They still in Minnesota?" Wes cherished this talk between them. He wished that the world would stop turning for just a moment so they could continue their exploration of one another. He was starved to know more about what made Callie the incredible and heroic woman she was.

"Yes," Callie said softly. "They live in a nice little house up in International Falls. That's close to the Canadian border. We kids are trying to save enough money in a special bank account to buy them a small farm where they can live out their days. I think my dad would be better off if we could get him out of town and back on the land. He's so depressed because he lives in the city."

Wes nodded. "I understand that. Even though I was

raised in the 'burbs, I ran for the woods every chance I got. I liked being out in the rain, wind and elements.''

"As a civil engineer you're outdoors most of the time?"

"Yes." Wes gazed at her. "And your job in the Corps keeps you outdoors, too."

Callie grinned tiredly. "Maybe we're gluttons for punishment. I don't know about you, but I'm freezing to death. I'm really looking forward to getting a hot shower."

As Wes gave her a heated look, he heard the clump of boots nearing the tent. It was probably Bertram coming back with the baby bottle. "Just remember, there's an open invitation to take it with me, should you change your mind."

Just the way he said it made Callie feel good about herself. Wes wasn't pressuring her. His invitation was a compliment to her. A wonderful one.

"Thanks…" she whispered, suddenly emotional. His face blurred momentarily and Callie gulped back her tears. "You have no idea what you've done for my self-confidence. You're such a gift to me, Wes.…"

Chapter Eight

January 4: 0900

''Hey, Callie!''

A hand gripped her shoulder and gave her a good shake.

''It's 0900. Get up.''

The voice of Captain Susannah Wilson sliced abruptly into her deep sleep. Groaning, Callie forced open her eyes. She heard the rescue dogs barking out in the kennel. There was a flurry of people rushing around outside the small ready room. Forcing her eyelids open, she saw Susannah's dark-brown eyes narrowed on her as she leaned over her.

''Uhhh…yeah, okay…I'm up.''

Grinning a little, Susannah released her shoulder and stood by the bunk as Callie stirred beneath the blankets. "What's with you, Evans? You get twenty-four hours of R and R I'd die for, and you curl up in your wet clothes here at H.Q. instead of getting a nice, hot shower and a warm, dry bed over at the B.O.Q."

Rubbing her face tiredly, Callie threw off the covers. She was still damp, but at least she was slightly warm. Her eyes felt puffy and she scrubbed them with her fists for a moment, trying to wake up. The activity outside the ready room was evident.

"I dropped Dusty off here," she muttered thickly, "and I couldn't move another step."

"So you crashed and burned here," Susannah said, placing her hands on her hips. "Don't blame you. Well, get your butt outta here, Lieutenant. Go to your B.O.Q. room and get cleaned up. You smell awful."

Giving her a slight smile, Callie combed her hair back into place with her dirty fingers. "You're right— I smell like hell."

"More like a garbage dump. Get outta here. I don't want to see you back here until 1600. Private Snelling is takin' care of the dogs and feeding 'em. You do a disappearing act. Hear me?"

"Yeah…I hear you.…"

Callie watched her tall, shapely C.O., who was dressed in desert cammos, walk briskly out of the room. After Wes had taken her and the baby to the hospital, Callie had come over to the unit to drop Dusty off and care for him. It was then that she'd run out of gas, physically speaking, and she'd crashed on the ready room bunk. It was the last thing she remembered.

As she slowly pulled her dirty, muddy black boots toward her, Callie's awakening brain swung between Wes and the baby. They called her Baby Jane Fielding because no one knew her first name. Callie was sorry she hadn't asked the mother. At least they had a last name, and when the Red Cross got a chance, they'd try and track down the father, or the parents or other relatives of Tracy Fielding.

As Callie laced her boots with slow-moving, fumbling fingers, she thought of Wes. Instantly, her heart expanded with such a euphoria that it wiped out her sleepy state.

Had he waited for her to come to his room? She didn't know. She'd wanted to, but had been simply too exhausted. Somehow, Callie knew he'd understand. After she rose and tried to straighten her damp, rumpled cammos into some semblance of order, Callie took her crumpled cap and put it on her head. First she'd check on Dusty and then she'd head over to the B.O.Q. for a delicious hot shower.

January 4: 1000

After putting on a set of clean, pressed cammos after her hot shower, Callie began to feel human again. The B.O.Q. room was small, but it was clean. Outside the window of the four-story brick building, she saw an incredible sight. The B.O.Q. was less than a mile from the airport. The amount of air traffic was mind-boggling. She saw at least ten Lockheed C-130 Hercules, a midrange cargo plane with four turbo-prop engines, trundling into the revetment areas, no doubt filled with supplies. The huge C-141 Starlifters were the work horses of the relief effort, however. There were three of them on the runways right now. The air vibrated with the mighty engines at full throttle as one took off, probably with a load of medical emergencies,

Callie guessed. The facility was a beehive of activity, with people, Humvees and planes moving in a constant procession to a line of awaiting, dark-green cargo trucks that she was sure would be taking life-giving supplies off base to the surrounding civilian areas.

Brushing her recently washed hair, Callie grabbed her cap and settled it on her head. Her stomach growled. According to the instructions on the dresser in her room, a chow hall had been set up in a tent the east side of the B.O.Q. Should she try to locate Wes? She'd seen his name listed on the roster down in the foyer of the building and knew he was in room 210. She was in room 320. Seesawing over whether she should find him or not, Callie decided she was ultimately a coward. No, she needed time to gather herself emotionally; the stress was wearing on her normally good, sound judgment. Hurrying out the door and into the carpeted hall, she saw a number of other marine officers in desert cammos coming and going. They ranged from second lieutenants all the way up to colonel. The B.O.Q. was becoming the only place officers could stay, because no one was able to get off base to their homes with all the roads outside Camp Reed destroyed.

The day was dawning clear and cool. Callie appreciated the blue sky and knew it probably wouldn't rain for a week or so. That would make her job easier. Hurrying to the tent, she saw the olive-green flaps were up and at least fifty long tables were set up. A number of officers Callie recognized from the dog rescue unit called to her as she got in line and picked up an aluminum tray. The cooks behind the line had huge tubs of pancakes, real scrambled eggs, fragrant bacon, and an urn of hot black coffee. Callie's mouth watered. She was starving.

"There you are."

Callie sucked in a sharp breath. Turning awkwardly on her heel, she looked up to see him standing in line behind her, a welcoming smile on his mouth. "Wes…hi…" Instantly, all of Callie's doubts about herself melted away beneath his dark-green gaze. Wearing a set of clean, dry cammos, Wes was clean shaven, his short hair combed into place. But it was the look in his eyes that sent a sheet of need through Callie.

Feeling heat steal up her cheeks, she stammered, "I—I didn't even make it to the B.O.Q. last night. I crashed over at the dog unit ready room."

Just getting to see Callie lifted Wes's flagging spirits. As they moved slowly toward the cooks ladling out the food, he grinned crookedly. "Don't worry about it. I don't want what I said to make you feel pressured." Her eyes were clear and bright now, and Wes was beginning to grasp the amount of exhaustion Callie had endured over the last few days. Her hair was clean, her face scrubbed, her cheeks a heightened pink color. Most of all, he liked the soft way her lips curved upward. He wanted to kiss her breathless. He wanted to make love to her.

Reaching the food lineup, Callie turned around and greeted the cooks. She received heaping amounts of scrambled eggs, rashers of bacon, several thick slices of sourdough toast and some warm, sliced apples in a thick cinnamon sauce. Wes wasn't far behind, so she waited for him to get through the line. Spying a nearly empty table, Callie pointed to it. "Want to sit there?"

Wes came up to her. "Want to be seen with me?" he teased in an intimate tone.

Grinning, Callie said, "I'm game if you are."

"In a heartbeat. If a beautiful lady asks me to sit down and have breakfast with her, who am I to argue? Lead the way."

Sitting down at the picnic table made of redwood, Callie watched as Wes sat down opposite her. They ate hungrily, in silence. The voices of the hundred or so other people there rose congenially around them. Picking up the thick white ceramic mug filled with hot, black coffee, Callie savored every sip of it after she'd finished her meal.

"We ate like starving wolves," Wes noted ruefully, setting his empty tray aside.

Laughing, Callie said, "I think we were a little hungry."

"No kidding. MREs only go so far. Give me real food anytime." And he grinned at her.

She sat forward with her elbows resting on the table, the cup between her hands. She'd taken the cap off, and her tawny hair had wide streaks of gold through it, he discovered, emphasizing her square face and sparkling blue eyes. If Wes guessed correctly, she was happy to be sharing time and space with him. Picking up his own cup of coffee, he sipped it.

"This is a religious experience," he told her with a low growl of satisfaction.

Grinning, Callie said, "Yeah, isn't it, though? Who'd think a hot meal and good, strong coffee could ever taste so good?"

"And it didn't cost an arm and a leg at some five-star restaurant, either."

She sighed and simply allowed herself the pleasure

and privilege of absorbing his handsome face into her heart. The sensation was new to Callie, but satisfying in a way she'd never experienced before. "I wonder how Baby Jane is?"

"I was wondering the same thing." Wes looked out of the tent. Camp Reed was built on hills and valleys of desert land, the yellow-ocher color glowing golden in the rising sun. "I was going to go over to the hospital to check up on her." He looked at Callie. "Would you like to come with me and find out how she's doing?"

Heart pumping harder in her breast, Callie whispered, "Yes, I'd love to, Wes. The baby was one of the first things I thought about after my C.O. shook me awake this morning."

"Me, too," he confided. With a rueful look he added, "I don't know what the medical facility is going to do. They're already over the top on how many patients they can handle. They've set up several large tents nearby to handle triage cases—people less seriously injured."

"Did you see the airport? I've never seen it so crowded or busy."

"Yeah," he said grimly, moving the cup slowly between his large, lean hands. "I saw it earlier today. They're at max capacity, from what an air control officer told me."

"I'd think the real problem isn't getting supplies into the base, but rather getting them *out* of Camp Reed to the hard hit areas outside our gates."

"Bingo," Wes muttered. Frowning, he shook his head. "I realized yesterday that we're at just the beginning of a very, very long disaster sequence, Callie. We're in for the long haul...and we haven't even begun to see the worst of it. There's got to be a million people homeless out there...."

Callie felt his worry and sadness. "You're right," she said quietly as she finished the rest of her coffee.

He lifted his head and drowned in her blue gaze, which was shadowed now. "You're the expert on this. You've seen this kind of devastation over in Turkey."

"It was awful there," Callie agreed. "But this is worse. Worse than I've seen anywhere else in the world. You're right—we're in this for the long haul. I was talking to Captain Wilson, my C.O., earlier, and she was working with the quake logistics H.Q. to figure out a long-term approach to using our resources."

"Dogs and humans can work only so long and so hard," he murmured. Wanting to reach out and touch her hand, which rested on the table near her mug, Wes stopped himself. "And you overworked yourself out there, Callie. I won't let it happen again."

She shrugged. "How can we not work ourselves until we drop, Wes? What if it was your loved one buried beneath that rubble? Would you stop?"

"I understand," he murmured. "Morgan Trayhern didn't stop. The man was ready to keel over, but he found the guts, the energy, to keep going."

"My point precisely," Callie said archly. "Hey, if we're going over to the hospital, let's drop in and see how Laura is. I don't often get to visit the people we've rescued. It would be a nice upper in a world gone sour around us."

"Sounds like a plan. Let's do it."

January 4: 1100

Callie held Baby Jane Fielding in her arms. The little girl was now in a pink fleece romper and wrapped in a blue quilted blanket. Wes stood by Callie's shoulder, smiling down at her as she held the infant.

"She looks healthy and fine," he murmured, reaching out and gently touching the little girl's curly black hair.

Smiling softly, Callie continued to rock the infant in her arms. "Just looking at her gives me peace."

Wes looked around. The maternity ward was in a state of quiet panic. The nurses were dressed in white uniforms, the looks on their face harried and stressed. The ward was overcrowded with infants of all ages, even some newborns who had come into the world less than twenty-four hours ago. Every last crib was in use. The nurse on duty, Captain Barbara Loews, had given Callie permission to hold Baby Jane. Callie liked the gentle look on Wes's face as he leaned down and caressed the infant's pink cheek with the tip of his large index finger.

"She looks good compared to how we found her last night."

Nodding, Callie reluctantly placed the infant back into her tiny crib next to the wall. "Babies have amazing abilities to bounce back fast from the edge of disaster, unlike adults or the elderly."

Brightening, Wes said, "Well, this is one positive story. Let's go find the Trayherns. They're up on floor eight, the post-op ward."

January 4: 1300

Callie eased in the door of the private room. She saw Laura Trayhern sitting up in bed, her broken ankle

raised by a series of pulleys. At her side was her husband. When they saw her, they both broke into welcoming smiles. Callie opened the door and called to
Wes, who followed her into the whitewashed room.

"Hi," Callie greeted them as she took off her cap
and approached Laura's bed, her hand extended. "We
just thought we'd drop in and see how you were."

Laura gripped Callie's small hand and squeezed it.
"We're fine, Callie. Hi, Wes. How are you two doing?
Morgan and I were just talking about you a few
minutes ago."

Wes removed his cap and nodded to Morgan, who
stood with his hand on his wife's blue-gowned shoulder. "Fine, ma'am. We thought we'd look in on you
and see how your ankle was recovering."

Laura smiled tiredly and said, "Call me Laura. And
my ankle is, as you can see, coming along slowly but
surely." She looked over at Morgan. "We were just
commenting on how well the Marine Corps is handling this ongoing disaster operation."

Callie stood inches from Wes at the bedside. Laura
looked pale, and there were dark smudges beneath her
wide, intelligent eyes. The bruises where she'd been
struck during the building's collapse were turning a
deep purple-blue. Morgan's hands were still swathed
in bandages. Callie was sure that he'd received mul-
tiple stitches, what with all the gashes and cuts he'd
gotten trying to dig out his wife.

"I think we're geared up as much as we can be,"
Callie told them. "Camp Reed is the largest military
reservation in Southern California, but even it can do
only so much in a crisis of this magnitude."

Morgan studied them. "Are you two on R and R?"

"Yes, sir, we are," Wes said. "They're flying us

back out by Huey at 1630 today and we'll renew our rescue efforts at the Hoyt Hotel grid.''

Shaking his head, Morgan muttered, "This is an unfolding logistical nightmare. What are all those people out there in the basin going to do for water? That's the biggest priority now—getting them water.''

Laura patted his hand and then gave them a wry look. "My husband is working with the base general. He has a background in disaster-type situations. We've got a team from his company, Perseus, on their way here, to help the planners.''

Callie saw a warm, burning look pass between the couple. She recognized that look because it was the one Wes gave her when they were alone. Hungrily, Callie absorbed Wes's nearness now.

"We rescued a baby yesterday, Laura. Baby Jane Fielding." Her voice dropped with sadness. "The mother died before we could get her out…but the baby survived. If you get bored, I'll bet Mr. Trayhern here could go down to the maternity ward and pick her up and you could hold her and bottle-feed her. They're overwhelmed down there. I know they'd appreciate your help if you volunteered.''

"What a wonderful idea!" Laura gripped her husband's bandaged hand gently. "I'd love to help, Morgan. In any way possible. Besides, I just love little babies. Will you go down there and see about this later?''

Morgan grinned slightly. "Sure. You and babies are a natural. Besides, maybe you won't be so bored if you have a little tyke in your arms.''

"That must have been a pretty serious break to your ankle," Callie commented, pointing to it. Laura wore a cast up to her knee, a thick white sock over the toe.

"I was in surgery for three hours." She smiled a little sadly. "The bone was broken. Shattered, really. They said they had to put me together again with pins. Right now, I'm tired, but I'm not in pain, and that's a huge help."

"And will you be able to walk okay when it's all said and done?" Callie asked. She liked Laura's warm effervescence. Her blond hair had been recently washed and hung in sunny strands around her shoulders. It was the life, the warmth in her eyes, that drew Callie to her. There was something so positive and healing about Laura Trayhern.

"Yes," Morgan said with a scowl, "she will."

Laughing, Laura said, "The doctors are saying I'll have to do a lot of physical therapy and rehab. Under the circumstances, that seems like little penance compared to where I was a couple of days ago—flat on my back and wondering if I was going to live or die in that cold, dark place."

Callie nodded soberly at her emotionally charged words. She reached out and awkwardly patted the woman's shoulder. "It's a horrible thing to be trapped like that. I'm sure you'll have nightmares and memories from it for a long time…at least, that's what I hear. Post-traumatic stress disorder. That's what they call it."

Wrinkling her nose, Laura said, "I've got flashbacks by the ton already." She looked up at her husband. "And I don't sleep well at night." Then she brightened. "But compared to so many other people who are still out there, suffering and in need of medical help, painkillers or antibiotics, I'm in good shape, so I don't spend much time feeling sorry for myself."

Callie nodded again. "And when are you going home?"

"To Montana?" Laura asked.

"Not for a while," Morgan said grimly. "Right now, they're flying out only the worst triage cases. People need surgery, but this hospital simply can't meet the demand. They're using the Herks and the Starlifters and flying patients up the coast to San Francisco, Portland and Seattle. The whole hospital system on the West Coast has now initiated the FEMA triage system to cope with this disaster."

"And so you're stuck with us?" Callie teased warmly. She saw Laura rally and give her a wan smile. "We can come and visit again?"

"We'd love to see you two again. And I don't mind being here," Laura offered. "Morgan was able to use his cell phone and contact our family and friends to tell them we're okay. Right now, every available plane, every space aboard those planes, are for medical emergencies, food or supplies. I don't fall into any of those categories. I'm willing to wait."

"We'll be here at least a couple of weeks," Morgan warned her, "maybe longer. I'm working with Logistics to get us on a scheduled flight out of here. My team is flying in, and the plane will be used to take supplies into the basin. Reports are slowly filtering in by cell phone that there are some local airports where the runways haven't been totaled. Our jet can get in and out on their short landing strips, so we're handing it over to Logistics to help out. A lot of civilian pilots with planes or helicopters are being called to volunteer their services for this disaster. We need them because we only have so many military pilots, and they can't fly twenty-four hours a day. By law, they can fly only a certain number of hours in a twenty-four hour period. If they work longer, accidents happen and people get killed. So the civilian help is going to be absolutely essential to our ongoing, long-range efforts for the disaster planning.''

"Yes, sir, and also factor in the problem that every aircraft has to have certain maintenance performed on it every five, ten, twenty and thirty hours, so we lose them to the mechanics," Wes added.

"Right," Morgan said heavily. "You don't fly an unmaintained aircraft or helicopter. That will put you into possible danger and could cause loss of life, too. No, we need experienced civilian air mechanics. The only problem is reaching them. Without radio or telephone, it's nearly impossible.''

"We have our work cut out for us," Callie agreed, gloomy over the long-range logistics that Morgan and Wes were describing.

Wes saw how tired Laura was becoming. He settled his hand on Callie's shoulder briefly. "Let's let these folks get some rest, okay? We'll come back for another visit the next time they give us some R and R.''

Laura gripped Callie's hand before she left. "Thank you, Callie, from the bottom of my heart for what you did. I wouldn't be here now if not for you...." Her eyes welled up with tears.

Hot tears filled Callie's own eyes as she stood there, gripping Laura's small, strong hand. "I—I'm glad we could do it for you, Laura. I just hope we find more folks out there soon. Time's running out....''

Morgan rasped, "I've got your name and unit, Callie. I promise you, once this disaster is under control and things are getting back to a semblance of normalcy, you'll be hearing from us. You need to be properly thanked.''

Giving him a slight, self-conscious smile, Callie said, "Sir, you don't owe us a thing. We love what we do. Seeing someone come out of this mess alive is what we live for. Just seeing you two together makes me happier than you could ever know...."

Wes stood there listening to the emotion behind Callie's softly spoken words. She was so unassuming. Never did she use the word *I*. No, she said *we* and was incredibly humble about her own courage and capabilities. His heart swelled with pride for her. He could see by the look in Morgan's eyes that the man meant what he said. Callie and Dusty deserved to be singled out and rewarded. Under the military system, however, she was seen as simply doing her job, and that was all. There would be no medals for her heroism.

As they left the room and headed down the bustling, crowded passageway, Wes enjoyed the feel of her arm brushing his occasionally. The elevators were working. Luckily, the nuclear plant that had been built on Camp Reed had not sustained damage. It was the only plant in Southern California capable of continuous electrical supply at the moment. Luckily for the military base, the marine electricians had fixed the fallen power lines already. Camp Reed was the only place in the basin to have electricity, a miracle in itself.

Outside, the sun warmed them as they walked, avoiding the gurneys, paramedics, EMTs, and survivors and hustling personnel on errands of mercy. The neatly kept lawn that sloped toward the asphalt avenue was covered with tents now. Everywhere Wes looked there was frantic, ongoing activity. He looked down at Callie, who was absorbing all the nonstop action.

"How are *you* doing?"

She looked up as they continued down the cracked sidewalk toward the street. "Me? Good. Getting to see the baby and to talk with Laura has really lifted my spirits."

His eyes gleamed. "And seeing me, too?" Was he being too forward with her? In some ways, Wes couldn't help himself.

Her lips curved ruefully. "Yes, the second thought after I was so rudely pulled from sleep this morning was about you."

"Care to share?" He stopped at the bottom of the stairs. People were hurrying all around them. There were at least thirty noisy, smelly diesel-fueled trucks of military convoy rumbling slowly down the street toward the main gates of Camp Reed, packed with life-giving supplies for needy people outside the base.

Feeling his warmth, his care, Callie looked up at Wes. He had such a little-boy smile hovering across his mouth. A mouth that had cherished her lips and made her feel so incredibly happy. Callie had never realized she could feel like that. "I don't want to give you a swelled head."

"Oh, that's already a foregone conclusion."

She liked his teasing. It gave her the confidence to tease him in return. "That's what I was afraid of."

"But I can be rescued."

"Oh?" She saw his mouth broaden with a good-natured smile.

"A kiss will revive me."

"You're such a glutton for punishment, Lieutenant."

"But," Wes sighed, meeting her shining eyes, which were filled with laughter, "you can save me from a fate worse than death."

"Right," she chortled. "Instead of mouth-to-mouth CPR, you'll revive with a kiss."

"One kiss will do it all," he promised her solemnly. How Wes liked to see Callie brighten and become playful. This was a new side to her and one he liked immensely. He knew her work was hard and serious; yet she had a sense of humor, despite the grueling and grim career path she'd chosen.

As she stood with her hands in the pockets of her jacket, Callie said, "You know what? I'm a coward, Wes."

"What?" He stepped down off the curb so that they were nearly at eye level. By the way her brows knit, she was serious. "Not in my view you aren't. Not ever."

She shrugged unhappily. "No…I meant a coward in an emotional sense. Like…last night. After I got Dusty taken care of, I was afraid." Callie avoided his sharpened stare. "I was afraid to come over to the B.O.Q. because I really wanted to boldly walk up to your room, knock on it and go take that shower with you."

"I see…." Wes saw her struggling with a lot of emotions. She was so easy to read, and he found himself wanting to reach out and touch her, soothe her, but he couldn't.

"I'm a coward in that sense." Callie sighed. "I guess because what few relationships I've had were all certifiable disasters in one way or another. I got used to being hit on as a convenient piece of meat that was around to take to bed to gratify a guy's urges."

"Ouch," Wes muttered. He sighed. "Oh, boy...and I've been coming on strong to you, too. You probably thought the same thing?" He had tried to tell her that his desire for her was much more than sex.

Nodding, Callie added, "I feel this urgency to be with you. It's such a different feeling here, in my heart. You were so gut-wrenchingly honest with me last night in the tent that it scared me. I saw you were being honest. It wasn't a line with you." She gave him a twisted smile. "I think I've lived long enough and been around the block enough times to know the difference." Callie wanted to broach the subject of whether he still only felt desire or whether his heart was involved, but she was afraid. She could see the wariness in Wes's eyes and knew he was thinking of his loss of Allison. No, he wouldn't share his heart with her, and that broke hers.

"Okay," he murmured, "so where does that leave us?"

"Scared."

He grinned and nodded. "I am, too, Callie." Several cargo-laden trucks roared by, and Wes didn't try to speak until they'd passed.

The desire to reach out and grip his hand nearly overwhelmed Callie. "See? That's the part that's got me scared, Wes. Your brutal honesty. No man I've ever met was up front like you are. And I know it's not a line to get me in bed." She pressed her hand to her heart. "I just know it in here." And she did. The sizzling look he gave her, loaded with desire, sent her pulse soaring.

"So, let's take this a day at a time," Wes suggested. "God knows, we're going to be working until we drop out there at our assignment. Let's dream about going dancing over at the O Club. Or maybe even a picnic at the beach?''

''And if I can steal a moment with you alone, can I have that kiss?'' Callie gave him a soft, teasing smile. ''You think you're the only one who wants one? I do, too.''

Chapter Nine

January 6: 0600

Everything was quiet. Callie moved sluggishly around her tent after feeding Dusty. They had been out on their grid for two days now, and the R and R seemed like a dream. She was down on her hands and knees, putting the bright-red vest on Dusty, when Wes appeared at the opened flap of her tent.

"Got a minute?" he asked, his voice low.

Instantly, Callie's heart beat hard. "Sure. Come on in."

Wes gave her a grin and slipped inside. He sat down on her cot, which she'd just made up. "Everyone else is still asleep. I thought I'd be selfish and leave them in their tents for ten minutes and share the time with you."

Grinning sheepishly, Callie patted Dusty's head after she'd arranged the vest on the dog. "You must have heard me thinking about you."

Clasping his hands between his opened thighs, Wes caught and held her wide blue gaze. Since returning to the Hoyt location, she'd noted that demands on his time had tripled. And so had the number of tents and personnel. She now had her own tent. Callie had been over with his crew on Dexter Street, where a three-story apartment building had collapsed. Many of the people had already been dug out by neighbors, but there were some portions that only a crane or cherry picker could handle.

"So, you were thinking about me?" he teased.

"Yeah, I was." Callie watched as the gray light of dawn crept in on them. In the distance, fires were still in evidence, but most had burned themselves out over the last few days. The rain earlier in the week had helped to snuff out many of them. The sky was blanketed with a thick, black layer of smoke, though. Dusty sat next to her, and she continued to stroke his head and neck.

"Can I get nosy and ask what you were thinking?" Wes hungrily absorbed Callie's face, her expression and the way her mouth curved.

"Oh, it might swell your head some more."

Chuckling, Wes removed his cammo cap and ran his fingers through his short hair. He gave her a rueful look. "I had that coming."

"Yes, you did."

"Well, I was thinking about you all day yesterday and last night before I went to sleep. Want to hear my thoughts?"

"Sure, I'm a glutton for punishment." She laughed.

Wes made her feel hope. All day yesterday, Callie had worked nonstop with Dusty. They'd found five people—three dead, but two still alive. Sergeant Perkins had found five more in their absence and that made everyone search even harder. By midnight she'd been exhausted, and Wes had ordered her back to their little tent city, which had now grown to twenty tents.

"Actually," he said, "I had more questions than anything else."

"Oh?"

He watched how her small hands stroked the dog, who was lapping up her every touch. Wes found himself wishing Callie would one day stroke him with such fondness. "I was wondering what you hoped for in your life." He knew he had no right to ask her such private and intimate questions, but he couldn't help himself. He knew his feelings had moved dangerously beyond desire, but something was driving him and he was helpless to stop it.

She sat down on the floor and Dusty lay beside her, his head resting in her lap. Giving Wes a thoughtful look, she said, "I never dreamed of being in a dog rescue unit. I joined the Marine Corps because my father had been a marine, and his father before him. I saw it as a place to make a steady source of income for my family. There's too many corporations out in the civilian world that will fire you or get rid of you in favor of their shareholders. I wanted something more reliable than that."

"Are you saying you don't have a dream of what you want your life to be like?"

Callie grinned up at him. "I create it as I go on a daily basis. How's that?"

Laughing, Wes said, "My dad had my whole life planned for me. I guess we're opposites on this."

"You wanted to build things and help people," Callie pointed out, "so I feel you're following your dream. Just not the way your dad planned, is all."

Giving her a searching look, Wes asked, "Did you have any personal dreams for yourself? Ever? Or did your father's injury wipe them out?"

Moving her fingers along Dusty's golden coat, she murmured, "I guess not, Wes. My dad got injured when I was young, so I grew up knowing that I had to help my family in any way I could." Callie shrugged and said, "I guess I'm not very glamorous, am I?"

"In my eyes," he told her in a low, emotional tone, "you're incredible. You care for others. You aren't selfish." He leaned forward and slid his fingers beneath her chin. "There's so much good in you, Callie." He saw her eyes flare as he caressed her cheek, which was growing warm and pink. Wes was discovering that she had no way to shield her reactions from him, and that made him desire her even more. "You don't play games. You're the salt of the earth."

As his fingers left her cheek, Callie wanted to get up, throw her arms around him and kiss him until she drowned in his embrace, melted into his heart. There was no question that Wes was sincere and serious about a possible relationship with her. It hurt to remind herself that it was only desire, not love.

Outside, she heard some of the other marines talking as they woke and started moving around. Wes heard them, too.

He gave her a rueful look. "I think I'd better go."

"Yes…"

He got up and slipped out of her tent. Because she was the same rank as he, the others would expect them to be talking and planning together. Still, Callie was sensitive to what it looked like, and she knew Wes was, too. She saw him hesitate at the flap, turn and give her a wink.

"Be careful over at that apartment building this morning," he warned her.

"I will...."

Wes closed the flap to her tent and was gone. She felt bereft. Dusty whined as if in sympathy.

"You miss him, too?" she asked her dog softly as she leaned down and pressed her cheek against his silky head. "What am I going to do, Dusty? His heart is off-limits." Closing her eyes, Callie sighed brokenly. "It's like allowing myself only half of him. My heart wants him, but he only desires me."

Lifting her head, she gazed down into the dog's liquid eyes. "Can I do this? Can I just bring my desire and not my heart to him?"

Dusty whined.

With a sigh, Callie got up and buckled on his harness. The apartment building was about half a mile away. She knew the other marines would be over there after a quick MRE breakfast. Having already eaten, she gathered up a handful of dried dog biscuits and put them in the thigh pocket of her cammos to give to Dusty throughout the day. His work was as hard as hers, and he would need the extra food rations to keep going, probably well into the night.

January 6: 2200

Callie was in the middle of the apartment complex rubble, up at the top where the third floor had once been when Dusty's excited barking split the air. Below, the bulldozer and front-end loader were working to clear debris. Most of the people, civilians who lived in the area, had left the site, going to their makeshift headquarters for a meal. She and Dusty were all alone on top of the rubble in the cool night breeze.

Dropping to her hands and knees, Callie called down into the layers of splintered wooden walls, broken window frames and steel rebar that twisted up and outward like pretzels gone awry. Dusty was panting excitedly, all his attention directed to where she was crouching. He was digging frantically, telling her someone was under there.

"Hello...can you hear me? This is Callie."

She waited. The roar of the bulldozer and crane drifted toward her. Turning her head, Callie pressed her ear as close as she could to the debris, her heart thudding.

"...Help!...I'm trapped...get me out...get me out...." The weakened voice of a man drifted back toward her.

"What's your name, sir?"

Again Callie waited. Dusty whined excitedly. She shushed him and told him to sit down. Obediently, he sat, his tail thumping.

"...Al...Al Gordon. You gotta get me outta here...."

Callie yelled back, her hands cupped to her mouth. "Okay, Al. Hang on. Can you tell me what your medical condition is?"

"...My arm's broke. I can't move. I got a wall pushin' in on my left side...."

"I hear you, Al. Hold on, I'll get help." Callie sat

back on her heels and pulled the cell phone from her web belt. The procedure was the same: call Wes, report in, and then he'd direct people and equipment to help her.

Within minutes Wes had shown up, along with Private Bertram and Corporal Orlando. She was glad to see him with the crew. First, they set up four lights below, the small gasoline-powered generator providing the electricity to help with the rescue efforts. Then they clambered up the teetering mound of debris where she stood.

Hungrily, Callie absorbed Wes's exhausted features. The darkness of his beard accentuated his lean face. When their eyes met, Callie wanted to throw herself into his arms, but resisted. He gave her a lopsided smile. Leaning down, he patted Dusty's head.

"Got a live one?" he asked.

"Yes, down here. Name's Al Gordon. He sounds elderly. And weak."

"He's been stuck there for seven days," Wes muttered.

Nodding, Callie looked around. "I'm glad you came. I don't know where to begin here. Everything is really unstable on this third floor." It was unusual to find someone alive after day six, but Callie had seen it happen.

Wes gazed around. The aftershocks were becoming less frequent and less intense, thankfully. Compared to the first day, when they'd had eighty-three tremors, Wes was glad to see the numbers dropping to twenty or thirty.

Callie stood there looking bedraggled in her camouflage uniform. She was so small that no matter what she wore, it looked too big on her slender frame. Her

face was smudged with dirt, her hair damp and clinging to her temples. Even though it was in the fifties
tonight, her work was hard, and perspiration gleamed
across her face and neck.

Just as he was going to speak, the earth began to
roar. *Aftershock!* The tremor began shaking the entire
area. Wes was caught off guard by the sharp, jerking
motion. In a split second, he was thrown off his feet.
He heard Callie cry out, but he was flying through the
air and couldn't help her.

Wes crashed into the rubble on his back, the air
knocked out of his lungs momentarily. He heard other
members of his team shouting in surprise. As soon as
he could draw a breath, he quickly rolled over and
scrambled to his feet. In the grayish light, he saw that
Callie had been knocked down, too. She lay unmoving
above him. *No!*

Instantly, Wes climbed over to where she lay on her
side, her limbs inert. Terror ate at him. Dusty was at
her side, whining.

Another aftershock occurred. Again they were all
thrown off their feet, jerked about like puppets. Wes
cursed, threw his arms up over his head for protection
and slammed back into the wreckage with a loud
grunt. As soon as the aftershock rolled by, he lunged
to his feet again along with Bertram and Orlando, who
had also seen Callie go down.

Had she been punctured in the neck by that dangerous rebar? Although her flak jacket protected her
torso, it didn't reach her neck. Terror coursed through
Wes. He climbed up and over the debris toward her.
She lay unconscious.

Breathing hard, Wes fell to his knees. He knew
enough not to move Callie. If she had spinal injury,

moving her could paralyze her. She was lying on her side, and looked like a broken rag doll. Anxiously, Wes glanced around her. He saw a chunk of concrete nearby and noticed a dent on the side of the protective helmet she wore.

"Callie?" His voice was urgent as he gently laid his hand on her shoulder. Wes didn't shake her again, because of the danger of possible spinal injury. Instead, he squeezed her shoulder hard with his fingers. "Callie? Can you hear me? It's Wes. Wake up. Come on, wake up…please.…"

The other marines gathered around. Sergeant Cove, their EMT, came running up to them.

"Get up here, Sergeant. I need you," Wes ordered.

"Yes, sir!" he scrambled up the huge pile of debris. His face fell when he saw Callie lying there unconscious, and then he quietly got to work, setting his bright-red canvas medical bag down and pulling out a pair of latex gloves. Once the gloves were on, he settled down on his knees and gently picked up her limp wrist, placing two fingers against the inside to take her pulse. Bertram and Orlando leaned down near Cove to watch.

She couldn't be hurt! Wes tried to keep the emotion out of his voice as he spoke to her again. Her face was pale and washed out. He looked up at Cove. "Well?" He couldn't erase the desperation from his low voice.

"Pulse is good, Lieutenant. Ninety. That's normal." Cove pointed to her dented helmet. "She probably hit that block of concrete over there when the aftershock hit." He leaned over her, his ear near her nose and mouth. "And she's breathing okay. Sixteen to twenty respirations a minute is normal, and she's doing sixteen. We shouldn't move her in case there's spinal injury. Just keep talking to her and she'll probably come around in a minute or two.''

"A concussion, maybe?" Wes wondered aloud. How badly he wanted to grab Callie, hold her and keep her safe. Oh, he knew her job was dangerous, but this drove the truth home in his aching heart. He was so scared he didn't know what to do.

"Most likely, sir. That would be my first guess.''

Callie moaned. She felt Wes's steadying hand on her shoulder. His voice was taut and worried. She opened her eyes. The world spun before her.

"She's comin' around, sir,'' Barry said happily, and he flashed his lopsided grin.

Wes leaned down, his lips close to Callie's ear. "Callie? Can you hear me? Are you okay?''

Her head was spinning. She barely opened her eyes. Automatically, Callie lifted her gloved hand to her helmet. "Uhh, what happened?''

Wes sat back on his heels and watched her become more cognizant of her surroundings. "An aftershock hit and you were knocked off your feet. We think you hit that piece of concrete over there—'' he pointed to it "—as you fell. Are you okay?'' It took everything not to reach out and grip her hand or touch her.

Blinking rapidly to stop the dizziness, Callie struggled to sit up. Feeling badly bruised, she allowed Wes to help her into a sitting position. He was so close. She lifted her lashes and met his dark, terrified gaze. In that instant, Callie's reserves dissolved. This wasn't the look of a man wanting to just bed her and walk away.

Her senses were skewed. She felt nauseous. Gripping his forearm, she clung to his darkened, narrowed gaze.

"I—I'm okay...." she murmured in a strained tone. "Just...give me a minute." She looked anxiously toward the debris. "What about Al? Is he okay?"

Wes glanced at Orlando. "Try calling to him, Corporal. See if he's okay?"

"Yes, sir!" The corporal scrambled over to the spot where Dusty was still sitting.

Cove maneuvered around and kept his hand on her back to support her. "Ma'am? Are you feeling dizzy? Sick to your stomach at all?"

Callie whispered, "Yes..." and she placed her gloved hands against her eyes for a moment and took in a deep, ragged breath. The dizziness would not go away no matter what she did.

Cove shot a glance at Wes. "Concussion, sir." Then he devoted his attention to Callie. "Ma'am, let me examine you to make sure you don't have any broken bones, okay?"

Slowly licking her lips, Callie said, "Sure...I think I'm fine, though...."

"I'm sure you are, ma'am," Cove murmured sympathetically, "but this won't take long."

Wes moved aside to allow his sergeant to give her a more thorough examination, from head to toe. Inwardly, he was shaking. Fear was gutting him. His heart was screaming out in terror over the whole episode, which was bringing him flashbacks of his fiancée's death.

As he stood there, he realized he was feeling a lot more than just desire for Callie. But he couldn't go there yet. Wiping his mouth with the back of his hand,

Wes took a deep breath, refusing to look at this thunderbolt realization any more closely right now.

He heard Orlando calling out to Al Gordon. Private Bertram had worry written on his face as he stood nearby, ready to help. In the past week the team had bonded as a unit—a family—and Wes could see their concern for Callie was real.

"I got a voice!" Orlando yelped happily. "He's okay!"

Wes looked up and saw Orlando throw him a thumbs-up. "Good. Private Bertram, help Corporal Orlando start pulling that debris away so we can get to Mr. Gordon."

"Yes, sir." The marine hurried over to where Orlando was beginning to pull splintered wood away from where the man was buried.

Wes didn't leave Callie's side. He watched in anxious silence as Sergeant Cove expertly examined her. Wes's heart was twisting and knotting with such powerful feelings that he simply couldn't ignore them. Similar feelings had been there with Allison, too. But what he felt now was raw and gutting in comparison. Callie could have died just now. What would his life be like if she had? Shutting his eyes for a moment, Wes clamped his lips together until they became a hard, thin line.

"Take your helmet off, ma'am? I need to examine your head."

"…Oh…yeah…." Callie fumbled with the closure on her helmet. She felt shaky and weak, and her fingers wouldn't work. Frustrated, she glanced over at Wes and silently asked for his help.

He nodded and leaned forward, his fingertips brushing her chin as he loosened the strap. Callie tried to smile but didn't succeed; the dizziness was nearly overwhelming.

"T-thanks..." She eased the helmet off her head, and immediately felt warm blood trickling behind her ear and down her neck. "I guess I really hit my head," Callie told them as she gave Wes her helmet. Lifting her hand, she touched the aching spot.

Sergeant Cove examined that area very gently. "Yes, ma'am, you've got a two-inch laceration on your scalp from that knock on the head. And it's pretty swollen."

Frowning, Wes asked, "Do we need to get her back to Camp Reed, Sergeant?"

"Yes, sir, I think so. She's got a concussion. And this laceration needs stitches. She can't be out here with that injury open like that."

"No!" Callie whispered. "No, Wes. I want to stay.... We've got to get Al out...."

Grimly, Wes looked at her. The distraught expression in Callie's eyes tore at him. She sat there in the rubble, the dark stream of blood curving around her neck and soaking into the collar of her cammos. "Sergeant, you and I are going to take her back to H.Q. Once we get her there, I want you to dress the lieutenant's wound."

"Yes, sir."

"I don't want to leave!" Callie whispered, seeking out Wes's dark gaze. "Just patch me up, Sergeant. I'll be okay. I feel better already." That was a lie, but under no circumstances did Callie want to be sent away. She and Dusty were needed more than ever now. Knowing that most people died after their fifth day buried alive, Callie would hate to be ordered back to the base at this critical time.

"We'll talk later," Wes promised her in a grim tone. "Sergeant? Help me get her off this pile of rubble."

"Yes, sir!"

January 6: 2230

Callie lay on her cot, her head spinning. Dusty was stretched out on the floor, snoring heavily. Outside, the floodlights powered by the chuttering generator sent a grayish glow through her tent. Sergeant Cove had cleaned her head wound, placed a sterile dressing over it and then wrapped gauze around her head to hold it snugly in place. Now she needed Wes. He'd disappeared once they'd brought her back to her tent. Her heart needed him; she wanted his arms around her. But his heart was off-limits to her. The thought made her want to cry.

"You still awake?"

It was Wes, standing tentatively outside her tent. Raising up on her elbows, she said, "Yeah, come on in." Forcing herself to sit up, Callie closed her eyes and gripped the sides of her cot with her hands, afraid that she was going to fall off it. The dizziness was unrelenting. She heard Wes quietly enter. Looking up, she saw him drop the flap back into place. He looked at her grimly.

"I'm going to be okay," Callie muttered defiantly.

Wes stood there, torn. Hands on his hips, he perused Callie's upturned, pale face. "Sergeant Cove says you need stitches and a tetanus shot. Not to mention antibiotics. I've got to send you back on that helo tomorrow when it makes its morning run, Callie."

"No!"

Wes cursed softly beneath his breath and knelt down on one knee in front of her. As he placed his hands on her small shoulders, he saw the agony in her narrowed eyes. "Listen to me, Callie. You're hurt. I care for you too damn much to let you stay out here in this condition. What if you get tetanus? That stuff will kill you. You need to go back and get medical help."

Gripping his arm, she whispered, "No! I'll be okay. Gosh, Wes, I've banged my head a lot worse than this before out at quake sites and I didn't receive any medical help. I've just got to keep working. There're people in those buildings. We've got to use every minute we can! Every hour counts!" Her voice broke as she gripped his jacket in frustration. "You need me here, Wes. Please…let me stay…." Her voice broke tearfully.

"Dammit, Callie," he rasped harshly as he framed her face with his hands. "I care too much for you to let this go…to let you go…." And he leaned down and brushed her parted, trembling lips with his. He tasted the salt of her tears as he did so. He heard her moan. Her hands moved greedily across his shoulders and her arms slid around his neck. She wanted to kiss him as much as he wanted to kiss her. Just knowing that, Wes moved his mouth in a cherishing movement across hers, to let her know how much he needed her…. At that moment, he remembered the look on Morgan Trayhern's face, the love burning in the man's eyes for his wife. Wes felt the same way about Callie right now, but was afraid to admit it.

The thought came as a shock to him in one way, but in another, it felt like the most natural thing in the world. He felt Callie's arms tighten around his neck and he drew her into his arms, bringing her completely against him.

Callie's world was spinning again, but not because of her head injury. No, this was due to Wes's mouth pressed hotly to hers, worshiping her as if she were some fragile, priceless treasure. More tears squeezed from beneath her eyelids and streamed down her cheeks. Wes was powerful, and yet Callie could feel him holding back, carefully monitoring the amount of pressure he exerted. He didn't want to hurt her. He wanted to nurture her, take care of her. She felt his big hands stroke her shoulders, her back, before pinning her tightly against him once more.

Never had she felt more desired. As he eased his mouth from hers, their noses almost touching, she opened her eyes. Burning beneath his slitted gaze, she felt a heat uncoil within her lower body. This was how it felt to want to love someone, Callie realized for the first time in her life. And Wes wanted her; there was no mistaking that. She saw it in his narrowed eyes, the way his hands caressed her shoulders and back.

"Don't send me away," she pleaded brokenly.

"I'm going to, Callie. For your own good." Wes winced as he saw the pain in her features. He wanted to simply hold her and keep her safe. Right now, he was scared as never before. She could have fallen on a piece of rebar out there and been impaled. She could be dying or dead right now, not sitting here kissing him hungrily.

"No!" she sobbed. "You've *got* to let me stay, Wes. You've got to!" She pounded her fist against his chest in frustration. "You're reacting because of your past—your loss of Allison. I know it!" There, the truth was out. "I'm not Allison! I'm *me!* I'm Callie!"

His mouth tightened. Inwardly, he winced at her accusation. But he couldn't remain immune to her weeping or her tears. "Okay...okay, listen to me, dammit." He gripped her by the shoulders and forced her to look at him, though her tears still tore at his heart. "I'm sending you back tomorrow at 0600. You get to the hospital for treatment. If they say you can come back here, Callie, you come back. That's the best I can do. I *won't* let you stay here like this. I want you alive and well. I—I care for you too much to let you stay here. Do you understand that?" His voice was low and strained. "Do you?"

Shaken and hurting, Callie released his jacket. She reached up and wiped her cheek. "Y-yes...okay. I'll go back...but I'll be back on that flight coming in at 1600." Twice a day, the Huey helicopter arrived, bringing supplies and taking out anyone needing medical help.

"Angel, you own me." Wes gripped her small hand and pressed it to his chest, over his heart. "I know you want to be here with us...and I know you're needed...but not at the risk of your life." He shook his head, and saw the tender look of response in Callie's eyes.

Bowing her head, her hand pressed against his jacket, she whispered, "Okay...it's better than nothing...." And she swallowed her hurt at his orders.

"I've got to go," he muttered. "I don't want to, Callie, but I have to...."

"Go...go help the guys get Al Gordon out of there, Wes. I know you can do it." She gave him a broken smile. The words *I love you* almost slipped from her lips. How badly Callie wanted to say them! Wes had talked about desire, not love. Yet the anguish burning in his eyes looked exactly like the expression on Morgan Trayhern's face when she'd found Laura in the rubble. If that wasn't love, what was it?

Torn with emotions, dizzy and confused, she felt like a thunderstorm was brewing inside her. "Keep Dusty here?" she asked.

Wes looked down at the sleeping dog. "Yeah...I'll do that...."

"Good," Callie whispered, relieved. If Wes allowed Dusty to stay, that meant he was expecting her back here. Reaching up, she touched his sandpapery cheek. "Stay safe out there. I'm scared for you, too, you know."

Nodding, Wes caught her hand and pressed a long, fervent kiss to the back of it. "Just get medical help, Callie. That's all I ask...."

Chapter Ten

January 7: 1300

"Callie?"

Callie had been dozing, her head tipped back against the wall in the passageway of the first floor emergency room at Camp Reed, when she heard her name called. She was sitting on a wooden bench, squeezed in with three other people, yet she'd been so exhausted she'd fallen asleep despite her physical discomfort. She had arrived at 0630 to Camp Reed and had hitched a ride from the airport in an ambulance. Since that time, she'd been logged in at the busy hospital and assessed as the lowest medical priority in the triage system.

Because her injuries weren't considered life-threatening, Callie had already waited long hours without being seen by any medical staff. However, she could see that the emergency room was overwhelmed with civilians flown in from outside the base. Many of them were near death or had far more serious injuries than she, so she used the time to try and catch up on badly needed sleep.

Hearing her name called a second time jolted her out of her light sleep. Blinking, she lifted her head, confused. She had to be hearing things. That sounded like Wes's voice. She straightened, looking around the passageway, which was crowded with gurneys bearing people waiting their turn to be seen by an ER physician. The cries and groans of the injured mingled with the tense voice of nurses and doctors drifting around her.

Wes saw Callie slowly straighten up. She still wore the gauze dressing Sergeant Cove had applied. Her hair was uncombed, part of it flattened—with dried blood from her head injury? Anger sizzled through him as he moved down in the crowded passageway. She looked washed out. Her eyes didn't look quite right to him as he made his way to her side. Kneeling down at the end of the bench, Wes whispered, "Thought I'd come and check on you."

Callie gave him a soft smile of welcome and she sat up.

"Wes. What are you doing here?" She realized that all eyes were on them. They were both officers, of the same rank, but they couldn't show any affection toward one another.

He rested one hand on the wooden bench where she sat and the other on her shoulder. Not giving a damn about official military protocol, he held on to his anger as he searched her dirty, smudged face.

"I just brought in Mr. Gordon. We got him free a little while ago," he said. "He's in the ER right now. He had a broken leg and arm. The old guy is eighty, and he's not doing well. I thought I'd take the opportunity to fly in with him on the Huey and see how you were doing." He saw her eyes grow warm.

"So you went to the B.O.Q., thinking I was there resting?" Her voice contained amusement. She saw the anger flicker in his dark-green eyes. Wes was dirty and dusty. It was obvious to her that he'd had a big hand in freeing Al Gordon, from the looks of it.

"Yeah, and you weren't there. So I got worried, thinking that they were keeping you here at the hospital, or worse, had flown you out because your head injury was a lot more serious than we thought."

"Well, put your worry away," she soothed. Pointing to her injury, she said, "An admissions Corps Wave put me as a number three in their triage system. I'm the least wounded, so I wait my turn."

Giving her a look of exasperation, Wes muttered, "But you left at 0600 this morning! You're telling me you've sat here for seven hours now and no one has seen you yet?" His voice grew tight with barely concealed anger. Callie deserved better than that. Yet, as Wes looked around, he saw many others who had been similarly tagged and were also waiting for help.

"Yes. It's okay, Wes. This place is overwhelmed. I don't see how the medical people are handling this influx. It's pretty bad, and I'm really okay. I've got a headache...but my dizziness is pretty much gone."

Standing, he looked around. The navy provided all medical personnel to the Marine Corps. The orderlies, enlisted people, were in blue or green scrubs. Doctors were in white coats. The nurses, all officers, were in white slacks or dresses, depending upon their gender. Gripping Callie's shoulder for a moment, Wes growled, "Stay here. I'm going to get you some help."

Opening her mouth, Callie raised her hand to call him back, but Wes had already melted into the crowd, quickly swallowed up in the ceaseless activity that filled the passageway leading to the emergency facility.

Wes barely held on to his rage as he swung through the doors of the ER. He wanted a doctor—now. Spotting a woman bending over an older woman, a stethoscope in her ears as she listened to the patient's heart, he headed toward her. The doctor, who he saw was a lieutenant, had short red hair and a face liberally sprinkled with freckles. Wes intercepted her as she moved from the wheelchair bearing the older woman and turned to the next patient in the overcrowded room.

"Lieutenant?" He saw the black bar with white lettering across the left breast pocket of her blood-splattered white coat. "Lieutenant Andrews?"

She halted momentarily. "Yes?"

Wes saw how exhausted the tall navy doctor was. "I know you're busy, but I've got my dog rescue officer out here in the passageway. She's got a concussion…and she's been out there for seven hours now. Can you take a moment and help her? Please?"

Samantha Andrews gave him a grim look. Her full mouth flattened. "Lieutenant—" she glanced at his name tag, pinned above the left breast pocket of his cammies "—James…I'm sorry, but if she's a number three in our triage system, she waits."

"Hold on," Wes growled, and he stepped in front of her. "Five minutes, Doctor. That's all I'm asking.

This woman, Lieutenant Callie Evans, has saved more lives in the last five days, going through that rubble out there with her dog…. She deserves better than this.''

Nostrils flaring, Samantha Andrews looked back at her patient and then at Wes. ''Okay, Lieutenant. I hear you. I'm over my head in emergencies….''

''Please?'' Wes begged softly. He saw the doctor waver. Her light-green eyes narrowed on him.

''Okay, Lieutenant. Where is she?''

Callie tried to contain her surprise as the red-haired medical doctor came walking swiftly through the crowd toward her, with Wes on her heels. He had a pleased look on his face as the doctor began to examine her.

''How are you feeling, Lieutenant Evans?'' the doctor asked, quickly putting on a clean pair of latex gloves and examining Callie's head injury.

''Okay. A little dizzy…a little nauseous….''

''When did you get this head injury?'' Dr. Andrews crouched down in front of Callie and examined her eyes with her penlight. She watched her pupils enlarge and constrict as the light was flashed into them.

''Last night…late….'' Callie sat very still. She felt more than saw Wes move protectively to her side as the doctor continued to examine her.

Holding up her hand in front of Callie's face, she asked, ''How many fingers do you see, Lieutenant?''

''Two.''

''Good. Do you see them clearly?''

''Yes.''

''No distortion? No blurriness?''

''No…none….''

The doctor gave her a quick smile and rose. "Good. I'd say you have a bruised brain, a concussion, but nothing more serious." She looked up at Wes. "Your lady is going to be fine, Lieutenant. Let me find a nurse around here...." She looked around, waved to someone, then turned back.

Smiling down at Callie, Dr. Andrews said, "I'm going to authorize you forty-eight hours of sick leave, restricted to your B.O.Q. quarters, Lieutenant. You need to give that brain of yours time to rest and recoup. Besides, you look like hell warmed over, and you've been working too long with too little sleep."

"But—" Callie tried to protest.

Dr. Andrews was giving rapid orders to the nurse who'd miraculously appeared at her side. "Nurse Collins? Give the lieutenant a tetanus shot, sew up her head laceration, authorize a forty-eight-hour sick chit that confines her to this base. Oh, and give her a prescription for amoxicillin, a ten-day supply of tablets. Understand?"

"Yes, Doctor."

Dr. Andrews nodded. "And bring it to me for my signature."

"Yes, Doctor."

Great. Callie was then helped to her feet. Dizziness swept over her, and if Wes hadn't been right beside her like a protective guard dog, gripping her left elbow, she'd probably have pitched forward on her face. Nurse Collins took her other arm and firmly propelled her through the crowd to a side room. Pushing open the door, the dark-haired nurse guided Callie to the gurney sitting in the middle of the small, clean cubbyhole.

"Sit down, Lieutenant," the nurse ordered briskly as she went to the cabinet and got latex gloves.

Callie maneuvered around and sat, with Wes's help. She gave him a silent look of thanks. His hand never left her upper arm. How badly she wanted to lean toward him and feel his arms go around her. Right now, because of sleep deprivation, the pressures of her job, the loss of so many people and the knowledge that, without her in the field, more people would die, Callie felt close to tears.

The nurse scrubbed her head wound free of blood and debris, shaved the immediate area and then began the painful duty of sewing up the laceration. Thankfully, Nurse Collins was swift and competent, all-business. She was also harried and stressed out, Callie could tell. Who wasn't?

Within ten minutes, Callie was taken care of—a tetanus shot delivered to her arm, a new bandage on her wound and the sick leave form in hand. As the nurse rushed out to get the prescription, Wes took the chit and stuffed it in his pocket. Once Nurse Collins was gone he stood in front of Callie.

"Okay, to bed with you."

"First," Callie whispered, "I desperately want a hot shower."

Nodding, he murmured, "I know the feeling. Come on, I'll help you out of here. You're still unsteady, Callie."

Whether she wanted to admit to it or not, she was. Nurse Collins rushed back in and handed her the antibiotic prescription, which had been signed by Dr. Andrews. Callie thanked her, and Collins gave her a slight smile and hurried off.

Gratefully, Callie accepted Wes's hand beneath her

elbow. She didn't even try to put her cap on her head over the new dressing. Her steps were slow and a little unsteady.

"Right now," she whispered as Wes opened the door for her, "all I want is to get out of here."

He understood as they moved into the passageway stuffed with patients, gurneys and medical personnel. Placing himself in front of her, a bulwark against the turmoil, he said, "Just follow me, Angel. We'll get you home as soon as possible...."

Angel. Callie's heart lifted at his grittily spoken endearment. He held on to her left hand and used his body as a wedge to move through the crowds. *Home.* How good that sounded. Despite how exhausted she felt, Callie's heart sang. Wes hadn't had to come and try to find her. His thoughtfulness touched her as nothing else had so far, with the exception of the branding kisses he gave her. Because of his care, his kisses, she felt beautiful and loved.

Out in the Southern California sunlight, Wes walked beside her, firmly gripping her upper arm. She was walking carefully and he knew she was still dizzy. The cracked sidewalk was crowded with people hurrying past them. The eighth day of this disaster was pushing every resource to the outer limits. Wes saw the stress on every face. He looked down at Callie as she paid strict attention to where she was placing her booted feet.

"Okay?" he asked softly.

"Yeah...doing okay...thanks, Wes. Thanks for getting me the help."

"You'd have sat there another ten hours, wouldn't you?"

"No...I was getting ready to leave. I figured I'd go

to my room at the B.O.Q., clean up my head with soap and water, wash my hair, take a shower, change clothes and hop the next helo back to our grid of operation.''

His brow arched wryly. ''You would have, wouldn't you?'' Wes saw the set expression in her dulled blue eyes. The B.O.Q. was less than a quarter mile down the road from the hospital. It was an easy walking distance, especially since the day was warm, in the sixties and with a bright-blue sky above.

''Yes, in a heartbeat.''

''Something told me you were in trouble,'' he said as he slowly walked at her side. It felt good to have his hand on her.

''Intuition?'' Callie managed a ghost of a smile.

''Maybe. I've never had it with anyone else, so I don't know what it is, or what you call it.''

''I see. How's Dusty?''

''Oh, I brought him back on the Huey with me. After I took Mr. Gordon to the ER, I went back to the airport where I'd left a sergeant over in Ops taking care of Dusty. He's now back at your unit H.Q., fed and sleeping.''

Relief tunneled through Callie. ''Oh, good! Thanks, Wes. You're a real hero in my eyes, do you know that?'' She looked up, to see his dark-green eyes glittering with amusement.

''I don't think the Huey pilot was too happy with me—a Captain Nolan Galway. He was pissed off that I'd bring a dog on board his chopper.''

''Why?''

''I called in a special flight for Mr. Gordon. I used my muscle to get a flight diverted so we could get him here for medical help. At first, the pilot wasn't too keen about being diverted, or having a dog as a passenger. He was pretty stressed out by it all.''

"So, you just powered on through, like you did to get that doctor to look at me?'' she asked wryly.

Grinning lopsidedly, Wes said, "You might say that.''

They'd arrived at the four-story brick B.O.Q., with its semicircular drive surrounding a stand of California pin oaks in a red-brick planter. The building was old, from the thirties; the architecture somewhat gothic. Wes liked the old building and now appreciated how well it was built. Even though Camp Reed had escaped the brunt of the earthquake, the base had sustained a fair amount of damage. This building had stood proudly throughout the worst tremors. There were some minor cracks in the bricks here and there, but nothing that couldn't be repaired eventually.

Guiding Callie slowly into the foyer, he signed them in on the desk ledger and then helped her up the wide wooden staircase. There was no elevator in the old building. Marines were a physically fit group by nature, however, and climbing stairs was considered a healthy regime. In Callie's case, because of her dizzy, weakened state, it was an obstacle. Wes tempered his impatience and walked slowly at her side.

On the second floor, he found her room halfway down the passageway and opened the door for her. This time, she'd been assigned a different room.

"...Thanks....'' Callie moved into her quarters. The room was small, just a bed, a shower, a dresser and locker. It wasn't fancy. The window had gold drapes on it, the sunlight cascading in and making the redwood floor shine. A clean set of clothes hung in the closet, and a bathrobe and towels had been set at the end of the bed.

Wes closed the door. He saw how pale Callie had become. "Listen, I have the next twenty-four hours here on base. Logistics has ordered me to come over and help them set up a highway and rebuilding program for the L.A. basin." He glanced at his watch. "I'm due over there at 1400." He saw her sit down on her double bed, which was covered with a bright-red quilt. "Let me help you?"

She smiled wanly. "That's great news…they're using your talents, Wes. I didn't think they'd keep you out there bulldozing buildings for long."

"Well," he murmured, kneeling down and unlacing her boots for her, "I didn't, either. Logistics is just now getting a leg up on this huge disaster. They're working with FEMA, and beginning to pull in groups of engineers to begin the rescue and rebuilding efforts." He set her boots aside. Running his hands gently down her small feet, he took off her dark-green wool socks. Looking up, he smiled at her. Callie was so tired. He could see the gray smudges beneath her eyes.

"Let me get the shower ready for you? Can you undress yourself in there or do you need help?"

Callie felt heat move up her face. Right now, she knew Wes was doing his best to take care of her. She felt no pressure from him, only this wonderful feeling of protection. "If you could turn on the shower for me, I think I can get undressed the rest of the way."

"Okay," he whispered, giving her knee a pat as he rose to his full height. He'd like nothing better than to undress Callie and join her in the shower. But now was not the time, and Wes knew it. As he walked into the small, clean bathroom and adjusted the shower to a nice, warm temperature, he tabled his desires. Right now, more than anything, Callie needed to sleep off her injury.

She moved slowly into the bathroom and began to unbutton her cammo top. Wes halted and placed his hand gently against her wan cheek.

"I've got to go, Callie, and it's the last thing I want to do."

She looked shyly up through her lashes at him. "I know," she whispered, an ache in her voice.

"If you could have any wish, what would it be right now?" he asked her in a low, gritty tone, his eyes never leaving her. How badly he wanted to kiss her senseless and love her. Wes saw the same desire reflected in her eyes.

"That you could come to my room and, if I'm sleeping, just slip into bed and hold me? I could really use some holding at this point."

The quaver in her voice tore at him. Wes was beginning to understand the emotional toll her job took on her. He would never have realized it if he hadn't been working with Callie so closely over the past week.

Leaning down, he brushed her cheek with a feathery kiss. As he lifted his lips, he whispered against her ear, "I'll see if I can make that wish of yours come true, Angel...."

January 7: 1900

Callie felt warm and loved. As she groggily surfaced from the layers of a very deep, healing sleep, she sighed. Right now, she felt the warm, quiet strength of a man's body against her own beneath the covers where she slept. Not only that, but she was aware of a man's arm across her torso, tucking her solidly against him.

It took long moments in the darkness of the room to reorient herself. Callie's dreams had awakened her—voices calling for help from the rubble where she was looking for survivors. The dreams were not new to her; they always happened when she was searching a quake area. Lifting her hand, she slid it down the warm, hard length of the man's arm. Another sigh, one of utter surrender, slipped from her lips as she felt the curled fingers that lay so near her breast. She wore a pair of men's baggy cotton pajamas; it was all that Supply had had available.

Wes. It was Wes. Her mind was spongy. She was still half-asleep, the dream awakening her momentarily. Drifting drowsily, she registered another wonderful sensation—his moist breath moving rhythmically against her neck.

At some point, he'd come back to her. And now he was bringing her wish to life. Sleep tugged at Callie. How marvelous it felt to be held and protected by Wes! Her heart sang with joy.

She hadn't heard him return to her room. It was dark now, so she couldn't see much—could only feel the long length of his body curved against her back. Realizing that he was lying on top of the covers, and she beneath them, Callie felt an even stronger surge of love for Wes. He was being respectful of her. She'd ask for him to come back and hold her, not make love to her.

And he'd followed her request to the letter. Sluggishly, she wondered if he was still dressed in his uniform. Her hand ranged upward to his elbow, and felt only skin. It was possible that he'd shrugged out of his dirty cammo jacket and was wearing his pants and dark-green T-shirt. It didn't matter. Right now, all Callie wanted was to be held. She melted back into his sleep embrace. Somehow, in a world that had been shattered and destroyed, his arms around her made everything all right in the midst of chaos.

As she lay there drifting between sleep and wakefulness, Callie realized she had never felt this way before. Simply being held in this quiet, wonderful way opened her heart—and her trust of Wes—even more. If only his heart were not off-limits!

As she closed her eyes, sleep pulling her back into its warm, healing darkness, Callie sighed. Wes's soft breathing against her neck and shoulder was wonderfully soothing to her. She had never awakened with a man in her bed before, but she was looking forward to doing just that. With forty-eight hours off, Callie hungrily absorbed the gift of time given to her. Soon enough, she would be shipped out to another building, to begin the task of looking for survivors...and this time, Wes wouldn't be there. No, their time together was like precious pearls strung on a silk strand. Each pearl was a gift to be appreciated fully in that moment.

As she spiraled gently back into the folds of sleep, Callie's lips parted and a soft smile played on her mouth. Everything was perfect. She felt more cared for than ever before in her life. Finally, she'd found a man who respected her, who thought she was beautiful, who considered her an angel. Callie had never experienced such happiness or contentment, and considered it a miracle. Even if his heart wasn't involved.

Chapter Eleven

January 8: 1230

Callie awoke because she missed the nearness of Wes against her back. Muffled sounds of trucks passing the building drifted up to her. Forcing open her eyes, she reached out from beneath the covers. Wes? Where was he? She frowned and slowly turned over on her back and looked around. He was gone. Blinking to try and erase the fogginess of her half-awake state, Callie lifted her wrist and looked at her watch: 1230. Impossible! She couldn't have slept so long—nearly twenty-four hours!

Forcing herself into a sitting position, she saw that she'd accidentally rubbed off her bandage. Gingerly touching her injured head, she discovered it was tender, but healing. The swelling was almost gone.

Feeling much more energized, Callie pushed herself to the edge of the bed and hung her legs over it. Rubbing her face with her hands, she realized she felt no dizziness. In fact, her head felt fine, just a little sensitive.

Gazing around the room as the light poured through the window Callie missed Wes. Had she been dreaming he'd been here? Grimacing, Callie muttered, "Come on, Evans, get up. Have another shower. Where you're going in a couple days, there ain't no such thing...."

Trudging toward the bathroom, Callie tried to straighten her rumpled pajamas. The light-green, cotton men's p.j.s certainly weren't sexy looking. On the contrary! But she was grateful she had anything clean to wear at all. Now for a good, hot shower and shampoo... What a heavenly gift.

As she emerged from the shower, a pale-green towel over her clean, damp hair, Callie heard a soft knock at her door. Frowning, she looked at the clock on the dresser. It was 1300. Pulling the white fleece robe that hung to her ankles around her, she walked toward it. Who could it be? Opening the door, she smiled.

"Wes!" He stood there in his desert cammos, his cap low on his brow, his green eyes narrowed. In his hands he held an aluminum tray with a large white ceramic bowl on it, along with a mug of black coffee and a lot of soda crackers. His face thawed as he gazed down at her.

"You're up. Hungry?" He lifted the tray toward her. "Chicken soup, Callie. I got the gunny who runs the chow hall tent down below to make up something special for you."

Touched, she moved aside. "Come in, Wes." Her

heart tugged as he gave her a tender, intimate smile. Had she been imagining things or had he really slept with her last night? Callie wasn't sure at all. It was an embarrassing situation to be in. Touching the towel on her head, she quickly closed the door and scrubbed her hair with it, avoiding the injured area.

"Put it on the bed, will you? I just got out of the shower. I'll be only a moment...." She disappeared back inside the bathroom in search of a comb.

"Take your time," Wes said, removing his cap and placing it on the maple dresser opposite the bed. His heart took off in joy as Callie reappeared. She'd brushed her unruly, damp hair, he noted. And she was nervous, judging by the way she fumbled with the sash of the terry-cloth robe she wore.

"You look a lot better," he observed. "What time did you get up?"

Callie pulled the blankets up and smoothed out the spread on the bed. "About thirty minutes ago. I guess I slept the sleep of the dead," she murmured. Picking up the tray, she placed it on her lap as she sat down on the edge of the bed, her bare feet on the shining wooden floor. "Join me?" she asked, looking up at where he stood.

Something was different. Callie sensed it as well as felt it. There was a new tenderness in his eyes as Wes gave her a slight smile and settled down at the end of the bed, leaving a good two feet of space between them.

"How are you feeling?" he asked as he watched her pick up the soup spoon and dip it into the rich broth, which had carrots, onions, celery and big chunks of white chicken in it.

"Much better," she answered between sips of soup.

"Mmm, this is great, Wes. Thanks! Talk about angels…you've been a guardian angel to me the last couple of days."

"Glad I could do it."

"Are you on lunch hour from Logistics?" Callie guessed as she eagerly consumed the soup.

"Yeah, you might say that." He smiled thinly. "I took a late lunch, actually. I had the person on watch down below at the desk come up and knock on your door an hour ago to find out if you were up and around. She called me when she said she heard the shower going on."

Giving him a slight smile, Callie broke up some soda crackers and sprinkled them into the soup. "So that you could feed me?"

Wes rested his elbows on his long, hard thighs, his clasped hands draped between them. "Actually, I went down early this morning and found Gunny Prater. I told him I had this angel with eyes the color of a turquoise sky, with sunlight streaking her hair. And she was sick. Could he whip up a personal batch of his best chicken soup for her?" Wes grinned and held Callie's surprised look. "Gunny took pity on me. He said if I'd found a woman that good-looking, he'd make chicken soup for her. I think he was envious."

Coloring, Callie shook her head. "I like the way you see me."

"Isn't that how you see yourself?" He saw pain flash in her eyes, then disappear. Callie turned back to the soup, eating with obvious enjoyment, yet delicately. Wes would never tire of watching her graceful movements.

Quirking her mouth, Callie took another sip of the delicious soup. "No. I'm just a skinny kid from Swedish stock who was born on a corn and soybean farm in Minnesota. There, the girls are tough and strong. They have to be. I didn't grow up learning much about curling irons, makeup or what boys might like to see me wearing.''

''Well,'' Wes teased lightly, ''you're my angel of the morning. That's what I've decided to call you.''

Callie set down her spoon. A third of the soup was left, but she felt sated. ''That's so beautiful,'' she said, her voice wispy.

''I can hardly wait until you see yourself like that,'' he murmured seriously. He saw Callie flush and then get up and put the tray on the dresser next to his cammo cap. Moving back to the bed, she sat down and faced him, her legs crossed in front of her. She patiently rearranged the white robe over her legs so that she was properly covered.

''It's time to be honest,'' Callie said, her heart beating hard. She felt anxious and unsure as Wes held her stare. Opening her small hands, which had numerous cuts in various stages of healing, she whispered, ''This is so hard to say, Wes. I'm really embarrassed. I *thought* you were sleeping with me last night, but I'm not sure.'' She gave him a strained look of apology. ''I could have dreamed it. I woke up once…at least I thought I did…and I felt you curved along my backside, your arm around me. I ran my hand down your arm…felt your warmth.…'' Gulping, she searched his hooded eyes. ''Was it a dream?''

The silence strung tautly between them. Wes saw the uncertainty in Callie's eyes and heard it in her soft voice. ''Didn't you tell me that your wish was to be held?''

Gulping, she choked out, ''Y-yes.…''

"I got off duty around midnight last night, Callie. To tell you the truth, with what I saw and heard over in Logistics, my stomach was in knots. The deaths…they're estimating a million people who have no homes, no water…and food is growing short. After hearing all that…well, I needed you last night. I just needed something *good* in the midst of all this mounting horror staring us in the face. Something safe. I wanted you. I came to your room. You were sound asleep." He smiled slightly. "I don't think a tank rumbling through your room would have awakened you. Anyway, I took a shower and climbed into a clean T-shirt and boxer shorts. I crawled into bed, on top of the covers, and fitted myself against you." Giving her a warm look, Wes murmured, "You never woke once. When I slid an arm beneath your head and wrapped my other arm around your middle, you snuggled right into my arms."

"Then—I didn't dream it. It was real.…"

Nodding, he held her wide blue eyes, which shone with desire for him. Callie seemed innocent and without worldly charm, yet that was exactly why Wes was drawn to her—she didn't put on airs or play games. No, Callie was the salt of the earth—pragmatic, practical and bone-wrenchingly honest with him.

"In one way," Wes teased gently, "it was a dream—a dream come true for me, Callie. I really needed to be with someone that I lo—er, liked last night. Emotionally, I was totaled by what's going on and what will happen. I'm in the middle of the planning board in Logistics and I've got to tell you, we're in a situation that's going to get a helluva lot worse before it gets better." Reaching out, he slid his fingers over her clasped hands, which rested in the lap of her robe. Shyly, Callie curled her fingers around his. Heart soaring with joy, he added, "You felt so good to me last night. Just getting to hold you while you slept…your breathing so light and easy, the smell of your skin…it was heaven to me, and you were an angel in my arms. My angel…"

She moved her fingers wonderingly across the thick, large knuckles of his left hand. "I like being your angel." Lifting her head, she gazed at him. There was such naked vulnerability in Wes right now. "You could have taken advantage of me…."

Shrugging, he said, "And who would that have served, Callie? That would have been pretty selfish of me, wouldn't it? You said you wanted me to hold you, not make love to you. There's a difference, and I respect that difference." Managing a wry, one-cornered smile, Wes admitted, "To be brutally honest about it, I wanted to love you, but I knew it wasn't consensual. Loving a person is special. It's a two-way street. It has to be mutual."

"Always," Callie whispered as she felt his fingers close gently around hers. "You're the first man I've met that didn't try to go all the way."

"Maybe all you knew were boys, not men."

Nodding, Callie admitted in a painful whisper, "I don't pretend to be worldly, Wes. In fact, I'm pretty limited in my experiences with guys in general. After being burned twice—used—I said enough was enough."

"I understand." And he did.

Wryly, she laughed and said, "What you see is what you get. No frills. No pretty packaging."

His smile faded, and he lifted her hand and placed

a warm, gentle kiss on the back. Then, watching her eyes soften, he released it.

Her hand tingled pleasantly where Wes had kissed it. "It's nice to know I've got company going through the emotional mill," Callie murmured. Gazing at him, she added, "I just never would have believed a man like you existed. Maybe that's why I thought I was dreaming you were here, holding me last night—because I didn't think any man could do just that."

"I want your trust, Callie. You have mine, but I know you're skittish because of your past experiences. I guess I want to prove to you that I'm good at my word." His eyes danced with self-deprecating humor. "Not that I didn't want to love you, to please you, to be with you in every way. I did. But the price would have been too high for me to pay. And whatever trust we have between us now, would have been shattered." Shaking his head, Wes muttered, "I know men think a lot about sex, and we definitely see things in sexual terms, but there's got to be balance to it, too. I learned the hard way that a good relationship is about two people's needs, wants and desires."

"I'm so hungry to know everything about you, Wes...."

"Same here." He looked at his watch. "I've got another half hour before I've got to go. Tell me about your college years. What did you major in?"

Giving him a laughing look, Callie said, "I majored in business. I was in the cadet corps and I found I liked the military. Because I wanted a career that would bring me a good paycheck to help my folks, with little chance of layoffs, I chose the marines. When I went through officers candidate school, I took a lot of tests to determine my career slot. At the time, the commandant of the Marine Corps was putting together an idea of having a rescue dog unit at each division. With my farm background, plus my degree in business, I got pulled for the project.''

"So, you created the template for the rescue units?" Wes was impressed. He saw Callie blush at his whispered words.

"It wasn't that hard, really. Pretty simple and straightforward.''

"Only because you think that way. That's why it's easy for you."

"Common sense, really. Farm people have a lot of that or they'd be in big trouble fast.'' She laughed softly.

"Common sense isn't so common,'' Wes growled. "So, you've helped build this concept into reality. That's really impressive.''

"I like helping people, Wes. And I love animals." She opened her hands and shrugged. "On the farm, we relied on each other. Farmers in the region would always help each other out. It was a community that worked and lived together. That's how I see the Marine Corps—a big family of sorts, where we all help one another. It gives me a good feeling to know one of the dogs that I trained could help to save a life somewhere in the world.''

"You really are an angel," he murmured.

"Oh, not really!" Callie laughed, embarrassed. "Sometimes I cuss when I get upset. Or I get mad. I'm not all sweetness and light, Wes, believe me.''

"You're an earthy angel," he chuckled, "and I wouldn't want you any other way than how you are.''

"What about you?" Callie asked. "Are you a career man?''

"Yeah, I want to put in my twenty. I figured I'd get a lot of experience in the corps, and then, around age forty, retire and start up my own construction business."

"You want the feel of earth in your hands," she murmured. Seeing the glint in his green eyes sharpen, Callie felt her heart squeeze with a delicious rush of desire.

"I like building and shaping things. Maybe I've got more of my father in me than I thought."

Callie heard the sadness in his tone. She intuitively felt that Wes still had a lot to work out with his dad. "Time seems to heal rifts between parents and children, from what I've seen," she told him gently.

His mouth worked, as if he were dealing with emotions he was withholding from her. "I hope you're right," he finally answered in a strained tone, and then tried to smile.

"He's got to be proud of you now, Wes. I know your knowledge and experience is going to help Logistics solve a lot of problems for folks out there beyond the military reservation. *I'm* proud of you...."

Getting up, he moved closer until her knees rested against his thigh. Taking her hands in his, he said in a low tone, "Callie, I want you to always be proud of me. I like what we have. I never expected to meet you...or to feel the way I have been since I first saw your face. It's a miracle, in all this death and destruction that's around us right now." Wes smoothed his thumbs across her small hands. There were so many scars across her tanned skin. Her skin was rough and Wes knew why: Callie thrived out in the elements—the sun, the wind, the rain, the heat and cold. She was a woman of the earth.

With a sigh, Callie leaned forward and rested her brow against his broad shoulder. A shoulder that could bear a lot of responsibility and weight. Closing her eyes, she whispered, "Wes, I have to admit I was scared before. You're so handsome, and I didn't see how someone as good-looking and obviously successful as you could be interested in someone like me. But now—" she lifted her chin, her voice tender "—the past two days, things have shifted in me. Maybe it's the trauma around us. Maybe I'm growing and maturing, or maybe it's just the magic of you. We need to talk about our desire. I know you said you wanted to explore a relationship with me." Looking away for a moment, Callie gathered her courage. "But after getting to know you, I can't pretend to be able to keep it light and strictly on the level of desire with you, Wes. My heart is involved in this. And I know your heart is off-limits." Holding his darkening stare, she saw his mouth go taut.

Sighing, Wes eased his hands upward, cupping them around Callie's face. "Let's keep talking, Angel. It's our lifeline to one another. I'd given up on finding someone, Callie," he added. "I wanted someone 'safe' this time. Allison wasn't in a safe job and you aren't, either. But I didn't think there was a woman on the face of this earth to fit my dreams until you walked into my life." He gazed deep into her widening blue eyes, which sparkled with gold highlights. "What we have is precious, Callie. I don't want to waste it. I don't want to hurry it. In one sense, we have the time. In another, I get scared just thinking of you going out there to do your work again. I'll be back here, stuck at Camp Reed. I won't know what's going on with you, and I'll worry...."

Sliding her fingers over his hands, she closed her eyes for a second, then opened them again. "Does this mean you want to explore life with me on a deeper level? To let your heart get involved?" Inwardly, she held her breath as she anxiously searched his closed features.

"Yes," he murmured, "what I feel for you is more than desire. I've been fighting you, Callie. Part of me has, I mean. I tried to keep my heart out of this equation with you. I was scared. When you got knocked unconscious out there, something snapped deep inside me. I still can't explain it, but I know I was forced to look at how I was trying to keep you at arm's length. It made me realize how stupid I was being."

"Then...what we feel for one another is serious."

"From my end, it is. Are you game?" He stared into her glistening eyes. How badly he wanted to kiss her! Just the way her lips curved upward at his last words made his heart fly on wings of joy.

"Oh, yes...I am."

"I'm going to worry myself sick over you being out there without me."

"I'll be okay, Wes...I really will. I'm an old pro at this. What I'll miss most of all is you. I know I'll be out there for three or four days at a time before I get any R and R." Callie drowned in his gaze. Wes was so close, so incredibly vulnerable and open to her. She absorbed the strength of his warm hands against her cheeks. "Kiss me?"

He heard the quaver in her voice. "I never thought you'd ask," he declared, leaning down and capturing her soft, parted lips.

Callie moaned as his mouth closed commandingly over hers. He was at once strong and cajoling, asking her to participate in their newfound joy. The gates to her heart flew open and a heat, startling and pleasurable, flowed through her and down into her belly. An ache settled there, as hungry and consuming as the flames of her need for him. She was breathless beneath his tender assault.

As he angled her head to drink more deeply of all she offered, her moist breath caressed her cheek. Arms sliding around his shoulders, Callie pressed her breasts against his chest. Though the thick robe was a barrier, she felt him stiffen as she told him in a nonverbal way what she wanted of him.

Groaning, Wes tore his mouth from Callie's. Her lips were softly pouted and wet from his onslaught. Her eyes were drowsy and dazed looking, desire sparkling in their cobalt depths. Her mouth… Wes groaned again. He had to resist. He had to get back to work! Time was their enemy now. Gripping her by the shoulders, he rasped, "Tonight…I'll be done at 1800. Let's plan to have dinner together?"

Her body throbbed with a wildfire of need that consumed her ability to think. Clinging to him, Callie heard the growl in his tone, the promise of things to come. "Y-yes…but I want more than dinner, Wes. I want you…all night. Here. With me. It will be our last night and I don't want to spend it alone…please?"

Cupping her chin, he gazed into her eyes as tears beaded on her thick, sandy lashes. "That's a promise, Angel. We'll spend the night together, in each other's arms. And I want to love you breathless. I want to please you…and make you as happy as you've already made me…."

Chapter Twelve

January 8: 2100

Callie busied herself at the dog rescue unit after receiving a call from Wes at 1800. Logistics was deep into a planning session, and General Wilson had ordered him to remain on to help the team complete their initial strategy for helping civilians find water in their given grid areas. She was disappointed, but understood. Her love would wait, she thought as she walked Dusty around the edges of the manmade lake a quarter mile from their facility. She and Wes had the time.

Still, as Dusty bounded among the tall brown cattails that hugged a curved inlet of the placid lake, Callie felt lonely. It was a new sensation to her. She no longer tried to fool herself or sidestep the truth of how she felt toward Wes. And he was willing to move beyond his fear, the pain of his past, to meet her halfway.

From where she stood on the lakeshore, a gentle slope littered with rocks and desert vegetation, she could see Dusty eagerly sniffing and wagging his tail as he hunted in and out of the cattails. This was one of his favorite places. He loved looking for frogs, sending them leaping away into the water. Being the water dog he was, he really wasn't interested in catching the frogs, he simply loved pouncing into the lake after them. It was a happy game for him, and she was glad she could give him some playtime like this.

Callie hoped Dusty wouldn't be too disappointed that in January, even in Southern California, the frogs were hibernating, and there would be none to be found among the cattails. Smiling, she clapped her hands and called him back. Dusty came promptly, sopping wet from being in the water, his eyes bright with happiness as he galloped up to where she was standing.

Leaning down, Callie grinned and petted his damp head. "Time to go in, Dust." She reattached the leash to his leather collar. Walking back to the kennel, Callie could see that it was a beehive of activity. Her C.O., Susannah, was busy working out the final details on where to send the twenty-two rescue units now that they were nine days into the disaster. Few people would be found alive at this point, so the dogs and their handlers had a more gruesome task: finding and locating the dead and getting them out from beneath the debris and properly buried so that disease would not become rampant.

The lights were bright and made Callie squint as she walked into the rear of the huge kennel building. People were coming and going, every one of them in a hurry. Dogs were barking. Humvees would arrive

and then speed off. After putting Dusty away, Callie
went to her C.O.'s office.

Her brow furrowed, Susannah was bent over her
green metal desk, writing furiously on a set of orders.
A private was standing at attention nearby, and Callie
waited until the marine was given the orders, did an
about-face and left.

"Phew," Susannah growled, "this is getting rug-
ged. You got a minute?"

Callie nodded and closed the door. Outside, the
sounds of barking, the people talking, made her edgy.
It was probably because of her concussion. Ever since
the injury, sounds bothered her a lot more than usual.

"What's up?" Callie asked as she sat down on the
red plastic chair in the corner of the room. Susannah's
office was small and spartan. Her desk was a disaster,
with papers, files and computer CDs scattered across
it. She looked drawn and tired. Who wasn't?

"Logistics just called me. They're gearing up for a
major—and I mean *major*—effort to create teams con-
sisting of marines in the engineering and other
trades—plumbing, welding and such—with a dog handler and a medic, though there's limited availability of
all these types of personnel. Logistics is trying to get
into a specific grid area of five square miles of the
L.A. basin by helo or Humvee—whatever it takes—
to help the civilian populace organize." She rubbed
her face tiredly. "Geez, Callie, I'll tell you, this is an
unraveling nightmare... Camp Reed has only so many
people to help. All the roads leading into the basin are
destroyed. It will take weeks and months to create
even dirt roads where highways once ran, so we can
bring trucks with food and water. This thing is going
critical mass. There's a million people out there with-

out proper water and food supplies. The whole country is mobilizing to help us.'' She became grim and gave Callie a hard look. "This is going to get ugly.''

"Logistics is trying to set up a chain of command so that civilians can work within those parameters, in the hope that it will stop mob rule activity?''

"Bingo. You hit the nail on the head.'' Susannah rummaged around on her desk. "As much as I'd like you to stay here and help me, I'm going to need you out in the field. We need every available handler and dog out there right now. I know you've got a forty-eight-hour sick chit. By the way, how *are* you feeling?'' she asked belatedly as she riffled through a set of orders on her desk.

"Better. No more dizziness. I'll be fine by tomorrow morning. What have you got for me?''

"I want you back at the Hoyt Hotel grid. You've already established liaisons with the civilians there and they know you. I'm sending you in with that team. They leave at 0700 tomorrow morning in front of the B.O.Q. by Humvee. Engineering has bulldozed enough dirt roads into the outer areas of the basin, and Grid Alpha, just outside our gates. Ah…here it is. Damn, I need to get this desk cleaned up. It looks how I feel.'' She grinned and walked around the desk and gave Callie her orders.

"I'll be there with bells on,'' Callie promised. "I'll come over and get Dusty at 0600.''

Nodding, Susannah sighed and put her hands on her hips. "Damn, Callie…this is a horrible catastrophe. A lot more people are going to die before it's over. I feel so helpless. I wish we could do more.…''

Getting up, Callie put her hand on her C.O.'s slumped shoulder. "Listen, we're all going to the max on this. The key right now is to get enough sleep every night so we can do our job to the best of our ability.''

Nodding, Susannah sighed. ''Yeah, you're right. I've had five hours in the last forty-eight.'' She grimaced. ''Listen, you get out of here. Get some shut-eye, okay? Your orders leave you on-site for four days, with the fifth day back here for twenty-four hours of R and R.''

''Right. See you later....''

January 8: 2300

Wes moved quietly from Callie's bathroom, a towel draped around his narrow hips. The hot water had revived him after a brutal day that had demanded all his time, knowledge and experience. Light filtered in from the small window and outlined where Callie lay sleeping beneath the covers. Barefoot, his feet still damp, he pushed wet tendrils of hair off his brow and approached the edge of the bed where she slept so soundly.

In the light, he could see that her hair was softly mussed. Her hand was beneath her cheek, her lips parted, her breathing light and shallow. When he'd quietly entered her room less than an hour ago, he'd seen the note on the dresser she'd written: ''Please come in and sleep with me. Love, Callie.''

Love. The word resonated deeply within him as Wes reached down and tugged the towel from around his hips. How like her to be so painfully honest. Wes had resisted that word when it came to Callie, but the last couple of days had shown him what a fool he'd been. No longer. Lifting the towel, he wiped his hair and face once more. Callie looked beautiful in sleep, so small in the big bed. So small, and yet she had such a courageous and giving heart. How badly he wanted her. His heart thrummed with anticipation as he hung up the towel and made his way to the other side. Lifting the covers, he slipped beneath them. The sheets felt cool as Wes eased his body toward hers. To his surprise, she was wearing nothing!

A grin creased his face as he propped himself up on his elbow and drank in the sight and feel of her sleeping form. "You really are an angel, Callie," he told her in a low, quiet voice. Lifting his hand, he ran his finger down the smooth line of her cheek. Her lashes were thick and long against her flesh. She was so feminine, and yet so strong. His heart expanded with warmth and awe. There was no question in his heart or mind that she was the woman of his dreams come to life. Somehow, Callie's practical qualities had soothed the fear within him. Yes, she had a dangerous job. No, he wasn't going to project what had happened to Allison onto Callie. That wasn't fair.

Who would have thought that she'd be in the guise of a rescue dog handler on the very base where he worked? Shaking his head, Wes pursed his lips as he gently stroked her cheek and her silky hair.

Callie moaned softly. She felt a hand, the hand of someone who loved her, stroking her cheek and her hair. The warmth of a man's body against her back penetrated her senses. And as she slowly twisted around onto her back, she raised her eyelids sleepily and looked up—into Wes's dark face. Drowning in the heat and desire in his eyes, she lifted her hand and rubbed her forehead.

"...Hi, stranger..."

"Hi." Wes smiled slightly as she blinked several

times and then turned over so that she was facing him. Her knees met his, and he felt humbled as she snuggled up against him, her arm around his torso. Callie was bold in a way that made him want to love her even more fiercely. She always downplayed herself as a simple country girl, but he knew better. This was a woman with solid confidence in herself, in her world, and he wanted to share that world now...tonight.

Whispering her name against her ear as he drew her fully against him, her small breasts pressed against his hairy chest, Wes heard her sigh. It was a sigh of surrender and utter enjoyment. As he slid his hand down her slim, strong back, he absorbed her soft, womanly curves and felt the surprising strength of her legs as they entwined with his. He shouldn't be surprised, he told himself, as he felt Callie's lips move like a burning brand along his collarbone and up the column of his neck. Her entire life was devoted to demanding and dangerous kinds of physical activity.

How much he loved her! The feeling was like a fierce river of lava that flowed through his heart, radiating outward. Easing back, Wes looked down into her sleepy, beautiful face. "You really are an angel come to earth to save the soul of this poor marine you're holding now. Do you know that?"

Callie laughed quietly. She lifted her hand and slid her fingers up the side of his jaw. Wes had just showered and shaved, and she liked the way he felt beneath her hands. Meeting and holding his dark gaze, she whispered, "I'm in need of saving, too...." Then she watched with fascination and joy as, at her touch, his body hardened against hers. There was no doubt that Wes wanted her. "You're such a hero in my eyes, my heart, Wes. You do so much good for so many...."

His ego soared at her whispered compliment. He liked being thought of as a hero, and he relished the look in Callie's wide, dark-blue eyes as she studied him in the lulling silence. When she moved sinuously against him, he grinned wolfishly. "All I want right now is you...to love you, share with you, Callie. All day today you were in my heart. Every time I took even the briefest break from planning, you were there." Tangling his fingers in her silky hair, he rasped, "I love you.... I want you to know how I feel."

He searched her widening eyes, which flared at his emotional statement. "We've got the time..." he added. "I just want you to know that coming to your bed, holding you—loving you—isn't a one-night stand for me. It's a long-term commitment to you...to us. To where I hope this ends up down the road." Easing his fingertips across her flushed cheek, Wes watched as her lashes fluttered shut at his caress. "Right now, we're at ground zero of a hell on earth." Grimly he looked up and stared across the quiet, darkened room. "We've got months of hard, unending work ahead of us, Callie. Dangerous work. But just know that, through it all, I'm here for you. I'll make every effort to be with you when I can. I'll steal every possible moment to be with you, Angel."

As Callie opened her eyes, he saw tears beading her thick lashes at his quietly spoken words. Leaning down, he brushed her parted lips with his, and tasted the salt of her tears. Barely touching her lips, Wes whispered brokenly, "Callie, I love you. It's that simple. It's that scary. I'm scared for you out there in the basin. Already there're gangs and insurrection starting to happen. There's gunfire, and people are fighting for their lives over scraps of food and cups of water. And you're going to be in the midst of it all.... I worry so much for you. I've just found you, and I don't want to lose you, beloved...."

There, it was out—everything he felt, everything Wes had ever wanted to say to Callie, now lay naked before her. As he eased away, feeling the delicious warmth of her body against his, Wes searched her damp eyes. There was such love for him burning in their depths. How could he have been so blind to love? Because his fear kept him from seeing it in her eyes before this, that was why. Caressing her brow and the strands of hair that drifted across it, he smiled at her uncertainly.

The strength and hardness of his male body against her own gave Callie the courage to speak. Her voice was low and husky, off-key with tears. "Where have you been all my life? In my dreams, Wes, I always hoped for a man like you. Only, you're better than any man in my dreams. Your honest..." Callie choked. "Your honesty opens my heart, opens me in such a way that I feel healed and whole." She reached up and grazed his mouth with her lips. Instantly, his arms tightened around her.

"And you gave words to what I was feeling in my heart," she added. "I want the same things you do, darling.... Yes, I know it's soon...but I think what we've discovered, what we have, is worth working on and waiting for. I know the months ahead are going to be brutal—and dangerous sometimes—but I have you now. Just knowing that will give me the courage I need to survive it."

Callie brushed his mouth with another kiss and heard him groan. "I love you, Wes...and I want every possible minute with you when we can steal them together. I know it won't be easy. We're going to have more separations than time together...."

His heart swelled with such warmth Wes thought he might suffocate with happiness. Could a man die from too much joy? Having Callie in his arms, her body molding against his, her husky voice flowing over him like hot, molten lava, made him feel as if nothing in the world could harm either of them. He caught her mouth and parted her lips in a hungry, searching kiss. As Wes eased from her and looked down into her half-closed, sultry eyes, he growled. "Then we'll make the most of the time we do have together...."

Her lips parted in a playful smile. "Oh, yes..." And Callie took his mouth in a hot, caressing kiss to let him know just how badly she needed him—all of him—in that moment.

Her world spun out of control, into a rainbow of light, heat and tactile sensations. Although Callie was not as experienced as Wes, it didn't matter. He drew her to him and moved the covers aside to expose her fully in the dim light. As he broke their kiss and moved his hand down her back, then around to cup and caress her breast, her breath caught. And as his lips found and caressed the hardened peak of her breast, she thought she'd die of incredible heat and pleasure. Desire spun raggedly downward through her body, fanning the fire that erupted deep within her. Callie felt helpless, out of control, arching and moaning against him as he suckled her and ran his hand across her hip. Then he slid his fingers between her curved thighs.

The violence of heat erupting within her caught Callie completely off guard, for no man had ever evoked such a powerful and swift response in her. She felt her heart contract as he raised his head, his eyes narrowed and a knowing smile pulling at the corners of his mouth. Because she was so petite compared to him, he was able to shift her onto her back in one smooth motion.

Feeling the bulk and heat of Wes's body move across hers reminded Callie of a huge warm blanket, protecting her. Lifting her arms, she slipped them around his shoulders as he eased over her. Wes slid his knee between hers. Her heart hammered in anticipation, her gaze clinging to his as he looked at her tenderly. The waiting was almost painful to Callie as she lifted her hips to receive him, all of him, into her waiting body, which was slick with anticipation.

She wasn't disappointed. As he eased into her wet, hot confines, a soft gasp of pleasure tore from her lips, and she pressed her face against the damp column of his neck. Callie clung to him, the exquisite heat weaving and winding throughout her as he began the gentle rhythm.

The world spun in dazzling colors, the sounds of his groans mingling with her soft moans of response. Their bodies were damp with perspiration, their breathing ragged. Callie absorbed every sensation in a way she never had before. Wes was asking her to be a partner in their lovemaking. He wasn't taking; no, he was sharing. And that empowered Callie as little else would have. She felt like a full-fledged partner as their bodies twined, moved, grew sleek and ultra sensuous against one another. As he leaned down and caught her mouth, taming her into rhythm with himself, an unexpected and startling sensation occurred

deep within her body. She had never reached climax
before, but now, as this heat and scalding intensity
throbbed in waves of intense pleasure through her, she
knew that was what was happening to her. And Wes
was prolonging the sensation, straining to hold her and
cherish her as he felt her body contracting wildly
against his.

As Callie felt her climax rip throughout her singing
body, she felt Wes tense. His growl deepened. His
head lifted; his lips pulled away from his clenched
teeth. His arms tightened like bands around Callie. In-
stinctively, she knew his life was flowing into her, and
she prolonged it for him by moving her hips in a flowing, continuous motion against his hard, rigid male
body.

They collapsed against one another moments later.
Their breathing was chaotic. Callie smiled softly and
ran her hands across Wes's strong, sleek back. He was
so powerful and yet he'd been so gentle with her.
Strength with gentleness. Yes, she'd always dreamed
of a man being both of those at once. Somehow, deep
in her heart, she'd known that such a thing existed.
And now, in Wes, she'd found it. Moving her head,
she pressed small kisses against his damp jaw and
thickly corded neck. Her body was throbbing with
such unbounded pleasure that she simply wanted to lie
quietly in his arms and absorb the incredible, golden
sensations still pulsing through her because of the love
they'd shared.

Eventually, Wes rolled off Callie and gathered her
into his arms. The satiation, the joy dancing in her
slumberous eyes told him how much she'd enjoyed
what they'd shared. That made his heart soar. ''Come
here,'' he rasped, pulling up the covers and holding

her close. Callie snuggled against him, her head resting against the juncture of his shoulder and neck.

Everything was perfect. Wes lay back, sighed and closed his eyes. The woman he loved was in his arms. The world around them might be hellish, but right in this moment, everything was exquisitely perfect in a way he had never felt before.

Within minutes, Wes felt exhaustion claim him. He wanted to talk, to share his feelings with Callie in the aftermath, but the long, demanding hours he'd worked due to the disaster had taken their toll. He closed his eyes, his arms around his woman, and spiraled into a deep, healing sleep.

January 9: 0530

"I'm going to let Dusty have a run down at the lake before we have to leave," Callie confided, smiling up at Wes as they walked out of the noisy kennel area. The day was dawning, the sky a brackish gray with a seam of red along the horizon as they sauntered down the desert slope toward the lake below.

"Yeah, let the guy have a run," he said. Now that they were out in public, Wes didn't dare touch Callie; military regulations forbade it. As she glanced up at him, dressed in her uniform and cap, he saw the joy in her eyes. He ached to reach out and take her in his arms and kiss her breathless, but now was not the time or place.

Behind them, the rescue unit was moving into high gear. All twenty-two handlers and dogs were being assigned to grids today, and were slated to leave either by helicopter or Humvee for their respective new missions in the escalating disaster. Wes tried to put his worry, his trepidation behind him. At least where Callie was going, the civilians knew her, and they were kind people. He didn't think there would be too many gangs or looting sprees, desperate people trying to steal one another's food. No, he'd laid a good groundwork in the surrounding neighborhoods before he'd left the Hoyt area.

Wes watched as Callie knelt down and petted Dusty, who was more than eager for his morning run to the lake. Wes's heart expanded fiercely with love for her. Her cheeks were flushed, her eyes shining—with love for him. As she unsnapped the leash, she shouted, "Run!"

Dusty took off at a wild gallop down the hill, and Callie smiled, knowing the dog would soon be searching for nonexistent frogs in the cattails. As she turned and looked up at Wes, she smiled because she liked the smoldering look she saw in his eyes.

"I like what you're thinking," she teased huskily. She gripped the leash in her hands, because if she didn't, she was going to blow military convention and throw her arms around Wes's neck and kiss him senseless. Her gaze anchored on that very male mouth of his, and her body responded hotly to it—and to him.

"Good," he replied. "Because if we weren't where we are right now, you'd be—"

Dusty's joyous barking interrupted their teasing. Callie smiled and turned on her heel.

"What?" Wes demanded as he looked up through the grayness toward where the dog was barking. Dawn was coming, but overhead the sky was still dark and he could still see stars fading in the west.

"He thinks he's found a hibernating frog, is all. I recognize that particular bark. A froggie bark." She chuckled. Giving Wes a tender look, she said, "He's happy, just like us."

"I know," he murmured. Reaching out, he slid his hand into hers for a moment. "Do you want to visit Laura Trayhern before you leave?" Instantly, he saw Callie's face brighten.

"I'd love to!" Callie felt like a beggar, taking every crumb of every moment that she could spend with Wes. Her body glowed from his lovemaking, and she wanted him all over again. Judging by the glint in his hooded eyes, he wanted her just as much. Calling to Dusty as he romped along the edge of the lake, she grinned up at Wes. "Come on, I'm not safe out here with you!"

Releasing her hand, Wes smiled. "No, you aren't."

Chapter Thirteen

January 9: 1200

Callie hurried down the hall of the hospital toward Laura Trayhern's room. Wes had been snagged by a Logistics officer as soon as he showed up on the sidewalk in front of the hospital and was asked to come to H.Q. He'd promised he'd try to see Callie before she left. Disheartened but understanding, she made her way into the hospital.

The passageways were crowded and noisy. Callie was slightly out of breath as she halted in front of Laura's room and knocked lightly on the door. Then she poked her head in. Morgan was sitting in a chair next to his wife's bed. Laura looked pale, worse than before.

Worriedly, Callie said, ''Am I coming at a bad

time? I just wanted to say goodbye before we got shipped out.''

Laura smiled wanly and lifted her hand. ''Hi, Callie. No, come in....''

Frowning, Callie walked over to her bed and nodded deferentially to Morgan, who gave her a tired smile. He was dressed in a white, long-sleeved shirt, his tie open at the collar and his dark pinstripe suit coat hanging on the chair behind him. A lot of files were spread across his lap.

''Hi, Callie,'' he said, greeting her warmly.

''Sir.'' Callie halted and reached out and touched Laura's hand. The woman's fingers felt cold. ''How are you doing, Laura? You look a little whipped.''

''Oh,'' she muttered, one corner of her mouth pulling inward, ''I developed a blood clot in my right leg late last night. They're worried it might break loose and flow up my bloodstream to my lungs, and then to my heart. If it does, I could die of a heart attack.''

Gripping her cool fingers, Callie whispered, ''That's awful...''

''She was in a lot of pain last night,'' Morgan said, shutting the folder he was holding and devoting his attention to Callie. ''I rousted out a very tired doctor and had her come in and check. She said it was phlebitis.''

''What can they do about that?''

Laura raised her blond brows. ''If they had the right drug, it would thin my blood and dissolve the clot.''

''But,'' Morgan muttered darkly, ''the hospital is running out of all drugs because of demands here and utside Camp Reed.''

''That's awful!'' Callie said again, devoting her attention to Laura, who lay back, her eyes murky looking. "What happens next?" She knew Morgan had his own jet coming and going to Camp Reed, hauling supplies to the basin. It could handle the shorter runways and land and take off without problems.

"Logistics is doing the best they can," Morgan said. He set his paperwork on the edge of the bed and slowly stood up. "I've authorized the Perseus pilot to go to a pharmacy up in Seattle, with a list of the most crucial drugs this hospital needs, blood thinners among them." He scowled and looked at the watch on his thick, hairy wrist. "By 1500 today, the jet will be back, and then Laura will get the Coumadin to start thinning her blood and dissolve that damn clot."

Laura reached out and caught her husband's hand. "The doctor said that as long as I had this leg suspended, and didn't try to walk, which I can't yet, anyway, I'd be fine. Don't look so worried...."

Callie understood Morgan's concern. She squeezed Laura's fingers. "That's really good news. I'll bet you'll be fine."

Laura studied her. "You look really happy, Callie. What's going on? And where's your shadow, Wes?"

Laughing and slightly embarrassed by Laura's gentle teasing, Callie released her hand and touched her own flushed cheek. "Gosh, does it show?"

"What?" Morgan demanded, standing at his wife's bedside, one hand on her slight shoulder.

"Morgan...we talked about Wes and Callie yesterday, remember?" Laura murmured.

"What?" His brows rose. "Oh...oh, yes. That..."

"Has he proposed yet?" Laura asked Callie with a knowing smile.

"How could you *know?*" Callie was mystified by

Laura's question. "Did Wes come here and tell you yesterday?"

Chuckling softly, Laura shook her head. She gave her husband a warm look and then studied Callie. "The fact that you love each other was written all over the two of you."

"Oh…" Callie cleared her throat nervously. "Gosh, if you saw it…I'd hate to think that other officers and our enlisted people will see it, too. We've tried to be really careful and not show any affection in public. Regs and all, you know?"

Wryly, Morgan grinned. "Yeah, we know. Laura's a matchmaker by genetics." His mouth spread into a tender smile as he held his wife's amused look. "She can sense these things like a bloodhound on a scent."

Relief rushed through Callie. "Then it's not obvious?" She was truly worried about appearing correct in the military world. She and Wes could get into a lot of trouble, legally speaking, and that wasn't what she wanted right now.

"No," Laura reassured her. "Not to anyone but us. I think people who love one another pick up on it in others, is all." She patted Callie's hand, which had curled into a fist on the bedside. "So relax."

"Whew…!" Callie smiled unsteadily. "Yes, we love one another…. It happened so fast, we're both spinning from it…."

"You have the time," Morgan counseled wisely. "Take it."

"Don't worry, sir, we are. We're looking long term." Callie lifted her hands. "This disaster is going to be going on for months before things even begin to start getting straightened out. Wes and I know that, and we're just grateful we have one another right now.

So many people..." She frowned. "Well, there's going to be so much more dying out there, more disease. "It's awful...."

Morgan nodded grimly. "You've seen it all, Callie, because you've been in major quake rescues in other countries."

"Yes, sir, I have...but this one is worse than any I've ever seen to date."

"How are you and Wes going to get together?" Laura wondered. "We hear he's been attached to Logistics and is heading up one of the main planning sections to start reconstructing highways and bridges. Morgan is working connections between Logistics and Supply, to coordinate flights coming in with specific needs for specific jobs being implemented right now."

Nodding, Callie said, "Wes will be here at Camp Reed from now on. That's great he'll get to work with you, sir. I'll be out there, in the basin, with my team." She brightened a little. "Every fourth day, I'll be rotated back to Camp Reed for twenty-four hours of R and R. That's when we'll see one another." She shrugged. "It's going to be tough, but the love we have is the durable kind—not a flash in the pan." And then Callie smiled widely. "Even if it hit us like a sledgehammer."

"Well," Laura murmured, "I knew I was in love with this guy from the moment he leaned down on that wet highway after I'd been struck and blinded by a car. And when he so generously stayed with me, and then brought me home from the hospital to take care of me, my love just deepened daily." She gripped Morgan's hand and squeezed it. "He finally realized he loved me, too."

Chuckling, Callie saw the warmth in their eyes. She

and Wes had the same look, she knew now. It made her feel good that what they had was indeed durable, just like Morgan and Laura. "I told Wes that I wanted what you two have. The love you hold for one another."

Laura nodded. "You work at it a day at a time, Callie."

"First you have to be best friends," Morgan rumbled. "And you've got to respect one another from the get-go."

"And," Laura said, "you don't try and change your partner, Callie. Work on your own inner growth, yourself, and things will go amazingly well."

"Good advice. Thanks." Callie looked at her watch. "It's time to go," she said regretfully. Reaching out, she gripped Laura's hand again. "You get better. And keep Baby Jane Fielding company."

With a smile, Laura said, "Me and the baby are becoming inseparable. The nurses down in Maternity are thrilled that I can take care of her, feed her, change her diapers. Did you know that the mother was a single mom?"

Callie shook her head. She knew that the body of the woman had been flown back to base for identification. "No. Does that mean the baby doesn't have a father?"

"That's right," Laura said. "Right now, Morgan is putting in a call to the Red Cross to try and find grandparents." She smiled tenderly. "Until then, I can be her mama of sorts." Giving her husband a teasing look, she said, "In fact, Morgan needs to go down and pick her up because her next feeding is in about ten minutes. Dear?"

Morgan nodded. "I'm going right now," he prom-

ised with a grin. Moving around the bed, he offered
his hand to Callie. "Stay safe out there. And if you
need *anything,* here's my cell phone number. Sometimes the military doesn't move as fast as your needs.
If you need something, you call me *first.*" He pinned
her with a look of command as he handed her a Perseus business card with his cell phone number scrib-
bled on it.

"Thank you, sir." Callie put the precious card into
her pocket. "Well, I'll see you all later...." She had
noted the hope in Laura's eyes as they spoke about
Baby Jane Fielding. Laura would make a wonderful
godmother for the infant.

"I'll walk you out," Morgan murmured, and
opened the door for Callie. "I have baby-sitting responsibilities right now." And he winked back at his
wife.

In the passageway, Callie turned left, and Morgan
went right, to the bank of the elevators that would take
him to Maternity. Happy that the little baby had two
angels to look over her, Callie's heart swelled with
hope and joy.

Just as she opened the emergency stairwell door, she
met Wes climbing up them. He smiled genially and
stopped on the stairs next to her. "Great minds think
alike," he whispered, closing the door behind her.
"I've got ten minutes to say goodbye to you, Angel....
We can have some privacy," he muttered.

The door leading to the hospital floor was made of
metal, with only a small glass window. No one could
see them unless they stopped to gawk, and Wes was
fairly sure no one had that kind of time to waste right
now, judging from the frantic, urgent pace of the hospital staff.

"Mmm, this is what I needed...you," Callie whispered, and snuggled in his arms, nuzzling the hollow of his shoulder and closing her eyes. Her arms went around Wes's torso. She felt his lips on her hair and sighed. "I love you so much, Wes James, that I think my heart is going to burst because it holds so much feeling for you...."

Caressing her shoulder, he whispered, "I love you so much it hurts." And then he added, "Last night was...a miracle. I've never felt love like you gave me, Callie. Not ever. You're incredible, Angel."

She sighed, running her fingers knowingly along his taut, long rib cage. "I'm embarrassed to admit this, but I've always heard of women having orgasms, and I'd never had one...until now...with you." She lifted her head and grinned wickedly up at his pleased expression. "It makes me want more. A *lot* more..."

Just being around Callie soothed Wes, fed him and nurtured him in ways that he wanted to continue to explore with her for the rest of their lives. "I kinda like that idea."

"More is better."

His laugher was hearty, echoing up and down the enclosed stairwell. "I think I've created a hungry angel of sorts. But I don't mind at all."

"No?" she teased, drowning in his forest-green gaze, which shimmered with love for her. Callie hadn't known how happy she could be—until now. Just spending time with Wes, talking, teasing, laughing, and wrestling with the darkness of the world around them, made her feel incredibly safe and protected.

"No." Wes stroked his fingers down the soft, tawny hair falling across her wide brow. He liked the light dancing in her turquoise eyes. ''This duty of yours is going to find you very busy during that fourth day— your R and R.''

''Oh? And how do you propose you're going to get that day off?'' In Logistics he was on a seven day a week schedule with no rest. Not under the circumstances.

''Long lunch hour, long breakfast, long supper,'' he proposed, a glint in his eye.

Callie didn't want to, but she looked at her watch. It was time to go. She held her wrist up so that Wes could see it. He nodded, his mouth tight. Straightening, he pulled her close, eased his arms around her slender body and brought her against him once more. Callie flowed like liquid sunlight against his tall, powerful frame.

''I like what we have, Wes,'' she whispered as she slid her arms around his neck.

''Me, too. Be safe out there, Angel?''

''Always. Look what I have to come home to. I'm the luckiest woman in the world.''

Threading his fingers lovingly through the strands of her hair, he whispered tenderly, ''And there's not a man on the face of this earth who has what I have, Callie. I'm going to love you—forever....''

*   *   *   *   *

Next month look for

RIDE THE THUNDER,

when

MORGAN'S MERCENARIES:
ULTIMATE RESCUE

continues in the
Silhouette Desire line!

Only from USA TODAY
bestselling author
LINDSAY McKENNA

Turn the page for a sneak preview....

One

Nolan scowled as the first light of dawn sent a gray ribbon across the eastern horizon. He was walking down the flight line toward his Huey when he saw another pilot standing by the opened door of the fuselage, looking in at his load of water. He rubbed his sleep-ridden eyes. The shadowy morning light was playing tricks on him, he thought, trying to make out the figure by his Huey. It had to be his new co-pilot.

Hope threaded through him as he quickened his pace toward the chopper. He had a new co-pilot. A permanent one. For Nolan, things didn't get any better than this. He saw the guy leaning over the cargo in the opened fuselage, making sure the netting was holding the boxes down and in place. Good, he liked a co-pilot who was thorough and efficient and didn't miss such details. Yes, life was looking good to Nolan. His step lightened considerably as he drew up behind his new co-pilot.

"Lieutenant McGregor?" he demanded.

Rhona gasped. The man's voice was practically in her ear. She straightened and whirled around.

Nolan's mouth fell open. It was the woman pilot he'd seen heading for Logistics the other day. This time, her black hair was caught up in a French twist and her gray eyes were huge and startled looking.

"Who are *you?*" he demanded, taking a step away from her. This couldn't be his co-pilot! Yet as Nolan raked his eyes over her upper body, he saw a set of gold aviator's wings stitched to her flight, and the name *R. McGregor* in gold letters on that black leather name patch above the left-hand pocket. No! This couldn't be happening! Not to him! He couldn't work with a woman co-pilot!

Rhona stared at the six-foot-tall Marine Corps officer. He was looking at her like she was a snake ready to bite him. Gathering her nerves, which were frazzled by his booming voice, Rhona thrust out her hand toward him.

"I'm Rhona McGregor, Lieutenant Galway. I'm your permanent replacement co-pilot. Nice to meet you."

Nolan stared at her long, thin hand. Her fingers were slender, graceful, but her nails were bluntly cut—these were no nonsense hands. Flight hands. All those realizations ran through his shocked mind before he could stop them. Even worse, he was discovering she was even more attractive looking to him than when he had first seen her. Her face was oval and narrow, her eyes warm, a slight smile pulling at the corners of her soft mouth. There wasn't anything to dislike about this woman. Not a damn thing. Except that she was his co-pilot.

"I'm Galway, all right," he snarled. "But you can't be R. McGregor. I'm looking for a *male* co-pilot."

Rhona was taken aback. She saw the dark cloud of anger in Lieutenant Galway's strong, square face. Nolan Galway wasn't pretty-boy handsome, but he had strength in his face that she instantly liked. Maybe it was the stubborn set of his jaw, or his large-set, intelligent eyes. Or his mouth, which was now thinned in complete disapproval of her.

"Gender has no place in this, Lieutenant Galway," she gritted out between clenched teeth. Great! He was a Neanderthal! Rhona's heart sank. Not another one! She'd left the Navy precisely because of men like the one standing in front of her right now.

"This has to be a mistake," he began.

"Look, the real reason I'm here," Rhona told him, "was that I walked in from Bonsall yesterday. I saw the devastation. I know you're running short-handed. I volunteered, Lieutenant Galway, because I *care* for the people out there," she said, jabbing her finger toward the Basin in the distance. "And I *can* make a difference. Now if you have a problem with me being a woman, that's *your* personal problem. Not the Marine Corps's. Not mine. Why are you flying these missions anyway? Just to fly? To get more flight hours under your belt?" That was an insult and Rhona knew it.

Anger sizzled through him. Especially when Nolan saw that they'd given her lieutenant rank; the same as him. She was his equal in every way under military law. Running his hands distractedly through his short brown hair, he glared at her.

"Climb down off your high horse, will you, McGregor? Okay, you're my co. I don't like it, but I'm not gonna argue any further under the circumstances." In the distance, he saw his crew chief ambling toward them. "It's time to turn and burn McGregor. You say you know Hueys. Well, I'll be watching your every move until *I'm* satisfied you know what the hell you're doing in that cockpit with me. Got it?"

Hurt wound through Rhona, but she dug her fingers into her hips to stop the anger from spilling out of her mouth. "Yeah, I hear you, Lieutenant Galway."

* * * * *

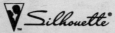

If you enjoyed what you just read,
then we've got an offer you can't resist!

Take 2 bestselling love stories FREE!
Plus get a FREE surprise gift!

Clip this page and mail it to Silhouette Reader Service™

IN U.S.A.
3010 Walden Ave.
P.O. Box 1867
Buffalo, N.Y. 14240-1867

IN CANADA
P.O. Box 609
Fort Erie, Ontario
L2A 5X3

YES! Please send me 2 free Silhouette Special Edition® novels and my free surprise gift. After receiving them, if I don't wish to receive anymore, I can return the shipping statement marked cancel. If I don't cancel, I will receive 6 brand-new novels every month, before they're available in stores! In the U.S.A., bill me at the bargain price of $3.99 plus 25¢ shipping and handling per book and applicable sales tax, if any*. In Canada, bill me at the bargain price of $4.74 plus 25¢ shipping and handling per book and applicable taxes**. That's the complete price and a savings of at least 10% off the cover prices—what a great deal! I understand that accepting the 2 free books and gift places me under no obligation ever to buy any books. I can always return a shipment and cancel at any time. Even if I never buy another book from Silhouette, the 2 free books and gift are mine to keep forever.

235 SDN DNUR
335 SDN DNUS

Name	(PLEASE PRINT)	
Address	Apt.#	
City	State/Prov.	Zip/Postal Code

* Terms and prices subject to change without notice. Sales tax applicable in N.Y.
** Canadian residents will be charged applicable provincial taxes and GST.
  All orders subject to approval. Offer limited to one per household and not valid to current Silhouette Special Edition® subscribers.
  ® are registered trademarks of Harlequin Books S.A., used under license.

Silhouette®

COMING NEXT MONTH

#1489 RYAN'S PLACE—Sherryl Woods
The Devaneys
Abandoned by his parents and separated from his brothers, Ryan Devaney was careful not to let anyone get too close. Then spunky Maggie O'Brien waltzed into his Irish pub. And Ryan's matchmaking best friend, a kindly priest, began to suspect that the warmhearted redhead could melt the icicles around Ryan's heart....

#1490 WILLOW IN BLOOM—Victoria Pade
The Coltons
Rodeo star Tyler Chadwick had amnesia, so he didn't remember his wild tryst with tomboyish Willow Colton. But then Willow learned she was pregnant. Before telling Tyler the big news, she decided to get to know the handsome rodeo man first. Could spending time together make Tyler realize that the mystery lover who'd been haunting his dreams was...*Willow?*

#1491 BIG SKY COWBOY—Jennifer Mikels
Montana Mavericks
With an intriguing mystery to solve, rancher Colby Holmes turned to psychic Tessa Madison for help—even though he didn't quite believe in her powers. Then Tessa became embroiled in a little intrigue of her own. Colby found himself rushing to protect her...and helpless to resist her passionate embrace. But when Colby's ex-fiancée came to town, not even Tessa could foresee their future!

#1492 MAC'S BEDSIDE MANNER—Marie Ferrarella
The Bachelors of Blair Memorial
Nurse Jolene DeLuca had been burned by a doctor before, so the last thing she wanted was to fall in love with plastic surgeon Harrison MacKenzie. Even though Harrison was handsome. And charming. And *sexy.* Would seeing caring "Dr. Mac" treat a helpless child break through Jolene's wary reserve...and prove to her that this man was the real deal?

#1493 HERS TO PROTECT—Penny Richards
Widower Cullen McGyver needed a bodyguard—but he didn't expect his old flame, tough-as-nails private eye Kate Labiche, to sign up for the dangerous job! Working together to stop a stalker, Cullen and Kate tried to fight their fierce attraction. When the dust settled, would the two be able to overcome past traumas and take a chance on love?

#1494 THE COME-BACK COWBOY—Jodi O'Donnell
Bridgewater Bachelors
It was time. Brooding rancher Deke Larrabie was ready to return to Texas to make amends for his father's mistake. Only, Deke hadn't bargained on bumping into spirited rancher's daughter Addie Gentry, whom he'd once loved with a passion that had threatened to consume him. A passion that had led to a fiery affair...and created a baby boy that Deke had never known existed!